The *Killing Tree*

The *Killing Tree*

A Novel

Rachel Keener

CENTER
STREET.

New York   Boston   Nashville

Center Street
Hachette Book Group
237 Park Avenue
New York, NY 10017

Visit our Web site at www.centerstreet.com.

Center Street is a division of Hachette Book Group, Inc.
The Center Street name and logo are trademarks of
Hachette Book Group, Inc.

Printed in the United States of America

First Edition: March 2009
10 9 8 7 6 5 4 3 2

Text design by Meryl Sussman Levavi

Library of Congress Cataloging-in-Publication Data
Keener, Rachel.
   The killing tree / Rachel Keener. — 1st ed.
      p. cm.
   ISBN: 978-1-59995-111-9
   1. Young women—Fiction.   2. Appalachian Region—Fiction.   3. Mentally ill—Family relationships—Fiction.   4. Domestic fiction.   I. Title.
   PS3611.E345K55 2009
   813'.6—dc22
                                        2008019574

For Kip, and his promise

And thanks to Andrea Somberg

The *Killing Tree*

PART ONE

Beneath the Peonies

*T*he chickens began to creep on a steamy day in June. They were used to walking and pecking. But on that day, they learned the same thing that I had. You have to creep around the silence to survive it.

My grandfather, Father Heron, sat and stared out the front-room window. His black eyes searched the gravel road that wound around Crooked Top Mountain, Crooktop to the locals. It was a twisted road that cut through squirrel-filled trees, blackberry hollers, and past his house, the one he was born in. The one that I was born behind.

I had studied his silence many times. And learned that people speak the loudest when they're quiet. They create words, even conversations, just with the twitch of their brow or the grit of their teeth. Sometimes his silence screamed so loud I wanted to cover my ears. "Be quiet!" I

wanted to shout at his unmoving mouth. But I didn't, because I knew that he was telling me things. About locked
doors, blood, and murder.

I spent my time waiting for a look, a sign, that would
tell me what to do to survive. I was born waiting on him.
My momma didn't live long enough to teach me anything
herself, so I had to soak up my lessons from her in the
womb. And she taught me that her daddy, my grandfather,
was a man that women should dance around, but never
with.

"She say when she's coming back?" he asked without
looking at me. His words were simple. But the dance
wasn't.

"Yes sir. Not 'til you promise not to kill any more of
her chickens."

"*Her* chickens?" he asked, leaning forward.

"Your chickens, sir, 'til you promise not to kill any more
of your chickens." *Around . . . dance around, not with.*

"And why? Why does that crazy woman think I
shouldn't kill my own chickens?"

"'Cause she's sick and tired of making your chickens
happy just to have to chop off their heads and fry 'em," I
whispered, my eyes lowered to the ground.

"God gave man dominion over every creeping thing on
the earth," he hissed.

I nodded my head.

"Mercy, does a chicken creep?"

I knew that chickens could walk, strut, peck, and scurry.
But from that day on, they would creep too. Because the
silence told them to.

"Yes sir, I reckon it does," I said with perfect rhythm. *I knew his dance.*

He jerked his eyes off of me and turned them back to the road, daring the sun that squinted them to tell him that chickens don't creep. I hurried outside of the house that rose defiantly on the side of the mountain. It was a crooked mountain. Like its top was broken. Not its peak, there weren't any mountain peaks in the Appalachians. Just slopes that rose rounded and wide. Like giant hills really.

But the people there didn't mind. It didn't bother them to live on a broken mountain. Most of them were born there. Some left in their youth, but most returned. Not for the jobs. When the boom of coal left Crooktop, so did most of its jobs. There was still a little for truckers to haul away to other sites. Just enough to cover the town with its dust. Coal was the god we could all see. It had built our little town in the valley. And it's why the most fundamental rule of Crooktop etiquette was to take your shoes off before you walked on carpet. Otherwise, all the rugs of Crooktop would quickly turn black.

People didn't stay on Crooktop for its entertainment either. Its valley had two clothing stores, Ima's Boutique and the Discount Family Shopper. The nearest shopping center was over the mountain, at the Magic Mart. And Crooktop only had three restaurants. A hamburger joint, a meat and three, and a barbecue diner. Only the diner served beer. There was no theater. No swimming pool. No skating rink. And if you bought a radio you wasted your money. The mountains blocked reception so the only stations that could be picked up were ones from nearby mountains. And those were only AM bluegrass or gospel stations. If you wanted to listen to FM music, then you had to buy tapes. You had to guess at what music was new and cool, because the radio couldn't tell you. So young people stuck with the safe bets. Lynyrd Skynyrd and Aerosmith were always new and cool on Crooktop.

People stayed on Crooktop because it was a way of life that couldn't be found outside the mountains. And it was protected. Hidden by the giant hills from the eyes of the world. Hidden by its poverty from the interest of the world. Outsiders never knew of the love or wars that festered on the side of that crooked mountain.

And in the middle of all the festering rose the Heron house. It was a small two-bedroom-one-bath house, painted white and topped with dingy green shingles. Built in a nearly perfect square, it seemed to say, "Every angle of the Heron family fits neatly together." But it was a lying house. It was his house. And though I spent all my days and nights there, it never felt like mine.

Sometimes to escape it all I would go to Mamma Rutha's tomato patch, touch the prickly leaves, and breathe the heavy scent—an earthy mix of moist dirt, sweet ripeness, and green, green, green. It was a smell that soothed me nearly as much as the smell of seng on Mamma Rutha's hands made me ache. At age six, when I learned Mamma Rutha was crazy, I saw her standing fierce-eyed and naked in the garden, with the stain and mystery of ginseng on her hands. Hair as thick and shiny brown as molasses spilled down her back in wild tangles. Small breasts, shaped like fists, barely rose away from the ribs that jutted from her chest. Her legs were scraped and scarred from running through thorn-filled woods. Her small wiry frame burned such an image in my mind that when I think about that night I have to remind myself that she was a speck of a woman and not the tower I remember.

Why I consider that the day I learned about Mamma Rutha, I really don't know. Looking back, it seems she had always been crazy. Planting her peonies haphazardly through the yard, like some sort of random connect-the-peony-dot game. Or religiously watching the early spring moon to know when to plant her garden, carefully sowing the seeds and then refusing to harvest it. When I was little she poured a dizzy, heated sort of love on me, crowning me with honeysuckle headbands and then forgetting to feed me supper. She was a woman who talked to the moon, who took her clothes off and stood naked amidst her pile of seng, who forgot to make sure that I had clean clothes for the first day of school, who never noticed when I went barefoot well past Indian summer. But she loved me breathlessly. Clung to me. Cradled my head and sang to me, strange songs about dragonflies and june bugs. Cried when I cried. Scoured the mountainside for a soothing remedy for my every complaint. My crazy Mamma Rutha, a woman who fell in love with her chickens and couldn't kill them anymore.

Folks down in the valley whispered that Mamma Rutha hadn't always been crazy. Father Heron, though, he had never changed. He was raised on Crooktop, graduated high school down in the valley, took a wife, and began establishing himself as a hardworking, levelheaded man.

He was the sort of man that made a list of the things he must accomplish in life and then set about to check them off. Graduate—check. Wife—check. Deacon in church—check. Raise granddaughter—check. He felt humiliated by Mamma Rutha, until he realized that staying with his crazy wife made him look like a martyr in the eyes of the valley. His fellow deacons muttered their sympathies and called him loyal for staying with her, and brave for trying to raise me. So it was stay with crazy wife—check, and continue raising granddaughter—check.

But raising is different than loving. So different that it sent me running to my mirror searching for a sign that I belonged to another family, even though the whole valley still talked about how my momma had died and my daddy ran off. But my eyes were always there staring back at me with the same black of Father Heron's. I could avoid my lips, that twisted into the same slightly crooked smile of Mamma Rutha. Or my nose that was a little too round—like my momma's, Mamma Rutha always said. But I could never avoid my eyes. Proof that I belonged, even when I didn't want to.

Chapter II

Why Mamma Rutha fell in love with her chickens was a mystery. Early in their marriage Father Heron would proudly take her fried chicken to his deacon fellowship dinners. She said the secret to her recipe was to raise a happy chicken, and then use an iron skillet to fry it in. And she spent many hours making sure her chickens were happy. She sang to them, petted them, and fed them more often than she fed herself.

The day she sobbed over her iron skillet was the day I knew that her chickens would soon be as sacred as her unharvested garden. Her eyes were red and swollen as she served supper that night. Father Heron noticed too. But we were too busy stuffing ourselves to care. She paced the length of the kitchen, wringing her hands and murmuring beneath her breath.

"Sit down and eat," Father Heron growled. "Or at least get out of here so I can eat in peace."

Her red eyes flashed wild and she began to murmur again. Father Heron picked up a drumstick and slowly took a bite. He smiled at her, bits of happy chicken peeking from between his teeth. She put her hands over her face and strangled a sob. I laid my fork down, but I didn't go to her. Even though I knew that I should cradle her head the way she had so often cradled mine. But what did she want? To take away the only decent meal we had had after weeks of living off barbecue from the diner I worked at?

"Shhhhhh," she said to our silent room before running out the back door. She had heard our thoughts, or felt them at least.

We finished our supper. Savoring the chicken. I knew that it was seasoned with her tears. And I knew that it would probably be the last happy chicken I ever ate. A suspicion which was confirmed later that night, when I awoke to see her pale blue eyes staring down on me.

"Mercy baby," she whispered.

"Mamma Rutha? What's wrong?"

"Please don't eat no more of my chickens!" she gushed, her eyes glowing with intensity.

Strangely, I asked her why. I had stopped asking that question a long time ago. Her eyes began searching me, asking me why I didn't know better than to eat the chickens she loved. She expected me to understand her, and I couldn't.

I sighed. "I won't eat 'em no more."

The next morning I found her burying the chicken bones under the June apple tree.

"Morning, Mamma Rutha." She didn't answer. "Looks like it's going to be a hot day, huh?" I asked. Still no answer.

I sat down across from her and watched. Her dress was covered with the dirt that her hands were slinging. Beads of sweat began to form on her face as she feverishly clawed the ground. She was silent. But it was a different sort of silence than Father Heron's. Sometimes she just felt things too deeply for conversation. Or she felt them as they really were, hot emotions too jumbled to organize into words.

After she had clawed a hole a foot deep into the ground she gently placed the bones side by side, making sure each had its own resting place before covering them over with dirt.

"Let's pray now," she said as she reached for my hands. I bowed my head.

"God," she said with her face uplifted, "please take care of my dear friend. Don't forget to feed him. He likes dried corn a lot. Pet him a little too. His favorite song is 'Turkey in the Straw,' but when you sing it to him, could you change the words to 'chicken in the straw'? And Lord, please forgive Mercy baby, for she knew not what she eateth. Amen." She squeezed my hands. "Say a blessing verse."

Mamma Rutha knew all the blessing verses by heart, the ones in the Bible and the ones she made up herself. Sometimes she spoke them as though they were her own special language, which always disgusted Father Heron.

"Holy scripture ain't meant to be used by the likes of a crazy woman and her peonies," he would mutter when he would see her singing them to her flowers. What bothered him the most was that she knew every word of those verses by heart. They were a part of her. I loved to hear her whisper them over me as I slept, or over the picture of my momma that she kept by her bed. I loved to watch her kneeling in the middle of her garden whispering, *"The mountains and the hills shall break forth into singing before you, and all the trees of the field shall clap their hands. Instead of the thorn shall come the cypress tree, and instead of the briar shall come the myrtle tree."* And her garden always produced an unharvested bounty, the envy of all other gardeners.

"What should I say, Mamma Rutha?"

"I think the one about bones would do nicely," she said as she ran her hand over the patch of fresh dirt.

The bone blessing. It was the one she had taught me to say anytime we came across death. When my baby possum died, we whispered the bone blessing. When Father Heron's dogs killed a stray cat, we whispered the bone blessing. And now that the happy chicken was buried, it was time to whisper the bone blessing.

"The Lord will guide you continually," I said solemnly, "and satisfy your soul in drought. And strengthen your bones. You shall be like a watered garden, like a spring of waters, whose waters do not fail."

"Amen," she whispered as she leaned forward and pressed her forehead on the ground. I heard her kiss the grave.

After that day, things were peaceful for a little while. I

kept bringing home barbecue and Mamma Rutha kept her chickens happy. But even hickory-smoked pork becomes unappetizing after several meals. Especially to Father Heron, who always had to swallow a Tums after he ate. So one evening he took my brown bag filled with barbecue, dumped it in the trash, walked outside, and chopped off the head of a happy chicken.

Mamma Rutha was sitting in her garden, singing to her okra when it happened. We both heard the noise. The whack, the shrill squawk, the sudden silence. Her eyes grew wide and wild. We both ran to him. As he tossed the limp chicken head to his dog, the body jerked violently and hopped around the yard for a few more seconds. I can still smell the hot blood that squirted from that head-less chicken. And I will always hear the wild scream that escaped from that tiny bit of a woman. It scared me. It scared him too.

She chased the chicken's body until she cradled it in her arms. "You're okay. You're okay," she cried to it. Her face and neck were flecked with warm blood. She ripped the mangled chicken head from his dog. "You're going to be okay. You're okay," she said to the head. The dog didn't protest, she scared him too. Then she ran far and fast, up the mountain. Long after the woods had swallowed her body we could still hear her.

She didn't come home that night or the next. It wasn't the first time she had disappeared. There were rumors about families living high on the mountain, back in the thickest part of the woods. Families that never came down in the valley, not even to send their children to school. Some said they were remnants of the Cherokee tribe that used to live there. Nobody had actually seen anyone, but I believed Mamma Rutha had. There was a reason why she would come down from the mountain carrying a pint of shine, or carry supplies back up and return without them.

When a week passed with no Mamma Rutha I went to look for her. More out of desperation for some real noise, some laughter and song, than out of concern for a woman who seemed to need only the mountain to survive. I heard her blessing verse before I saw her. She sang to the trees about knowing the wind, the rain, and the secrets of the owl.

She lovingly placed her thin hand upon each of their trunks. I longed to be one of those trees. To be content with the love she offered, without hoping for anything more.

"Mamma Rutha," I whispered, like we were in church. She looked at the tree as though it had spoken.

"Mamma Rutha, it's Mercy."

"Hi Mercy baby," she said, still looking at the tree. She didn't ask why I had come, or how I found her. She never took her hand from that tree or her eyes off its bark. She simply gave me her message for Father Heron and then walked further into the woods, sending me home alone to dance around him over her chickens.

I did her bidding. I gave Father Heron her message, and the chickens began to creep. But she waited for a sign that her chickens were safe. Waited for a reaction from a man who rarely reacted. I began to fear that she might have to wait forever.

I picked up double shifts at the diner so that my only

hours at home were spent sleeping. It was the diner in the valley. The only one that served beer, earning it the reputation of being a place where men hid out from their families on Saturday night and then ushered them in after church on Sunday. And the smokers were always going full speed on the weekends, sending me home smelling like a smoked pig. No matter how much detergent or fabric softener I used, it was a smell that married my clothes.

After I graduated high school the month before, the diner became a welcome escape for me. Between serving up pulled-pork platters and mugs of beer, I felt connected to something outside of that tidy little house up on Crooktop. When groups of rowdy teenagers came in on Saturday night, there were brief moments when I actually felt like I was a part of their world. One where everyone ached to be older. So as the boys smoked and the girls showed off their push-up bras, I ran to smear on Plum Passion lipstick before sneaking them half mugs of beer. They would roll their eyes, swear about curfews or being forced to go to college in the fall. And then I would feel our difference. As they strolled out arm in arm, whispering, "Thanks for the brew, Mercy," I knew how different we were. While they raced home to beat their curfew and count the days until classes began at the community college over the mountain, nobody waited at home for me and I had never even seen a college application. Though my grades were fairly decent, I knew college wasn't an option for me. I didn't have any money and it had never crossed my grandparents' minds to send me. And even if money hadn't been a problem, I had no idea how to go about getting into college. All the things I heard the Saturday night crew groan about—the tests, the application fee, the campus tour, picking a "major"—it was all foreign to me. So the highlight of my graduation was "picking a shift schedule" at the diner, since school no longer interfered with my work.

I wasn't angry. Anger is the child of surprise, and the fact that Father Heron never spoke the word "college" to me didn't surprise me. As my black eyes stared back at me in my mirror, I knew that Crooktop had its fist around me.

On Sundays the diner would become respectable. After attending First Baptist of Crooktop on the arm of Deacon Heron I would change into my grease-stained apron. The tipsy teens and seeking adults of Saturday night were replaced by children in pastel frills, mothers with hot-rolled hair, and fathers tugging at their neckties. The beer was exchanged for sweet tea. On my break in between shifts I would sit and watch them. The wife playing with the curl on her husband's neck, the sleepy baby starting to cry. Sometimes I would imagine what it would feel like to go home with them. To be safely tucked away in the backseat of a four-door family car.

The Sunday after Mamma Rutha ran away the diner was especially crowded. My boss, Rusty, was busy barking orders while we waitresses were busy taking them. When the crowd finally began to thin, I took a seat at the bar to count my tips. But my eyes drifted from my skimpy pile of change to a family in a back booth, and I soon lost count. There were three of them. And they sat together, on the same side of one booth. The man had his arm wrapped around the woman as she nursed a baby beneath a blan-

ket. It was a picture so intimate that I felt both embarrassed to spy and forced to at the same time.

"Pretty gross ain't it," Rusty said. "If the lunch rush
wasn't over, I'd tell her to step into the ladies' room. You
can get away with that stuff in a lot of places, but this
here is a respectable eating establishment. The last thing
families want to see is swollen nipples and hot milk right
before they eat."

His words tried to sully the moment I had stolen from
them. I asked him why, if this was an eating establishment,
that little baby couldn't eat right along with everyone else.
He looked surprised, started to reply, but saw the look on
my face and decided not to.

"Well, simmer down, Miss Sass, and come have a
smoke." He grinned.

"Can't. Got one table I'm still waiting on to leave."

"See, Mercy, that's the difference between having just
anybody ask you to come and smoke, and having your boss
ask you to," he said as he called for another girl to watch
my table.

I never enjoyed my daily smoke session with Rusty. He
was sweaty, fat, out of breath, and always calling himself
the boss. But for the sake of a decent shift schedule I
puffed away on his Camels and forced some conversation.
Besides, I had seen Rusty get angry, seen him turn red all
over and throw dirty dishes at the cooks. If all it took was
a smoke break to keep me away from that side of Rusty, it
was a small price to pay.

"Busy day ain't it?" he asked.

"Sure is."

"Hot too," he murmured.

"Yup," I answered, trying to sound interested as I leaned forward to light my cigarette.

"Sorry about your grandma."

I didn't respond.

"Sure is a shame," he continued, "poor Deacon Heron and you stuck with somebody so crazy. Just ain't right to run off like that. I reckon nobody ever knows what old Rutha Heron's gonna do next."

"How'd you know?" I asked softly.

"Shoot, Mercy, you know that everybody in the valley knows about everything up on that mountain, just like everybody on that mountain sees everything going on down here in the valley."

I had long since quit trying to excuse Mamma Rutha to anyone. So I sucked in my breath and held the hot smoke until I thought my chest would explode. My eyes started to water.

"Mercy, I didn't mean to make you cry, sugar," he said softly as he placed his greasy hand on my knee. My eyes fell to it, red and puffy, cupping my knee.

"It's the smoke, Russ. There's just too much pig smoke in this air to be smoking cigarettes too," I said as I jerked myself up, throwing his fat fingers off of my leg.

"But it's damn fine pig smoke! The finest pig smoke in these here mountains!" he yelled out after me.

Back inside the diner, my little family had left. As I wiped down their table I thought about Rusty's hand on my leg. It seemed so different from the gentle embrace of the man who had sat at the table I was cleaning. It seemed greedy. Most of my experiences with men came from Father Heron, and the rest came from my conversa-

tions with Rusty. The other girls at the diner said that
he wanted me. That he wanted to be my boyfriend. The
thought made me queasy.

"Wanna ride home?" he whispered over my shoulder.

I wanted to say no. But how could I feel superior to
Rusty, manager of his daddy's pig-smoking diner? I waited
by his truck while he locked the building up. He usually
closed early on Sundays, so the sun was still out. I looked
up at the sky, but I didn't see much of it. The view from
the valley always made the sky look like a puzzle. Pieces
of green and brown mountain closing off and locking in
the blue and white.

"How do you breathe?" an outsider asked me once. "It
feels so claustrophobic," she explained, "looking up only to
see more land, and no open air."

Her words sent me digging beneath my bed for an old
shoe box stuffed with magazine clippings of the ocean. I
had collected them for years, ever since my second grade
teacher told me there was a body of water deeper than
Crooktop and bigger than all my mountains put together. I
sorted through my clippings and noticed for the first time
that yes, my sky was different. Peeking between swells of
land once rich with coal. My sky was a busy one. Not the
empty sky filled only with an occasional white puff and a
bird. There was movement in the sway of the trees. In the
daring trespass of the mountaintops. In the shadow of the
hawk. It was a living sky.

The squall of Rusty's horn pulled me back to earth.
"C'mon, dreamer, let's get outta here!" he yelled.

I tried not to wince as the vinyl of his seats scorched
the back of my legs. The thought of his hand on my knee

made me uneasy and embarrassed around him. Figuring
that the more I puffed the less I was expected to talk, I
asked for a smoke.

"Gawd o'mighty!" he swore. "This heat's hell on earth."

As I agreed with him, I added to myself that so was
his truck. Smelling of stale Camels, sweat, and pig smoke,
his truck made my stomach turn. He pulled up by Father
Heron's mailbox, grinned at me, and started to speak.

"Thanks for the ride. I better get in and check on my
grandfather," I said, jumping out of the truck. I could feel
his eyes watching me run. I took special care not to sway
my hips as I ran to the backyard.

Father Heron sat whittling on the back porch.

"Brought you some supper," I told him.

He didn't look up, but I wasn't expecting a response.
I sat for a long time staring at him. Sitting there whittling. Looking old. Maybe even feeble, with his mussed-
up white hair, tinged yellow from pipe smoke. Sitting a
little slumped, his round belly straining against his belt.
The man who as a child I swore could smell my fear. I
wondered what he'd do if I challenged him, whether he'd
become my felled Goliath. I imagined standing over him,
patting a pocket filled with five smooth stones.

But I was a coward. I wouldn't even bend down to pick
up stones for my pocket, much less build a sling.

"Rusty asked about Mamma Rutha. He said everybody
knows. He said he heard some of the deacons at church
mention that maybe we should have a search party for
her, in case she's lost. Said it would be like a mission, you
know, reaching out in Christian love to a lamb lost in the
wilderness. He wanted me to tell you he would be willing

to help, since you're so busy you can't really be expected to be her shepherd," I said, carefully watching him as the rhythm of his knife steadily slowed.

My dance was short. But the shrill sound of metal pounding metal that woke me the next day showed me that the steps were perfect. I peeked out of my little window and saw Father Heron hammering metal rods down into the ground near his garden, the one that we harvested. A few feet from where he was standing I saw a bundle of chicken wire. He was building a new chicken coop.

It had only been a few years since he had planted a new garden. The baby ears of sweet corn had just ripened, and Mamma Rutha had stood guarding her garden from any harvest, butcher knife in hand. Father Heron swore at her and quoted scripture about how the ground was cursed for man's sake, that he may toil in it and eat from it. His voice rose and stressed the word "eat." She never moved. All through the day and night she stood planted amidst her corn. Whenever Father Heron approached her, she would calmly raise her knife and whisper, "An eye for an eye, a tooth for a tooth, an arm for a stalk, a hand for a fruit."

Father Heron wisely chose his limbs over sweet corn. And that day another garden was planted. One that wasn't sacred. One that wasn't sung to or blessed. One that to his great frustration, and the amusement of the valley, was never quite as bountiful.

Once the coop was built, I heard him start his old Chevy and head down the mountain. I knew that he was going to get his chickens. Unhappy chickens. Chickens that Mamma Rutha could cook without tears. Chickens I had never tasted, but already knew would not be as good as the old ones.

I was in a good mood at work that day. I freely accepted Rusty's offers of smoke breaks. I didn't even count my tips. And when Della, my best friend, came to the diner I let her convince me to go to the docks that night.

Della and I had been friends since my freshman year in high school. We bonded through shared misery. High school had taken me by surprise. For eight grades I had faced the same school and same faces every day. My first day at high school left me breathless. The cafeteria seemed bigger than the whole building of my old school. I went through the lunch line that day only to face endless rows of tables and strange people. How was I supposed to pick where to sit? Where had all my old friends gone? After glancing at my plate of pasty lukewarm spaghetti, I tossed it in the garbage can and ducked outside. I leaned hard against the brick wall, feeling its support.

"Wanna apple?" a voice spoke.

"No thanks, not hungry," I replied to a tall curvy girl, with hair as red as the apple she held out.

"Don't blame you. Me neither. Lunchtime is a ridiculous tradition. I don't observe it out of principle," she said, looking at me with approval.

I was unable to resist asking her to explain, and she told me that eating involved a celebration of death—death of the apple, death of the cow, preventing death of the human—and that therefore hunger alone and not tradition should justify meals.

Della continued to defy tradition throughout high school. She bloomed into a beauty that frenzied the boys.

But like me, she never seemed to fit in the world of her classmates. Instead, she preferred to hang out with older boys. She cut as much class as she attended. And she despised the "tradition" of grades, as "useless numbers that only limit us." She craved attention the way I craved to be hidden. Often teased for being a drama queen, she justified her sassiness by calling herself a revolutionary. Fifteen-year-old Della was a wannabe hippie, two decades too late, in a region too removed, and with a face that wore too much makeup. But despite her boisterous ways, she had a glow. A glow that outshone the dirt floor that she was raised on. Della's father was killed in a mining accident when she was three, leaving behind a hungry mother with five children. All of her siblings fled the mountains the day they became old enough to escape their mother's clutch. But not Della. Even after she quit high school the day Mr. Hillbert called her writing style "too inflammatory," I knew that she would stay. She had promised me so.

It's hard growing up alone on a big mountain. So when we found each other at fourteen, we gulped a sigh of relief and swore we'd always stick together. "Girls like us have to love each other," Della said. "Ain't no one else around to do it."

She was always in some sort of trouble, either as the victim or the perpetrator. She changed boyfriends as frequently as she changed her hairstyle. In fact, she had a theory about that. She always said that you could predict a girl's love life by the way she wore her hair. A girl that was always willing to spice up her look with new colors, new cuts, and new styles wasn't afraid to spice up her life with a new man. And a girl that was always content with the same old look would be willing to settle for the same old boy. So with every new man, she got a new do. Whether it was golden streaks or a swingy bob, a new man meant a new Della. And according to her, that was the problem with my love life.

"I'm telling you, Mercy," she'd say, "as long as you stay straight, long, and brown that's what your love life is going to be, *boring*. You gotta spice it up. I could put some real wham into your life if you'd just let me put a few streaks in your hair."

But it wasn't *my* love life that was on her mind the day she ran into the diner to beg me to come to the docks with her. With fresh highlights in her hair, I knew that she was eyeing a new fling. Going down to the docks was never my idea of fun. But her timing was right. If my good mood could make me a willing smoke pal for Rusty, it could certainly make me game for some of Della's sport. So I told her I would meet her at eight, to give me time to run home and find Mamma Rutha.

Chapter III

Underneath the June apple tree, freshly cut flowers were laid across the chicken grave. Mamma Rutha was sitting by her garden, singing to it.

"I've missed you," I told her as she cupped my face in her leathery hands.

"My Mercy baby," she said, smiling. She patted her lap and I laid my head across it. My eyes closed as her hand gently tugged through the tangles in my hair. There was someone to love me again. Even if it was crazy love. It was finally home.

"I found a new blackberry thicket. Do you remember the baby deer and his momma that used to come eat from the garden? Well he's clean grown up now. Starting to get little points for antlers. He showed me the blackberries."

I opened my eyes and looked at her. Her hair spilling

in curls and tangles around her. Her blue eyes shining. No one would know that she had spent fourteen days in the wilderness.

"Where do you go?" I asked.

"In the mountain."

"Do you have a shelter?"

"I have my sisters, the oaks," she said, smiling. "And a soft bed of brown mountain earth. The mountain takes good care of me, don't you worry."

She was a fairy-tale grandma who spoke of sister oaks and blackberry thickets. Her life was a poem. But sometimes the poetry was too much. I craved some real answers.

"Mamma Rutha," I said as I sat up and faced her, "you were gone for two weeks. You never came home for food. You didn't have a blanket. But you look fine."

She didn't respond.

"Is there somebody else up there?" I finally demanded.

"God," she said, the smile fading from her face. "You know that."

"Who else?" I asked, just as Father Heron appeared.

He stopped and looked at us. He was pleased she was home, though he'd never voice it. It was another milestone on his list. Rescue wife from the wilderness—check.

Mamma Rutha's hands froze in my hair.

"Evening, Rutha."

"I put your barbecue in the fridge," I told him, trying to distract them from each other.

"I was thinking we could have some chicken . . . one of my chickens, tonight," he replied.

I looked at Mamma Rutha. Would the new chicken coop work? Were all chickens sacred?

"Sounds fine, Wallace," she said calmly as she rose to her feet. "Mercy baby, go pick some okra."

Father Heron stood looking at me after she went inside.

"Thank that boy Rusty for his kind offer to help with the, uhmm, the situation. Tell him that I took care of everything."

That night at dinner, we picked up where we left off two weeks ago. Eating chicken. But without the tears. I stared at my plate, at the mosquito on the wall, anything to distract myself from the tension that filled the room. I always wanted to make dinnertime a moment where the Heron family fit the house it lived in, pleasant and neat. I chattered about the new sauce at the diner and Della's new hair color. Mamma Rutha tried to act interested, though her eyes were distant. And Father Heron forbade me to do something so whorish as to use hair dye.

"I have to go back to work tonight," I lied, knowing Father Heron despised the docks. "Gotta help paint the back room."

The mosquito flew away.

"I don't know what color, though. Rusty picked it out. I haven't seen it yet."

"I think a shiny yellow would be lovely. Like the belly of that tree frog that lives in the apple tree," Mamma Rutha suddenly said.

"For heaven's sake, Rutha, I don't really think people want to have frogs on their minds when they go to a place to eat. I reckon a nice clean white would do just fine. Clean and simple, tell Rusty that's what a diner should aim for," Father Heron grumbled.

They were actually speaking. We were having dinner conversation over my lie.

"Then how about an orangey red, like that bucket of nails we left out in the rain. I reckon that would suit a barbecue joint," she said, smiling.

Father Heron just grunted and shook his head.

"Cleanliness. All people need to see in a diner is cleanliness. Something you might want to consider, Rutha, next time you walk through that disease trap you call a kitchen."

It was true too. Mamma Rutha never bothered with what she felt were unessential details—like throwing out old food, or washing up dishes. When I worked double shifts at the diner, the dishes would stack in the sink until the whole house smelled sour. If it wasn't alive, then Mamma Rutha didn't notice it. And if it wasn't "man's work" then Father Heron would die before he touched it.

"Well maybe the best color would be a blend of those two. Like a pale peachy rose. Light enough to be clean but still with enough color to look lively," I offered.

Father Heron grew even more disgusted, started to speak, and then decided just to shake his head and continue eating. Mamma Rutha began to hum to herself. "Pleasant and tidy" dinnertime was over. I cleared the table and started walking down the mountain.

Halfway there I met Della, driving her momma's car.

"Boy are we gonna have some fun tonight!" she squealed as she ground the gears, desperately searching for third. "Wanna beer?" She used her teeth to twist off the cap of a bottle.

"No, what's going on at the docks?"

"You know me, I don't plan. I just prepare the way for fate," she said, handing me her beer.

I took a sip and tried not to gag as I swallowed. Beans. Beer always tasted like ice-cold bean soup to me. She laughed at the face I made.

"It takes time to get use to. Maybe you should try wine coolers. Those taste just like Kool-Aid. But with patience and effort, you can train yourself to like beer. My momma started training me the day she bought me my first bra. You need to learn too, because beer and hair are the keys to men! That's some of Momma's wisdom." She laughed as she took an extra-long gulp of beer to show me how it's done.

I took her beer back, tried again, and then gave up. She rolled her eyes at me and laughed.

"Why'd you break up with Carl?" I asked. "I thought he was rich. Your momma must be awfully mad. Bet her wisdom never taught you to break up with a rich man."

"Carl was handsome, had money and everything. But I realized something important. You need to know this too, so you don't make the same mistake," she said seriously. "Poor girls can't ever marry rich men. Ever." She paused to let the impact of her words sink in.

"I know my momma always said, 'Della, you can marry rich as easy as you can poor.' But that just ain't true. How does someone like me, who never had nothing, talk to a man who always had anything he wanted? How do I say to him, 'Carl, I never had a white dress when I was little because if I wore it inside my house it'd turn brown with dirt'? He couldn't see where I had come from, or where I was at. Lord knows I tried to go up to his level. I talked about travel. I read up on new cars. And you know what I learned? Being rich is boring as hell. Nothing to think about, or wish for, or dream. Like us, we may dream about flying off to paradise on a big shiny plane wearing new Calvin Kleins and red sunglasses. But rich people, Mercy, rich people don't dream. They just die at night. Why I would wake up from some wild dream, roll over and tell Carl about it, and he'd just look at me. So I asked him to tell me about his dreams. For a solid week, every morning I'd say, 'What'd you dream last night?' You know what he always said? He shrugged his shoulders and said *nothing*. People like us, Mercy, we live through our dreams. We see things in our dreams that we can never see in our lives. But rich people, they don't have the need like we do. They lay there like a dead person dreaming nothing. And the last thing I want to do is sleep with a dead person." She took another gulp of her beer before tossing it out the window.

"But maybe," I said, "Carl could tell you whether your dreams were true. Like my dreams of the ocean. Ever since I held that seashell to my ear in second grade, I've been dreaming about that ocean. I have a shoe box stuffed with magazine clippings of it. But I still haven't really seen it. Only in my dreams have I heard it, smelled it, or felt it. But a rich man, a man that has seen outside these mountains, he could tell me if my dreams were true. He could tell me whether you can stand next to the ocean, lick your lips, and taste the salt."

"If you are trying to twist me back into dating Carl . . ." she began.

"All I'm saying is maybe he deserved a better chance. I mean he's no Jake. After what Jake did to you, I think sleeping with dead people sounds pretty good."

She grew quiet for a moment, her eyes saddened. "But what if I told you that you had to stay with a man who thought you were crazy for dreaming about that ocean? Who made you feel small for your dreams. Could you do it?" she asked. "Beat me or don't beat me, I just don't think I could stay with that kind of man. You couldn't either."

She was right. I couldn't love a man that made me feel small for my dreams. Or that had never spent a moment searching his mirror to see if he really belonged.

"Well," Della said, laughing, "tonight's not the night for us to be worrying about it all anyway, rich or poor, cute or ugly, we are going to have us a little fun!"

I had my doubts. The docks always felt like a bad high school dance for people too old for high school. It began as the political dream of an old mayor of Crooktop. As the whole world began to shift to other forms of energy, towns built around the coal industry began to worry. There was an election that year, and the election was won or lost on the issue of what was going to happen to Crooktop after coal. Tourism was the proposed solution. And a big part of that solution was the docks. The voters were told that people loved to come to the mountains. But Crooktop lacked one important essential to being a tourist magnet—water. We needed a lake, the mayor said. And the perfect spot was found in an old quarry where the ground had been stripped and blasted so much that a lake was the only thing that could hide the destruction. So there, in between the mountains, a small, muddy lake was born.

The tourists never came. Eventually the docks became known as a place where you could still find people selling their moonshine and pot. Go parking. Blast Lynyrd Skynyrd out of your car. Nice people were warned that the docks was where a rough crowd hung out. Sometimes that was true, but usually it was just young people doing grown-up things and old people that didn't realize they weren't young anymore.

We got out of the car and I stood awkward and stiff while Della looked around, deciding which direction to head in. She blended in perfectly. Looking casual and careless as she scanned the crowd. After four years of high school, I was still unsure of how to be cool. So I did what I felt like doing. I crossed my arms and folded them across my chest—awkward and stiff.

Della pulled me toward a group huddled around a grill. The crowd absorbed her, while I hung on the outskirts. I watched her laughing, flirting, talking up her "theories" on life. They were all watching her too. There was something about Della that you just had to watch. Swinging between dreadfully serious and pitifully shallow, you just couldn't help but like her. Whether she was angry, sad, hurt, or hungry, her glow shined through. If I hadn't loved her so much, I would have envied her. Instead, I just stood in awe.

She slid up to a tall muscular man flipping burgers. Mr. Next-in-line. She smiled at him, and ran her hands through her hair to show off her new highlights. With her attention fully taken, I walked to the end of a dock and lit a cigarette. Normally, I didn't smoke unless I was with Rusty or Della. But I felt how alone I was. When everyone else had hidden themselves in the crowd, they could see my back turned to them. So I smoked to show them that I was just a girl enjoying a cigarette. I wasn't a girl scared to feel alone in the middle of a crowd.

"Gotta light?" a voice asked me. A male voice.

I didn't turn around. My heart pulsed in my toes and I hated myself for feeling all jittery just because I heard a man's voice.

"How do you think this got lit, see anyone else around?" I asked, trying to hide the shake in my voice with brave words.

He stopped suddenly, and I cringed inside. I had wanted to sound like I didn't care that a man walked out to me. But I ended up sounding childish and mean.

"Awright then," he said lowly, more to himself than me, as he began walking away.

"Here," I said, turning around and offering my lighter.

My eyes quickly searched him and I guessed that he wasn't from Crooktop. There were two types of Crooktop boys. Ones that dreamed only of driving coal trucks like their daddies. And ones that didn't care what they did, as long as it didn't have the scent of coal dust on it. I could usually pick either kind out with one glance. The coal boys looked like fresh versions of their daddies. Wearing caps that proudly advertised their future trucking company. Hanging around the trucks, tuning them up and making them shiny. They took cues from their parents and only looked worried when the threat of another strike loomed, or when coal prices began to dive. The other boys, the dreamers, didn't wear a consistent uniform. They were the ones that felt in their bones that they were born for something other than coal. And if you looked closely enough, their faces betrayed their worry. Their fear that even if they were born for something else, coal was all that Crooktop could give them. And as far I could tell, the man walking toward me was neither. He just didn't seem to carry the pride or the worry over coal that all Crooktop boys seemed to be born with.

"Thanks," he said, taking the lighter from my hands.

He faced the last bit of the day's sun. And the burn of it on his skin showed that he was as brown as any white man could be. He stood before me, showing me his skin, his frayed jeans and stained T-shirt, but he didn't speak. I wondered why. Maybe he just wanted to smoke. Or maybe he was disappointed in me, now that he was close.

He tucked the end of his cigarette into a bottle and hurled it into the lake. We watched how far it sailed before plunking into little muddy ripples. He shuffled backwards from the edge of the dock, and I noticed how worn and muddy his shoes were. It was time for him to go. And if I didn't want him to, I was going to have to speak.

I held out my pack of Camels. "Need another?"

He shook his head, still looking out at the water.

"You looking for something?" I asked, trying to sound casual. Trying to be Della.

He nodded. "Fire trout."

Father Heron frequently fished, bringing home rainbow trout and brown trout. And occasionally, Crooktop Baptist would have a fish fry, and the tables would be loaded with catfish, brown trout, and rainbow trout. He didn't look crazy. I *lived* with crazy. But there was no such thing as fire trout.

"You mean rainbow?" I offered. "Those can't be caught in this dirty lake. You gotta go up to the mountain streams, or even down to the riverbottom."

"Huh-uh, I mean fire trout," he said evenly.

"No such thing."

He shrugged his shoulders and stepped up to the edge of the dock again. He moved so close to the water that if I looked at him just from the waist up, I could see water rising out from him, rippling all around him.

"Well, what's a fire trout then anyway?" I asked, my voice trying to make peace, trying to become a thing he wouldn't shrug off. He turned and looked at me. His eyes were a troubled mixture of green and brown, like dark sunflowers floating on green river pools. I held up my pack of Camels again. He took one and I waited.

"You ever hear of foxfire?" he asked, once he was half finished with his cigarette.

I nodded. Foxfire was a strange glow in the woods at night. A pale yellow light that outshone the moon. Some said it was ghosts, my high school biology teacher said it was a fungal reaction on the wood, and Mamma Rutha said it was the soul of the mountain, revealed to a chosen few. Not many people had ever seen it on Crooktop. But I had once when I was thirteen, after the worst thunderstorm I could remember. I hid in my room as the lightning lit up the sky and ripped through the trunks of old, mighty trees. When it was over I looked out my window and saw the glow in the woods. I crept through wet weeds and bur briars until I was standing in front of a twisted hickory

slain by the storm. Its exposed wood glowed. So bright
that I could see the tears shining on Mamma Rutha's face
on the other side of the tree.

"It's the soul of the mountain, Mercy baby. You've seen
its soul," she whispered with reverence.

The sound of his voice when he spoke again was so
even that he seemed quiet, even when he wasn't. It was
like river water. A constant flow that you can forget you're
hearing if you don't pay close attention.

"I was fishin'," he said. "Fell asleep, got woke up by the
light." He paused and kicked a pebble off the end of the
dock. "Light where there ain't supposed to be."

"I've seen it too," I said. "Once, in the woods."

He looked at me again, and I saw the subtle stir of his
eyes. The mixing of the green and brown.

"You touch it?"

"No. You?"

He nodded his head. "Made sure I wasn't dreamin'."

"What'd it feel like?"

"Nothin'. Just rotted wood fallin' in my hand," he
said.

"It wasn't hot?"

"Huh-uh." I had been scared to touch it. The soul of
the mountain should have been hot, the same way that it
looked.

"I always figured it'd burn."

"Nah, it just set in my hand a shinin'," he said, holding
his hand out over the water.

"You keep it?" I asked.

"Dropped it in the water. Lit it up too."

"It still glowed in the water?"

He nodded, "Yup. 'Til an old brown trout ate it."

"A fish ate it?"

He nodded, "A big 'un. Swam up, and ate it all."

"Well, what happened then?"

"Still saw the light," he answered, his voice rising like a swell in the river. "That brown swam away with a belly of fire. Been lookin' for him ever since."

He smiled.

"Hey Trout! Burger's ready, man, c'mon!" someone yelled from the crowd.

He looked over his shoulder and nodded his head.

"Thanks for the smoke."

"No problem," I called out as he walked away. My cigarette had turned into a solid row of gray ash. I had forgotten to dust it. *He must think I am such a child*, I thought. I turned and looked one last time into the water. I saw a glimmer of my own reflection, and a memory of flowered eyes. But no fire trout.

Chapter IV

I dreamed of an ocean. Surrounded by a shore that rose like a wet desert in slopes and dunes. I stared down into a pool that cradled shells, my childhood idols. Their images were carved into soaps that sat dusty on the back of our toilet. How my dirty hands had ached to wash with a pink shell. Once, overcome with temptation, I held one. Too scared to lather it, my tongue darted out to lick it and the taste of cheap perfume filled my mouth. Hearing Father Heron approach, I threw the soap back and ran away.

But in my dream, I didn't lust for the shells. I only wanted to feel the water all around me. I fell forward and sank low. The pool's bottom was cold and full of shadows. The slippery snake wrapped itself around me, squeezing the air from my body. I woke up gasping for air.

For years the ocean had visited me in my dreams. Sometimes violent. Sometimes glassy smooth. That morning, his words haunted me. *Light where there ain't supposed to be.* It was like my ocean. Water where there shouldn't be water. It was in my mind, drowning my dreams.

I heard the shower cut off and knew that it was my turn. Father Heron always took his shower first on Sundays, to give him extra time to prepare for the service. He was a greeter at church. He stood on the front porch to shake hands and pass out bulletins. If visitors raised their hands when the preacher asked them to, then Father Heron would walk to them and hand them a copy of the church's mission statement, a book of matches with "First Baptist Crooktop" printed on it, and a paper copy of the Gospel of John. He always woke up early on Sundays, to organize his little piles of paper and matches.

"Young lady, you will not straggle into church today," Father Heron called through my closed door. His God had never promised *I am with you always.* He only visited Crooktop from the hour of eleven to noon on Sundays. And if I took the time to shave my legs in the shower, he might just disappear. Mamma Rutha always said that God would meet me anytime, any place that I would make myself available. Which was a good thing for her too, since Father Heron demanded she quit church after her incident over the withered fig. The preacher had been talking about how Jesus had pointed at a fig tree and told it that it would never bear fruit again. And how the next day the disciples found that fig tree withered away. As the preacher described how a lush green tree was disfigured into a dry, brown, worthless plant, and how at any minute one word from God could wither everything around us, Mamma Rutha's sobs broke through. Thinking she was having a moment of great spirituality, the preacher said, "Sister Rutha, do you have a word from the Lord?"

Mamma Rutha looked up, eyes open and sobbed, "*On the day you were born you were not washed in water to cleanse you, nor wrapped in cloths. You were thrown out into the open field. And when I passed by you, and saw you struggling in your own blood, I said to you, Live! Yes, I said to you in your blood, Live!*"

Kids covered their giggling mouths and grown-ups coughed to hide theirs. Father Heron's face turned purple with anger. Mine turned purple with shame. The preacher didn't know whether to laugh or shout. He didn't know she was Crazy Rutha, he was too new.

He wiped his brow with his sleeve and said, "Yes Sister Rutha, you're right. There's more to God than wrath. Those scriptures from Ezekiel show us some powerful mercy too. We all need to pray for such mercy." Then he quickly moved on to the next verse.

Father Heron was happy to leave Mamma Rutha at home, but he wasn't willing to let me stay behind too. He didn't want to be the only deacon with a pagan family. So every Sunday we were there together, dressed up on the third pew. A nice picture.

I pulled myself out of bed and into the shower. I wanted to wait longer, to let more hot water build up, but I knew better than to push Father Heron on Sundays. After my shower I picked out a dress. One of my three church dresses. Since one dress had to be worn twice in a month, I had a careful rotation system, to make sure that it wasn't the same one month after month. My closet wasn't empty. But most of my clothes were grubby diner clothes spotted with barbecue stains and still smelling like smoke. Since I had been working more after graduation I bought that third dress. The rest of the money I made went to gas for Della's mom's car, my girl stuff—since I would rather die than write "tampons," "Soft and Dri deodorant," and "Plum Passion lipstick" on Father Heron's grocery list—and a jelly jar hidden in the corner of my closet. So far that jelly jar had all of forty-three dollars in it. Pretty good considering my average tip was somewhere between zero and ninety-nine cents. There was an unspoken code on Crooktop that tips should never be paper money. If someone left me a dollar, I knew that they were an outsider.

Every other Friday people could hear me rattling with change as I walked down to the Miners' Credit Union to trade the coins in for bills. I loved having that money. I loved being able to walk into the Valley Pharmacy and look at all the different colors of lipsticks and know that I could buy forty-three dollars' worth. I never did. I always stuck with Plum Passion, but if I ever wanted to try Burnt Sunset I knew that I could.

I wasn't really sure what I was saving that money for. I knew that I'd be old or dead before it would be enough for college, or a car. I guess I just liked seeing that glass jar stuffed with thin green paper knowing that it was mine. My work earned it. My thriftiness saved it. My closet hid it. It was my jelly jar secret.

I pushed some clothes back over the jelly jar and put my dress on. It was the new one. I had gotten it on sale at Ima's Fashion Boutique, the only dress shop in the valley.

It was a warm dusty rose. The kind that was cut just below the knee and swirled when I spun around. And it made my skin just glow, Della had said. With that compliment, and the half-off price tag, I took sixteen dollars from my jelly jar. I didn't have any shoes that looked right with it, so I put on a little extra lipstick—to keep people's attention on my face and off my feet. I looked at myself in the mirror. *Della is right*, I thought, *my hair is boring.* Long straight and brown. But highlights? Or a cut? It just seemed so drastic. My figure was boring too. By the time Della was sixteen she was bursting out of her shirt and amply filling the seat of her jeans. But not me. I had the head of an eighteen-year-old, stuck on the body of an overly tall twelve-year-old. Della always laughed when I said that.

"You're slender and graceful," she would say. "Besides, it's pretty darn hard to look classy with boobs up to your neck. And you're too classy for big boobs." Looking in the mirror that morning, I preferred to be a little less classy.

Occasionally, during the week Father Heron and I could have a strained conversation about the garden, or work. But never on Sundays. We would ride listening only to the gospel music station. If his eye caught a glaring sin on the way, he would point it out to me.

"See that Sabbath-breaker mowing his lawn?" he would ask.

Or if he saw people headed over the mountain to the new Methodist church he would shake his head and mutter, "Bunch of sprinkling fools. Giving fake baptisms. I'd see you dead, Mercy, 'fore I'd see you a Methodist." Then he'd eye me suspiciously, as though I might secretly be a Methodist.

At church Father Heron's attention would be turned to his matches, papers, and handshaking. I was finally alone. There was no crazy grandmother to protect, no black-eyed grandfather to please. It was just me with my heart full of questions and doubts as I scanned the altar. With my heart full of hope.

I liked the new preacher, Preacher Grey. He wasn't as loud as some of the others had been. He seemed smarter too. He didn't just shout one phrase over and over, and tell everybody to say Amen. You could tell that he thought about his sermons in advance, what he was going to say, what he wanted you to hear. He seemed to know how to survive in a small church like this too. The first Sunday he was here, he invited Mrs. Esther out to lunch. Mrs. Esther was the ninety-one-year-old widow of the man that founded the church, and she held the deed to the land it sat on. If she was on the new preacher's side, it didn't matter who wasn't.

That Sunday the Lord's Supper was served. Methodists called it "communion," but at First Baptist Crooktop it was strictly *the Lord's Supper*. As the deacons filed across the front of the church to serve the members stale crackers, I noticed how much alike they all looked. All graying and stout. With somber looks on their faces. Father Heron stood next to the chair of the deacons, Sheriff Barnes. You could always see the bulge of a pistol beneath the sheriff's suit jacket.

"It's a sad day when the law can't be left behind at the door," he would shake his head and say, "but the sin of man doesn't respect the house of God, so you never know when you might need me to be Sheriff Barnes, instead of Chairman Deacon Barnes."

When he said that, women got goose bumps, children stared at him with eyes they reserved for heroes, and men became envious. I wanted to laugh. Anybody that read the *Crooked Top Herald* crime section would know that the most action the sheriff ever got was an occasional pot bust. And according to Della and the gang that hung around the docks even those reports weren't always real, but were cover-ups for old vendettas and dirty political tricks.

"The law on Crooktop ain't the Constitution, or the Congress, or even the governor," Della would say. "It's just homecooking, whatever it needs to be within these mountains to serve the powers that be. And Sheriff Barnes is the master chef."

I never bought it. Sheriff Barnes was one of the nicest men I knew. He called me Miss Mercy, had a warm smile and a hearty deep laugh. I couldn't help but smile when I was around him. He reminded me of a storybook grandpa. The opposite of the real one I knew. Besides, pot could be found any night down at the docks, so those crime reports couldn't be that far-fetched. I figured Della's "homecooking" theory was one filled with more bang than truth.

I took my stale cracker and ate it. Then drank my hot, sour grape juice, being careful not to spill it on my new dress. We rose to sing "Blessed Be the Tie That Binds" and then began filing out. I shook Preacher Grey's hand and told him I enjoyed the sermon. He looked tired and I wondered if it was draining to be filled with the Spirit. To be God's mouthpiece. His wife stood next to him, dutifully shaking hands too. She looked small standing there. Slightly behind him, stretching her thin hand out to mine. Her husband spent his week praying over and blessing us. I wondered who prayed for her.

"Lord bless you, Mercy, you tell your Mamma Rutha I said hello now," she said. During the three weeks she had been there she had never forgotten my name. And she knew about my Mamma Rutha too. But I still didn't know her name. Not many of us at church did. She was just "Preacher's wife" to everybody.

I waved to Father Heron, got a change of clothes out of the truck, and started walking to the diner.

"Running a little late," Rusty said when I walked in.

"Sorry, Lord's Supper today."

He nodded, mumbling something about not making a habit of it.

"New dress?"

"Yep," I replied, praying he wouldn't think I was wearing it for him.

"Pretty. All swirly too—like that Merlin Munroe. You should wear it today. Bet you'd make good tips."

"And I'd have to use 'em to buy a new dress too with all the stains I'd get on it," I replied as I headed to the bathroom to change.

Somewhere that day between sweet teas and pulled platters the lunch crowd disappeared, leaving me with a pocketful of change. I was wiping down tables when I heard Rusty exclaim, "Well well, Miss Della DeMar!" in his best French accent. I grinned to myself, knowing how bad she hated that. New teachers at school would always try to do the same, slurring a "dur" and drawing out a "mah."

"It's day-mar," she would always say, "like a cross between a mon-*day* and a *Mars* bar."

"Well hello there, Mr. Rusty Nail," I heard her reply
before breezing past him and plopping herself down in
the booth I was cleaning.

"You have a good time last night?" she asked.

"Mhmm. You find a replacement for Carl?"

"Found some potential. No sure bets, but some definite
potential," she replied. "You sure were quiet last night on
the way home. Weren't mad or nothing, were you?"

"Just tired I guess."

"What was the matter, Trout got your tongue?" she
asked, smiling.

I could feel heat burning my face and filling my ears.
Had he said something about me? I focused all my attention on a spot of dried barbecue stuck on the table.

"No reason to be as sour as a yellow SweetTart, Mercy.
You know I'm kidding. Besides, you're too good for Trout.
He's just a mater migrant."

Mater migrants were people that traveled every summer to work the tomato and strawberry crops of the
mountains' riverbottom lands. Most of them were Mexicans without green cards. They were a despised people
in Crooktop. Living in tents and pop-up campers around
the fields they worked. Blistering their hands and warping
their backs for a pitiful wage and all the maters they could
eat. There were always a few white mater migrants. Men
with bright red palms. Hands stained with the juice of the
fruits they picked, branding them a lower class than the
rest of Crooktop.

"Yep, those mater migrants," Della continued, "those

are love-'em-and-leave-'em men, you know. Here today, gone by October."

I tried to change the subject. "You get that job at the new Ben Franklin?"

"Uh-huh, gotta start tonight. I get ten percent off on makeup too. My boss, though, he's gonna need to be tamed. You oughta come see me later tonight. I'll sneak you a Coke."

I told her I might, but I knew that I wouldn't. Sunday night was Heron yard night. After Father Heron came home from church and I got home from the diner we would weed the gardens, harvest Father Heron's, and sometimes lightly prune the peonies—just to keep them healthy, not to "force" them into our idea of what the bush should look like. It was our only positive tradition. Mamma Rutha usually worked in her garden. Since we ate from Father Heron's I focused most of my energy on it. I always began with the potatoes. To see the love knots they made as they grew. Yellow vines twisted beneath thick green leaves. Mamma Rutha caught me pulling them when I was little and told me I was breaking the potato's heart, by untwisting its love knots.

I never worked with gloves on. Like Mamma Rutha I preferred to just sink my hands down into that rich mountain earth. Liking the gritty feel of it beneath my nails. I was more cautious working in the corn, where the packsaddles lived. Fat green worms blending in with the stalks and stinging worse than bees. But my favorite was always the tomatoes. Breathing that heavy green scent was my weekly tonic. I secured the ties that held them to their stakes, letting their fuzzy leaves prickle my skin.

We never talked much while we worked, other than "hand me that hoe" and "have you seen the size of those turnips?" But it was as close as the three of us ever came to complete harmony. Once the need for words was gone, the clank of the hoe and shovel said it all.

That night I lingered over the tomatoes. Wondered if the plant called to the mater migrants, the way it did me. If I were going to be a crop worker, I'd want to be a mater migrant, I thought. I watched Mamma Rutha and Father Heron. One working passionately, the other fiercely. *This is how it will always be*, I told myself. Pig-filled weeks, church and dirt-filled Sundays. Holding my breath around Father Heron, and over Mamma Rutha. I wanted something more. Something that stayed silent and unnamed in my heart. And without a name to call it, I knew it would never come.

Chapter V

I was eager for fall, when everything would smell better and feel more alive even as it started to die. Kind of like the mountain's last hurrah, before a long gray winter. But the coming season change also filled me with dread, or maybe desperation. For as long as I could remember, fall signaled not only the end of heat, but a change of pace and scenery as a new school year began. But that year my routine would stay the exact same. All the days of my life seemed to stretch out before me in one long, straight path. I was only eighteen years old, but that path made my feet ache.

I was grateful when the last August weekend brought rain, a sneak peak of the coming cooler weather. It wasn't an afternoon cloudburst or an evening storm, but a good steady rain. A potato-making rain, Mamma Rutha would call it. And though I hadn't brought an umbrella to work, I was still determined to walk to the Miners' Credit Union before five. I was almost a rich woman. My jelly jar was crammed with over a hundred dollars, and I was going to celebrate my wealth. Perhaps buy some new jeans. Some nice ones, maybe even Calvins. I wanted jeans that would hug my hips in the right places, making me seem like I had more curves than a straight sapling. Girls with money used to wear those kinds of jeans to school, driving the boys mad. The rest of us wore the cheap kind. Jeans made straight and square that made our bodies look straight and square, or even worse, straight, square, and wide. But I was close to buying some jelly jar jeans, so close that I could almost feel them cinching in my waist and shaping my hips as I headed out the diner door.

The rain surprised me. It was colder and wetter than I had expected. The drops more forceful. Sane people hid indoors. And I wondered about the sight I must have made. *Mercy Heron's as crazy as her grandma Rutha*, they would say. *Must run in the family*, they would laugh. They were probably right too. But if that August rain was what crazy felt like, then I was learning what Mamma Rutha had always known. Sometimes crazy is just the best choice.

And then there was someone else. Walking slowly toward me, head down, clothes soaked. I blinked hard in the rain, trying to see through the water. But the gray and silver masked everything, until I saw the red. Stubborn stains that even a heavy rain couldn't cleanse. I knew then that it was him.

I peered through the rain. Liking his hair twisting into wet loose ringlets. His unshaven face. The water that dripped off the tips of his ears. Liking the way he walked so slowly, as though it were a sunny spring morning.

"Excuse me, miss?" a lady called to me as I followed him into the Credit Union. "Miss, you're dripping all over our floors," she whined.

"Oh. Sorry. I forgot my umbrella today," I replied, wondering if he had noticed me, or if he even remembered me.

"Mhmm," she clucked. "Well, if you got business here, hurry it up before you water-spot the new rug."

As I watched her count out each nickel and dime, he left. I had planned what I would say when he spoke to me, how cool and easy I would be. *Hey there yourself*, or *Oh yeah, now I remember, I met you at the docks*. I left the Credit Union disappointed that I didn't get my chance.

But there he was again. Standing under the awning of the Credit Union. His eyes flashing recognition as the rain washed away my cool speeches. I stood there and looked back. My hair uncombed and tangled, my barbecue-stained clothes clinging to my wet skin. I was a wreck. Even by a mater migrant's standards.

"It's a mess out here," I said.

"Sure is."

"Guess it washes the coal dust out, though," I said. "Makes everything look all shiny again."

He nodded, his gaze falling to the puddle I was standing in.

"I'm soaked." I laughed, tossing my hands in the air.

"Look like you're standin' on a mirror."

I looked at my feet, and the silver pool that was growing around them. I could see my knees reflected in it.

"Ought not break it then, huh? That'd be seven years of bad luck."

"You trust in all that?" he asked, his voice betraying a note of surprise. I looked at the ground again and saw glassy pools all around us, like the windows of heaven had been broken.

"No. Don't understand it enough to believe in it. Don't see how black cats, ladders, or mirrors are supposed to change my life." He nodded his head in response, but I couldn't tell whether he agreed with me or not.

"You scared to be on these mirrors?" I asked.

"Nah. Ain't got nothin' to lose."

"Seven years of bad luck would seem like a loss to me." I laughed. He watched me laugh, and smiled back.

"Preacher once talked about seven years of famine. And then seven years of feast. Way I figure it, my famine's been goin' on so long, ain't no use in waitin' for the feast. And if the feast ain't comin', no broke mirror's gonna hurt me."

I knew of the feasts and the famines. Once in church all of the children had to march forward to say who we wanted to meet the most when we got to heaven. After a row of Jesus answers, I said Joseph. Not the most famous Joseph in the Bible, not the Joseph that was Mary's husband. But Joseph the dream interpreter. The man in the colorful coat that understood dreams and prophesized of famines and feasts. I wanted to ask him why I was beginning to dream of a crushing body of water that I had never seen.

"You're saying a curse can't hurt an already cursed person," I said.

He nodded. "I broke one big ol' mirror a long time ago. Reckon I can do what I want now. Can't put that mirror back whole again. There's no changin' my luck, but at least I'm free."

"Free to be a mater migrant?" I asked, wishing I had said "field hand" or "crop worker" instead. He held his hands palms up and looked at them.

There was a long silence, and I began to feel a deeper chill from the rain. He looked back up.

"Free to quit waitin' on the feast. And let any good thing shake me up, no matter how small."

"Like the fire trout?" I asked.

He smiled then. "That's right. Like seein' a fire trout and hopin' every day to get to see it again. Wanna see where he was?"

I didn't have to answer yes. There were some things that even the rain couldn't hide.

Inside his truck, I guessed that it was his home. Dirty clothes were piled around cans of Skoal that lay on the floorboard. Fishing line and little packets of feathers and animal fur were scattered on the seat. The air was filled with heavy, damp scents. The sweat and tomatoes of his dirty clothes, the yeast of warm beer, the wintergreen of Skoal, and the rain sitting on our skin. The vinyl of the seats was ripped in several places, exposing the wires that lay beneath. And there was a patch of rust growing in the floorboard through which I saw flashing bits of the road beneath. Realizing that our only conversation had skipped proper introductions, I asked him if his name was really Trout. He told me it was, since it was the only name he could remember being called.

"So it's not your birth name?" I asked.

"Huh-uh," he said. "I didn't ever get one of 'em."

"How could somebody not have a birth name?"

"If they got a young momma, I reckon. Mine's fourteen when she had me. And she was dead set against bringin' me into the world a bastard. She told my daddy that I was gonna have his name whether I was a girl or a boy and he'd better go on and claim me and marry her. So while I was in her belly they called me Earnest Grover Price. Good thing I was a boy, huh? Can't hardly see a girl being called Earnest Grover," he said, laughing. "But ol' Earnie ran off with Momma's sister, and set out for California to try and be in pictures. After that, Pap Red, man that lived next door, said she'd cuss anybody that'd say my daddy's name around her. She hollered that he's worse than dead to her. Swore he'd never even lived to her. But for all her hollerin' she couldn't keep his baby from comin'. Once I did, I didn't have a daddy's name to take. I'm the bastard son of a man that ain't ever lived. They all called me 'baby' for a while, and then 'boy.' Then one day at a river baptism, Pap Red said I started walkin' out in the river. Preacher saw me, and I reckon he thought I was bein' called to baptism. He started hollerin' about how even a child knows the curse of sin enough to fear hell and started yellin' for me to let the Holy Ghost carry me through the water to joy. I waded out a little ways to a pool, no higher than my knees. Then I reached right down and scooped up a little rainbow in my hands. Even Preacher was shocked at me, a little tike, scoopin' up a trout with my bare paws. That day on, they all called me Trout. Trout Price. It's the only one I know, so I reckon it's my name, even if my momma didn't give it to me," he said, studying my reaction.

"Pap Red took me home and cooked that rainbow up for me. Made me eat it all too. Eyes, brains, everything but the chokin' bones. He said the trout chose me, had claimed me. And I had to eat it all so I could think like one, so that I could see the things they see. Worked too. Was the best thing anybody ever done for me."

Maybe he was crazy after all. I had expected to hear that his name was John or Bob and that his friends just called him Trout. But instead I learned that the man who spoke of fire trout, feasts, famines, and broken mirrors *believed he was part trout.*

"How about you, what's your name?" he asked.

"I'm Mercy. Just plain ol' Mercy Heron. And that's my birth name. Though while I was in my momma's belly it was Naomi. She had wanted to call me Naomi, but my Father Heron refused. Said I shouldn't be named after a lady in the Bible when I was born of sin."

He looked at me, and I could tell he didn't quite understand, but was hesitant to ask.

"I'm a bastard too," I said, only half laughing. "Just like your momma wouldn't give you your daddy's name, my Father Heron wouldn't let me have a Bible name, or take my daddy's last name. So it was Mercy Heron."

As he pulled his truck off the road, he joked, "Just a couple a bastards ain't we, on our way to hunt the fire trout."

It was hard for me to smile, even though a great deal of people in my mountains were bastards. In a part of the world where the closest movie theater, skating rink, or bowling alley was at least two hours away, dating for most teens meant having sex. There was little else to do to fight the boredom. But it was still hard for me to grin and call myself a bastard, the insult reserved for despised, worthless people. He must have sensed that too, because he asked me if I liked my name.

"What do you mean? It's my name. It's just what people call me, it's not anything to like or dislike," I said. I could tell he disagreed.

"When a momma picks one word, out of all them words out there, it means somethin'. Somethin' near holy. I ain't got that kind of name. My momma didn't pick a word for me. It had to pick me. I reckon luck traded me up."

"Yep, I think Trout's better than Earnest Grover," I said.

"Maybe you was traded down."

"How?" I asked.

"Your momma chose a word. And maybe that word's what fits you. But it didn't fit your grandpa so he traded you down. To Mercy. 'Cause it's what he figured suits a bastard."

I looked away. Staring out the truck windows at anything that couldn't see my emotion.

"Mercy's a good name. But maybe it ain't your holy name," he said. "And a name's like walkin' shoes, if it don't fit, it's gonna blister."

I followed behind him while he held back briars and branches for me to pass through, wondering what he expected me to do, just tell people to start calling me Naomi? For the first time, I focused on my name. I whispered it to myself and listened to the way it sounded. Did it mark me as a child of sin? Is that why Mamma Rutha had never called me Mercy, but always Mercy baby? Would being called Naomi feel holy? It couldn't melt my cages. My cages were born of a birth, murder, and a locked door. Letters weren't strong enough to build those cages. Letters weren't strong enough to trade me down to where I was. *Were they?*

I heard the creek before I saw it. The rain had slowed to a misty drizzle, and little of it touched us beneath the shelter of the woods. He sat on a rock and motioned for me to join him.

"That's where light was comin' out," he whispered. "And I dropped it in the water here, watched that brown swim up and eat it."

The mood of excitement that had swept over him at the docks when he spoke of the fire trout didn't come. Instead he was quiet, almost reverent. We sat for a long time, neither of us speaking, watching the water. I felt privileged. He had taken me to the place where the fire trout was born. And for the moments I sat on that rock staring into the water I was a believer, *the fire trout was real.*

It gets dark more quickly in the woods. As though there are two sunsets. The first when the light becomes too weak to pierce through the leaves. The second when the sun actually disappears for the night. Soon I could only sense the heat off of his body, I couldn't see him.

"Say it," I whispered.

"What?"

"My holy name. I just want to hear what it sounds like," I said, thankful he couldn't see that my face was hot with the flush of blood.

"Naomi," he said, in a voice that washed over me as though he were holding me down in that stream. "Naomi," he whispered, his mouth brushing my ear. He was so close that I was sure I could smell the scent of crushed tomato vines.

I felt dizzy. Emotions swept through me so hot and jumbled I couldn't even name them. I tried not to cry, but tears spilled from my eyes. His arms slipped around me as I struggled for control. But it was no use. He had unbound me, and I ached to show him more of my bruises.

Later that night, in the safety of my bed, I wondered about my flood of tears. I whispered *Naomi* to myself in the dark. And then I knew. It wasn't the name that made me cry. It was the man who whispered it. It was the way he said it. Like it meant something.

Chapter VI

I broke three glasses at work. Spilled one pitcher of tea and turned my new apron red with barbecue. I kept hearing it. The word he spoke to me. Five little letters that sounded so different when he spoke them. Like a whole new word. I kept smelling him. The smell of those crushed tomato vines. My skin kept feeling him. The graze of his lips across my ear. My eyes saw him everywhere. In the tomato that I sliced for a sandwich. In the stain of barbecue that spilled over my hands. In the bathroom mirror that was slightly cracked at the corner.

I needed Della. I could always count on her to distract me. She came to see me that day at work, with a soft new crinkle in her hair.

"How's Ben Franklin?" I asked her as I filled her tea

glass with beer when no one was watching. She tossed a lemon in it to complete the disguise.

"Wonderful," she said, grinning. "I'm in love with Mr. Ben himself. He's perfect. Steady but with a wild streak, stable but still exciting, and cute, of course."

"What's his name?"

"Well, in front of the other employees it's Sir. When it's just the two of us it's Randy, though sometimes I still call him Sir, you know?" She winked. "But I'll tell you one thing, I am tired of having to drive down to the damn docks to do it."

Della was an expert on sex. And she knew more than any book could teach, because Della earned her knowledge the hard way—through old fashioned hands-on experience. My first week in high school she told me more about men in fifteen minutes than I had learned in fourteen years with my grandparents. And besides being a general expert on the subject, Della also considered herself my teacher. Knowing that if she didn't teach me nobody else would, she felt it her duty to inform me of all the details of what she called "the magic."

"The magic is wonderful, Mercy," she would tell me. "It's one of the only things in the world in which the woman is totally powerful. We can cast our spell over a man and make him do more tricks than any white rabbit in a hat."

I always listened, but I secretly believed that Della's powerful magic was a spell that only she could cast. There was nothing magical about me.

"Why don't you go to his house, I mean, he has one doesn't he? He *is* the manager."

"That's where his wife is," she whispered, leaning forward.

"Married! Della DeMar what in the hell are you thinking?" I shouted.

"SHHH!" she said. " She's practically *forcing* us to have an affair. She treats him just awful. Spends all of his money on her eighteen cats. She feeds them steak and she won't even let Randy sleep in her bed. No room for him and all the cats. Besides, he's good to me. I told him about a dream I had, and, you are gonna die when you hear this, Mercy," she said, leaning forward, "he had the *same* dream. The same one on the same night. He wasn't lying either. I can smell lies on the breath of men, and he wasn't lying."

"Nothing's as dangerous as a woman who knows the name of her husband's lover," I said.

She stared at the table and twisted her napkin. "I know it may be dangerous. And I know it sounds real sinful to a deacon's granddaughter. But I reckon I *am* sinful, Mercy. I know the way people talk about me. So why stop and care about what they say now? If my love for this man is some real bad sin, it's just because it comes from my black heart. But I found a man that dreams my dreams, a man that satisfies me, not my mind or even my body, but satisfies me right here," she said, placing her hand on her chest.

I couldn't help but smile. And I told her that Randy was lucky that she dished out love the way grandmas are supposed to dish out oatmeal. She had dished it out to the shy and scared Mercy Heron she found hugging a brick wall outside of the high school, to the old blind dog she adopted, to her mother that had tried to swallow her whole, and now to this tortured husband.

She finished her beer and told me about her new perm and I told her about the jelly jar jeans I was going to buy. Sitting there with her I felt like an invisible thread was sewing me together again. I felt like the old Mercy Heron. And then she unraveled me all over again.

"You remember that mater migrant, Trout?" she asked me, carefully eyeing my reaction. "He is one crazy man."

"Really?" I shrugged, doing my best to hide my interest. I was scared that he had told her about our walk in the woods. I had never told Della about the name I was supposed to have had. And I couldn't bring myself to describe how it felt to hear him say it.

"Randy's wife insisted that he bathe all them cats last night, so I went down to the docks to hang out," she said. "Anyway, we were all sitting around when Trout walks up. Daryl sort of knew him, so Trout sat down with us. Pretty soon Daryl starts complaining how there's nothing to do here. And Trout told him he just didn't know his mountain. Daryl got a little smart, and said, 'You mean the way you know maters?' And Trout didn't say anything. I felt bad for him too, 'cause he seemed sad after Daryl said that. So I suggested that we should all name one Crooktop thrill that other people might not know about. Daryl said, 'I *would* say laying with Della DeMar, but everybody already knows about that.' He can be such an ass. I can't believe I ever dated him. Then Trish said Daryl's daddy's pot patch. I said stealing makeup out of the drugstore. As long as you unwrap it before you put it in your pocket, the clerk can't be sure it's not really yours."

"But why'd you say Trout was crazy?" I asked, trying to focus her. "What did he say?" I hoped that he hadn't shared the secret of the fire trout with them, like he had with me.

"Nothing for a while. It was his turn, but he just sat there. Daryl got after him, asking him what Crooktop thrill he knew about if he knew our mountain so well, and telling him that mater women didn't count. All the sudden Trout looked up and said, 'I guess it'd be holdin' death but not dyin'.' Just like that, all low and quiet. It gave me the shivers. Daryl asked him what the hell he was talking about. And Trout told him you could hold death and not die on Crooktop. Sure we were drunk, but it was strange. Daryl said he didn't believe him. Thought Trout was stoned out of his mind and talking nonsense. So Trout said he'd show him if he wanted. Before I knew it, me and Trish and Daryl were all piled into the bed of Trout's truck, heading off into the night."

"Where did he take you?" I asked, feeling like I was about to learn something big.

"A place like none other. He was right. There's a place on Crooktop where people hold death but don't die."

"Well, tell me," I said, growing impatient. "Where did you go?"

"It was dark outside," she continued. "But I was sober enough to know we weren't on a real road. He was driving straight enough, but the three of us back there were getting tossed every which way. Trish was starting to cry and Daryl said he was gonna get sick. We had to hold our hands up over our face, to keep branches from smacking us. Trish cried out that she wanted to go home. Then Daryl hollered up at Trout to stop the truck, but Trout wouldn't, he just kept on driving into the trees. I was covering my face with my hands, when all of the sudden I saw light flashing between my fingers. Then everything grew still, and I heard it. My skin began to crawl and Trish started screaming."

"What was it?" I asked.

"People moaning and wailing. Some laughing. Some shouting. It was like every noise in the world, all mixed up together. Light was pouring out the doors of a little shack in the woods. And I swear, Mercy, that building was moving. It was smaller than your house and the whole thing seemed to breathe. Inhaling and exhaling, shaking with its noise."

"Where were you?"

"I will never be able to tell you. If I had a thousand years to figure that out, I couldn't find my way back there. It was like trees were growing out the side of the building, like trees were growing on it. We got out of the truck and Trish screamed that they had better take her home. She was crying and saying how her daddy would get them good if they didn't take her home."

"Didn't you want to leave too?" I asked her, noticing how flushed her face was becoming.

"Don't get me wrong, Mercy, I was scared to death. Them people, they were screaming like they were dying. But I couldn't move. All I could do is stand there and look at that shack."

"What'd Trout do?" I asked.

"He was like me. Standing there watching it. Daryl asked him how he found that place. 'Just did,' he said. Like we were the strange ones for not knowing it was there."

"Did he tell you what was inside?"

"He showed me," she said, her eyes growing wide. "I

told Trish to lock herself in the truck and we walked towards it. I knew I shouldn't. But I couldn't stop myself. My feet just kept carrying me closer, and I figured finding out what was in there just might be worth my life. I was so scared I don't see how I was standing. I had one hand on Trout's arm and another on Daryl. Kind of funny now that I think about it. A few minutes earlier I was thinking Trout was going to kill us all. And then later I was grabbing on to him for protection. At first all I saw was the doors. Somebody had carved crosses into 'em, and they were open wide. Then I started to hear this thumping noise. Boom. Boom. Boom. Just like that," she said tapping her hand on the diner table. "Boom. Boom. Boom."

"What was it?" I asked.

"I didn't know. I thought somebody might be chopping them people up in there, you know. Boom. Boom. Boom. And as I got a little closer I heard the clicking noise. Like a thousand woodpeckers were hammering away inside there. I felt like running but I was right in front of that shack. And I saw it all." She stopped to catch her breath.

"Them people were crazy. Hollering and screaming and twitching. And that thumping noise, that was them jumping. Boom. Boom. Up and down. Moaning like they were in such pain. I watched them but I couldn't for the life of me figure out what was happening to them. Nobody was touching them."

"People don't just scream out over nothing," I said.

"That's what I thought. And I couldn't find what that clicking noise was. 'Til I saw 'em crawling all around. In between their legs as they jumped. Over the pews. Twisted around their arms. And they weren't woodpeckers."

"What?" I asked her.

"Rattlers. Big ones too and their babies. That shack was a church. And them people were snake handlers."

It was a mountain myth, spoken of in whispers. People that believed they were ordered by God to hold poisonous snakes as a testament to their faith. Della's story had the effect she had aimed for. I was amazed that there was a place like that on Crooktop. And that a stranger would be the one to know of it.

"I hope you got outta there fast," I told her. "One bite from one of 'em and you're dead."

"I wanted to. But Trout started walking into the church. I grabbed hold of his arm to try and stop him, and he pushed my hand off. You should of seen him, Mercy. Imagine a man walking into a pit of rattlers surrounded by people dancing with the Holy Ghost."

"What happened to him?" I asked, trying not to sound too eager.

"The people never even saw him. They were too busy jumping up and down and hollering. The preacher was standing up front, a Bible in one hand and a thick snake in the other. Trout walked up to him and took it right out of the preacher's hand. Then he turned to me and Daryl, calm as he could be. He held it up, its tail just rattling away in his hands, and he looked at Daryl and smiled. He was holding death, and he was crazy as a man ever was. He makes your Mamma Rutha look sane."

Chapter VII

*P*reacher Grey's sermon was about heaven. A topic that disappointed many in the congregation. Most people enjoyed a good hellfire sermon much more than one about heaven. But I liked those sermons, though I could never really understand them. About streets of gold and a gate of pearl. What did all that have to do with happiness? Beauty didn't guarantee peace, Della was proof of that. But as I watched the preacher's face glow and listened to his voice break with emotion as he described it all, I knew that to him, it was everything.

I thought about the snake handlers. How shocked everyone around me would be to learn of it. If Father Heron thought Methodists were the devil's tool, I could only imagine what he'd think of the snake handlers.

Nobody went forward during the invitation. They

always did after the hell sermons. It was easier to run from hell than it was to run toward heaven. And when nobody went forward, the preacher always looked sad. Like he had failed. Sometimes I was tempted to go forward and make up a need, just to make him feel better.

I was on my way to the diner after church when I saw the truck. It was an old brown Ford, with worn tires, rust spots on the door, a dented bumper, and a missing tailgate. It was the type of truck that should have been retired years ago, but since it wasn't, had pledged itself to drive to the death. He was sitting in the back, his legs swinging out where the tailgate should have been, looking up the road that I was walking down.

"Hopin' I'd find you here," he said.

"What are you up to?" I asked.

"You gonna work?" he asked, looking at the apron I was clutching.

I told him I had to. That my boss was mean and that he'd throw a fit if I didn't show up. I told him that there was nobody that could cover my shift, and that Sunday was the diner's busiest day. And I told myself that I didn't really know this man. Then I hopped in his truck to go fishing. There were some things I couldn't talk myself out of. Trout Price was one of them.

He drove toward six and twenty mile holler. It was one of nature's strongholds, where she was winning the war against man. The people that lived up there were primitive too. Primitive at least in the eyes of the rest of Crooktop because they were so poor. *That's what happens when cousins marry cousins*, Father Heron would grumble about the six and twenty milers. But they took care of their own.

Growing and hunting for most of their own food. Coming
down the mountain only if they wanted to attend school,
or sell pot at the docks. The six and twenty mile boys were
valued by the coaches and ignored by the teachers. They
were bigger than most men, with well-ripened muscles.
The girls rarely finished high school before disappearing
back up the holler with swollen bellies. On the first day
of school the line for the free government lunch program
was always joked to be six and twenty miles long, an un-
fair statement since nearly half of the school qualified for
free lunch and were considered poor by any outsider's
standard. But the six and twenty mile poverty was of a
completely different level, even to us mountain people.
It was a level defined by crude shacks pasted together on
the side of the mountain, leaning with the direction of
the wind.

I had lived on Crooktop all of my life, but I had never
been to six and twenty mile holler. Most Crooktop folks
hadn't. In school I had stared at their dirty clothes and the
orange free lunch passes. I stared, but I didn't join in the
laughter. As a child my own clothes were often dirty, and
I would long for an orange pass when Mamma Rutha forgot to pack me any lunch. Sometimes I even envied their
sense of belonging. They were outside of everything, but
they were outside together. I was outside alone.

And now I was riding into their land. Crooks and bums
were supposed to line the road. But it didn't look dangerous. It just looked untamed and wretched, with crumpled
piles of wood that only slightly resembled homes.

"You know where you're going?" I asked him. "Into six
and twenty mile holler. Ever heard of it?"

"Didn't know the name. Just knew it ain't like the rest of your mountain."

"What do you mean?"

"Just feels like I'm on a whole new mountain. A wild one. It ain't all carved up like yours. With roads and a shoppin' valley."

"I've never been up here before," I said.

"Never knew you was neighbors with all this, huh?"

We drove past a small boy, around five years old. He was standing on the side of the road, naked except for a pair of boots, holding a dead squirrel by its tail. His eyes curiously followed our truck as it climbed further up the holler.

"Did you see him?" I asked. He nodded. "Poor little fella," I said.

He looked at me, and I could tell he didn't understand or agree with my statement. It all seemed normal to him.

"Where you from?" I asked, after we had driven for a while in silence.

"Down the riverbottom," he said, giving me the answer I already knew.

"Have you been up here much?"

"Been fishin' all summer in these parts. They got trout streams better than any place in these mountains," he said.

"You met any of the people here?"

"When they first seen me, they just looked at me like they couldn't figure me. It wasn't the same as the way your people look at me, though."

"My people?" I asked.

"Crooktop. The people of your mountain."

"How do they look at you?"

"Same as a skeeter, I reckon. I'm like a summer bug to y'all."

He had said "y'all." He had lumped me together with the rest of Crooktop. He didn't think that I looked at him like a summer mosquito, did he? I hadn't, had I?

I wanted to tell him that he was wrong. That I never knew how to be a part of the "y'all." But I couldn't decide which was worse, the assumption in his voice when he said "y'all" or telling him that I had never belonged anywhere, least of all Crooktop.

"Ever fish before?" he asked me.

I nodded. "I always bait my own hook too."

He smiled. "So you're a bait fisher, huh? Well you gotta learn somethin' new, 'cause I don't bait fish."

"What do you do, then, just scoop 'em up in your hands?" I laughed.

"Nah, I use a fly. More fair to 'em, rather than just sinkin' a fat meal down in their home."

I had never been fly fishing. Father Heron occasionally fly fished. But I was not his chosen company, and I had never gone. I wished that I had. I wished that Trout would look at my skill with surprise and approval.

"C'mon," he said as he hopped out of the truck and disappeared into the woods.

We walked far, but I don't know how far because I couldn't see anything but leaves and branches and briars. The air was thick and heavy with ripe moisture, and gnats bit at my ankles. I was still in my Sunday dress, cream with purple trim, since I left with him before changing. And my feet hurt as I shuffled through the undergrowth in my scuffed pumps, quickly turning black with dirt. Eventually, the thickness of the trees began to thin, and soon I heard the stream.

"Down here," he said as he walked over to a small clearing on the bank.

He took off his shirt and laid it on the ground so that I could sit down without ruining my dress. I liked what that told me. That he knew I had on a pretty dress.

I tried not to look at him, to stare at his nakedness. My eyes struggled to avoid the rise of his shoulders, the short little hairs around his belly button, the sweat covering his muscles. I watched the stream, the sun, the chain of ants marching onward, anything but that naked man in front of me. I had seen Father Heron without his shirt, an altogether different sight of sagging gray flesh. And I had seen other boys at the docks or at work without their shirts. But I had never been that close or that *alone* with a man. As he described to me how to hold the rod, how to stand, how to jerk my wrist forwards then backwards, I looked at his face, only his face. His prickly stubble that had tickled my ear. Those sunflowered eyes. And then he told me to watch him as he fished. To watch his arm. To watch his back. How his body worked together with the line and the rod to create one smooth rhythm.

I obeyed my teacher. With his back turned, my eyes satisfied their curiosity. But it wasn't just his nakedness that captivated me. It was the way he fished. He didn't hold the rod. He was the rod. It was a part of his arm, curling over the water, grazing the surface, snapping back with a slight whistle. Curl, graze, snap. It was as beautiful and strange as any of Mamma Rutha's blessings. And the fish couldn't help but bite.

"C'mon, give it a try," he said, without turning around or ever losing his rhythm.

As his hands covered mine, placing them where they were supposed to be, I realized that I had never really looked at them. I had looked at the stain, but not his hands. They felt rough, callused by the plants. They were hands that didn't swallow mine in largeness, but cradled them gently. Hands with little brown clusters of hair at the knuckles. Smooth lines at the joints. Traces of thick veins hidden beneath the skin. They were the hands of a man, a fisher, a mater migrant. And all of them were touching me.

"There you go," he said as I finally managed to hurl the line over the water after repeatedly getting tangled up in it. "Quit thinkin' about it, let the fish take over. They'll tell you what to do," he coached.

Don't think, I told myself. But it didn't work. I was stiff and self-conscious, silently counting *one two three* under my breath. I cast and cast, but the fish weren't fooled. Finally when my arm burned with fatigue, I let the line fall limp and tangled at my feet.

"I guess I'm not much of a fisher," I said as I walked over and sat next to him.

"Nah, you were great," he said, smiling. "You was lyin' about not knowin' how to fly, weren't you?"

I laughed and reminded him that I didn't catch a single fish.

"All the same, you got flyin' in you. Must be your

fancy fishin' outfit. I figured the fish would just leap out to you."

I blushed, knowing how ridiculous I must have looked, standing on the banks of wilderness in my cream and purple dress and bare feet. He looked at me, and his red hand softly touched my red face.

"Hungry?" he asked.

I nodded, rendered speechless by the moment that had just passed between us.

"Sit down and I'll see about rustlin' up somethin'." He pulled out a pocketknife and began filleting the fish he'd caught. One hand grasping the slippery skin, while the other skillfully carved its flesh.

"I'd ask for a light, but I'm afraid it might make you sassy like down at the docks," he joked as he pulled a lighter from his pocket and began building a small fire. He laid the fillets on wide slabs of bark that he had soaked in the stream, and placed them just at the edge of the fire where they could slowly roast.

The air filled with a delicious smell. It was a full salty scent, one of roasted meat mingling with burning wood. By the time he slid the pieces of bark away from the edge, my mouth was watering.

"This ain't no roasted pig or nothin', like you'd have if you weren't with me," he said shyly as he served me a fillet.

We ate with our hands. Greedy hands filling hungry mouths. Della would have been shocked and alarmed to see me, filling my mouth with that smoked trout, not caring about the pieces of dirt or bark that still clung to the skin.

"Never, never eat 'til you're full in front of a man that you're not related to or don't despise," she had instructed me. "Sexy women are hungry women, Mercy. It's hard for a man to see a woman as mysterious and erotic if he just watched her gulp down a whole rack of ribs. You gotta save your appetite for when you're out with other girls, or at home by yourself. Otherwise, you'll be a woman in the prime of your looks pigging out without a man anywhere around."

It wasn't that I didn't believe Della's lesson on men. I knew as I stuffed my mouth with fish that I wasn't attractive or feminine. But my hunger and the adventure of eating fish that had been swimming just a few minutes ago overwhelmed any feminine wisdom that I had acquired. I ate several fillets, never waving off any that he offered me.

"C'mon," he said, after we finished the last fillet.

I followed him to the edge of the stream and knelt beside him. He leaned forward and scooped water into his hands. I leaned forward too, cupped my hands together, and let the stream fill them. The water was cold, colder than I expected on that muggy summer day. It slid down my throat, more cool and comforting than sweet tea could ever be.

We were satisfied. We sat on the bank and talked about his job. How he was careful not to bruise the fruits he picked, how he was sad that he couldn't smell the plants anymore because he had worked in them so long. I wanted to ask him why he was a mater migrant, but I didn't. I was afraid he would think I looked at him like a mosquito. So we talked about my job, and Della. I told him she was my best friend. And I asked him about the snakes.

"You never done it?" he asked.

"I didn't even know places like that were around here. How did you?"

"You and me, we ain't the same," he said simply.

"I don't understand."

"You walk in your valley, people see Mercy Heron. You don't gotta go no other place for people to look at you. I walk through your valley and people see red hands. It don't bother me none, I ain't shamed by my hands. But that don't mean a man don't need to go places where people ain't always lookin' for 'em. Those places are out there, hidin' in these mountains. And when I find 'em, I ain't a mater migrant no more. I'm just a man."

We traced our way back to his truck.

"Where you live?" he asked.

"Up from the valley, on the mountain."

"Do I take a left at the end of the holler?"

"Oh, no. No. Just drop me off at the diner," I told him, careful to disguise the edge in my voice. He didn't answer me, and though I stared out the window as hard as I could, I could tell he was trying not to look at me. I was ashamed of myself.

"I have to face my boss eventually, and I might as well go ahead and do it tonight," I lied coolly.

He was quiet. And I wondered what questions he was asking himself. If he struggled between wanting to believe me and his suspicion that I didn't want my family to see me with a mater migrant. Did he think he couldn't take me home because I was a part of the "y'all"? Was he right?

"I had a lot of fun today, with the holler and the fish.

I had a real good time. Thank you," I stammered as he pulled up to the diner.

I awkwardly stared at my scuffed pumps as I spoke, not sure of how or what to say, but knowing that it just wouldn't be right not to thank the man that drove me to the wilderness, entertained, and fed me.

"Good," he said, still not looking at me. The easiness was gone. His silence had changed into something stiff.

"I really do have to see my boss tonight. I'm not what you think. I'm not like everybody else here."

"No," he said, before driving away. "You're a whole different kind of woman."

Chapter VIII

I went inside the diner. Chairs were turned up on the tables, and it smelled of dirty bleach water mingled with barbecue. It was quiet, except for water running in the kitchen where the dishes were being washed.

"Rusty?"

There was no answer, but his truck was still there. I guessed that he was out smoking so I hurried and scribbled a note. I wrote that something had come up with Mamma Rutha that I had to take care of, and that I would be in for work tomorrow. Then I called Della and told her to pick me up down at the Credit Union.

Her questions were relentless. As soon as she pulled up she knew I hadn't been at work.

"You're still dressed up! Where have you been?" she

demanded. I tried to act cool and calm. I told her I had just been taking care of errands.

"Errands, my ass! You have a clean apron in your hand, your shoes are filthy, and that's not how you go to the grocery!"

I didn't want to tell her. Not until I had a chance to sort it all out, like Father Heron's greeter papers, into neat little boxes of conversations, looks, and laughter. But I felt important, girlishly important. For the first time ever, it was me who had the story.

"It's not what you think," I began. "We just went fishing. That's all."

"Who, Mercy? Who!" she demanded.

"Trout. I ran into him on my way to work, and I like to fish so I went along with him. No big deal."

"Trout mater migrant? The snake handler! That's almost as bad as something I'd do!" she teased. "And fishing? I've known you forever and I don't remember you ever hankering to go fishing. The fish you were after just happened to be named Trout, huh?" She laughed. "Well, tell me what you did, what he said, how he looked!"

I gave her a very boring story. About a man that fished and fed me. As I talked I felt flushed and confused every time I thought about that curl, graze, and snap, about those hands with thick veins and smooth lines, about the salty smell of that smoked trout.

"Be careful, Mercy," she said before dropping me off. "Remember who you are. You're playing a dangerous game."

There weren't any lights on in the house. It was Heron

garden night. In the moonlight I saw neat little rows of vegetables, with leaves that looked silvery black in the darkness. Sounds, smells, and thoughts stirred within me. Like Polaroids. The image of his back. Of fish guts thrown into the woods. Of scuffed pumps.

"Young lady, I need a word with you," Father Heron's voice broke through the quiet night.

A word with me. Hello. That's a word. How was your day, Mercy? Five whole words. But I knew that none of them would be Father Heron's *word with me.* Father Heron never spoke *a word with me* in kindness.

He saw me riding home with Della, I told myself. *Della is a whore.* Those will be his words. *Your momma was a whore. You will not be a whore like Della and your momma.*

"Yes sir," I said lowly.

"Look at you," he said with disgust. "Standing here in your church clothes, but didn't go to evening services. May Flours is telling everybody she saw you hop in a truck with a man. Said she thought he might be a mater migrant. *A mater migrant, Mercy,*" he repeated through gritted teeth.

May Flours was a bitter little prune of a woman, with a shriveled-up face and bluish hair. A spiteful gossip who stirred up more trouble for new preachers than the devil himself could ever hope to. She had spread rumors about preachers having affairs with the woman who kept the nursery or pocketing change from the offering plate. And now I was her target. I imagined the sense of joy she must have felt, seeing me get into his truck. Knowing that for once she had a scandal she could spread that was actually true.

"You will not disgrace our name," Father Heron said sternly.

In his narrowed black eyes and set jaw I recognized danger. Tick tick ticking. Ready to explode with the slightest spark.

"No, I won't. I don't sneak around with mater migrants. I also don't listen to gossip from the likes of May Flours. Just as you taught me to, sir," I said, not daring to look him in the eye. "If you want me to explain why I'm dressed the way I am, if you need me to show you how May Flours is wrong, well, I can. If you believe the things she says."

Father Heron couldn't stand there and say he believed May Flours. Every good person in our church had rallied against *the lying lips* of May Flours. *Lying lips are an abomination*, Father Heron had declared.

He looked startled, a bit confused even.

"I don't need any explanations from the likes of you. And I don't need any of May Flours' rotten tongue either. I'm just letting you know what we stand for and what you will respect."

I breathed a sigh of relief and wondered what he would have done if I had said yes. I was out with a mater migrant. Yes, we drove together, *all by ourselves*, to the middle of six and twenty mile holler. Yes, we stood in the wilderness *together*. Yes, he was half naked. *Yes, I loved every single moment with him.*

I went inside and crawled into bed. The little details, hidden by the big events, surfaced in the darkness. We hadn't spoken of our first night together looking for the fire trout. And I hadn't felt embarrassed as I had thought I would. It had all disappeared in his carefree admission that he was waiting there for me. And what had he called me, a different kind of woman? Different from what? From pretty, popular girls? With swingy blonde hair and round full breasts? Or was I like the holler? He had called that a different kind of mountain. A wild one.

The next morning I felt like more of a woman, if not a different kind. I paid new attention to the soft curve of my calf and to the way breathing made my chest rise and fall in the shower. I studied myself in the mirror. Eyes the color of coal. Hair that no amount of Breck shampoo could ever make bounce. Lips sparkling with Plum Passion. Teeth just a little crooked on the bottom row, but fine on the top. Small breasts, shaped like Hershey's kisses.

"Mercy baby," Mamma Rutha called to me through my closed door. "I have something to show you."

"Just a minute," I cried as I pulled on my cutoffs and T-shirt.

We walked behind the shed where she reached into a tattered boot box and pulled out a bloodied baby squirrel, with a horrible gash in its back leg.

"Wallace's dogs killed its momma and about killed it too. I came out here and right underneath my feet was its poor mangled momma and this little thing. I'm gonna have to go hunt up a good salve for its little leg."

The squirrel was shaking and bleeding. I was certain it wouldn't live. At least, it wouldn't without Mamma Rutha to care for it.

"I need your help," she said seriously.

"What?" I asked, fearful of what she would say.

Once when I was sixteen, she had asked me to help her paint the house sun yellow so it would blend in with

"God's design" for the mountain. For two weeks I carried her a bucket of paint each day, until nearly every shadowy place in her garden was hiding a little bit of sunshine. Then, as soon as she had drugged Father Heron and he had stumbled to bed, we began painting. We painted without stopping through the night, until the next afternoon. When Father Heron woke up and saw the house, you would have thought we had painted curse words on it he was so choked with anger. It did look ridiculous. But I didn't care, it wasn't like anybody I knew, except for Della, ever came close to the house. Father Heron hired a whole crew of men to come repaint the house that very day. So before sunset, it was clean and white again.

When Mamma Rutha showed up at dinner that night, *she was sun yellow.* Everything, except her blue eyes that looked even more washed out by the contrast of her neon skin. When Father Heron asked *what in God's name had she done to herself,* she looked at him calmly and said, "This is your house, paint it what you like. My body is my house. And I will paint it what I like."

Father Heron didn't seem to mind at first. He just hoped she'd get poisoned and die from it all. But she didn't. And she even touched up any nicks or chips that she had. When she needed something from the valley, she just took her yellow self right on down there. That was the worst for me. Father Heron may have been called righteous for staying with Mamma Rutha, but I just felt hot shame when my classmates started calling me Sunny. As if I were the yellow one. *Hey Sunny, make the rain go away.* She stayed yellow for a long time, until finally one day she decided that she scared her animals. So she bathed, leaving a permanent tinge of yellow in the bottom of our bathtub.

"I need your help with his dogs. They torture my chickens. They mangle the squirrels, possums, and mice. They're unnatural. They don't even eat what they kill half the time," she said.

Father Heron's dogs were not pets, but hunting tools. He usually kept them in cages during the day, and set them loose at sunset. They were almost wild, obedient to Father Heron only half the time.

"What do you want to do?" I asked her. "Kill 'em?"

She looked shocked.

"Oh no. They can't help the way they are, how they've been raised. But this part of the mountain, where we live, I've worked hard to make it safe," she said, motioning to the woods as though she could see all of her beloved creatures. "And I'm not going to let them dogs destroy that. I want to take 'em far away, up the mountain. Let 'em be a part of what they try to destroy. Let 'em kill away from here and for a reason, a natural reason."

"How we gonna do all that?"

"Tonight, after he's asleep, we'll lead them away. Dogs can make maps in their heads, so we'll have to blindfold 'em. And we can't take the truck, it'd wake him. Today in the valley, get me some rope or chain to lead by. I'll fry him one of his chickens, slip some sleepy into his tea, and when he's asleep we'll put our walking shoes on. I already know where we'll be going, so you just be ready, okay?"

Fried chicken and sleepy tea, Mamma Rutha's famous mischief cocktail. She kept a small jar filled with a crumbly substance, hidden behind the cornmeal. I didn't know what it was. All I knew was that she returned from the mountain with it, and that whenever I saw a residue of crushed powder on the counter and the table loaded with Father Heron's favorites, I should brace myself for trouble, Mamma Rutha style. There were a thousand reasons why I shouldn't have agreed. But then there was Mamma Rutha, the reason I said yes.

When my shift at the diner ended, it was time for me to pick up the supplies. I went to the Ben Franklin to see Della and look for some rope. There was just one register open, and a small girl with a pimply face and shifty eyes working it. When I asked her if Della was working, she motioned toward the back and shrugged her shoulders.

I wasn't halfway through the store before I heard her teasing giggle. As I neared the back of the store, where the words "MANAGER'S OFFICE" hung importantly above a door, I heard a man's voice too. Nasal and pleading.

I could see him. Through a little slat window carved into the side of the door that helped him keep a better eye on the store. He was very skinny, and tall. Tufts of hair around his ears and neck, but none on top. He had a handsome face, with high cheekbones. But it was still a shock to picture Della with him. Della wasting all of her glow on *that*?

Since Della was busy, I started to leave and go search for my rope when he saw me.

"Can I help you, ma'am?" he called after me.

"Mercy?" Della said.

I stopped and slowly turned around, flushed with embarrassment. I had been caught spying on my best friend while she flirted with her boss.

He looked worried, and I guessed that he was wondering what I saw, whether I knew his wife.

"It's okay, Randy. She's my best friend," Della said, grinning at me.

His high cheekbones locked. "Call me Sir when we're at work!" he snapped. Then he turned to me. "You know?"

"Rope," I said. "I just need some rope."

"You've been spreading this around?" he asked Della.

"Not spreading it around, just telling my best friend. I tell her everything. She is my magic student!" she said, giggling again.

"Do you have any idea what this could do to me? Me, a married man? The boss of this store? Screwing around with an eighteen-year-old cashier, and you spread it around!" he asked, the top of his slick head turning scarlet.

"It's not like that, Randy," Della said softly. "She's the only one I've told. And she understands, I told her about your wife."

He turned toward me. "And how can I know, how can I be sure that you'll keep your mouth shut?" he asked.

"'Cause she loves me. And 'cause she's as bad as me. Dating a mater migrant is no better than dating a married man." Della laughed with a good-natured wink.

I protested, my ears burning red. *I was not dating a mater migrant.*

"Rope's on aisle four," he interrupted as he started walking back to his office. "And Della, I need to see you in my office."

"Oh, yes sir," Della said in her most sexy breathless voice.

"Not like that," he said, shooting her an angry glance.

"It's okay, Mercy. He's just so high-strung, you know? It's his wife. Any man would be high-strung living with the likes of her. Anyway, I'd help you pick out your rope, but duty calls, you know? I've got to put my forty hours in if I expect to draw a paycheck," she said as she grinned and whirled toward his office, skillfully bouncing all of her curves.

I made my way over to aisle four, vowing to wring Della's neck for telling him that I was dating a mater migrant. I had seen the look in his eyes when she said that. A look of victory.

Aisle four had three kinds of rope. Thin purple rope, the kind used in Vacation Bible School crafts, medium yellow rope, and thick red rope. I tugged on the medium yellow rope. It seemed sturdy, but those dogs were so big. I decided on the thick red rope and bought four lengths.

The distance to my house from the valley wasn't even two miles, but it was steep enough to give my calves a deep-down-in-the-bone burn. As I watched the sun slowly fizzle into darkness, I knew there was little time to waste. So I walked briskly, jogging at times, probably looking as crazy as Mamma Rutha, with four long pieces of red rope trailing behind me. When I arrived home, it was dark outside and smelled of fried chicken. After I hid the ropes beneath Mamma Rutha's potato plants, she met me on the back porch.

"Mercy baby," she whispered, "good news. The baby's doing okay. I put a salve on its wound, and I think its gonna be fine. But the dogs still must be moved. Your grandfather is drinking his tea now. Go change into something warm and stay back in your bedroom 'til I come and get you."

When Mamma Rutha had a plan, she could execute it with perfect sanity. She was calm and in control, while my hands shook as I tied my sneakers. I thought about how calculated she must have been that evening. Killing the chicken, frying it, brewing his tea, crushing the powder that she stirred with extra sugar into his glass, plotting a map in her head of where we would walk that night.

"He's been asleep for an hour now, so I don't think he'll wake up," Mamma Rutha whispered as she motioned me to follow her.

"Are you scared?" she asked me once we were outside.

"No. But I am hungry, got any more chicken?"

"I put it in the compost pile for the garden," she said matter-of-factly. Just like Mamma Rutha. Worried that I was scared, but forgetting that I hadn't eaten supper.

It took us longer than she had planned to round the four dogs up. They were too busy having fun, tearing up the night. We called them softly. *Wolf! Here boy! Bear! Here boy! Coon! Come here! Fox!* I was wildly running around with my two red ropes. Diving for their thick bodies, falling facedown in the dirt.

Finally, we managed to slip a rope around each one's neck. Then ripped T-shirts were bound around each dog's eyes. They seemed so different, tied up and blinded. They were nervous, skittish pups.

We began our journey. Mamma Rutha in the lead, pulling her two dogs behind her. I followed her and led the red dogs, Fox and Coon.

We walked, climbing upward and upward until my legs grew numb. I tried not to think of all the snakes, coyotes, and mountain lions that were watching me. Or maybe even bears. The dogs occasionally would growl, low and threatening. I knew they smelled things that my eyes couldn't see. I had never seen the mountain like that. We were traveling to its heart, deep into the woods. It was crawling, rattling, and shaking with life. The mountain itself seemed to breathe.

Mamma Rutha never stopped to rest. I followed her soft rustling as she passed through leaves and branches. The four dogs and me huffed and puffed and struggled to keep up. She didn't even seem winded as we climbed and climbed. I wondered how old she was. Maybe as old as her mountain.

"Almost there, just a little further," she called back to me after hours of following.

The dogs were worn out and thoroughly confused by the time she suddenly stopped and announced that we had walked far enough. The six of us sat down. Not caring whether we sat on unseen anthills. The dogs stretched their tired limbs and began breathing deeply. I wanted to stay like that forever. The six of us, in a half circle, in the heart of the mountain. The hunger, the fatigue, my aching muscles and rope-burned hands all held me to the ground.

I dozed in and out, until I became aware of Mamma Rutha gently pulling the blindfolds and red rope from the dogs. She stroked the tops of their heads and told them to live a good, peaceful life. She told them that she could not bless them after what they had done to the baby squirrel, but that she wished good things for them. She took my hands and pulled me from the ground. I followed her back toward home, dragging my two loose red ropes, feeling much lighter walking downhill without Fox and Coon to pull along.

As we neared home there was no yellow or orange light in the sky yet, but night was beginning to fade from black, to navy, then to a purplish blue. I was beyond tired. I was floating toward home and my bed. The woods began to thin and suddenly stopped. I was standing at the edge of Mamma Rutha's garden.

"Mercy baby."

I turned and looked at her. Her eyes shining victorious, no sign of exhaustion.

"You are happy," she said.

"What do you mean?" my sleepy voice asked.

"I can feel it. It's new."

"I'm just really tired. That's what you see," I murmured, not daring to meet her eyes.

I was too tired to think anymore. Too tired to ask myself what Mamma Rutha saw. I fell asleep fully clothed on top of my bed, curled around my pillow, hands clenched to pull and tug my two blind red dogs.

Chapter IX

M

y hunger woke me. It was a painful gnawing in my stomach. My body had soaked up a few hours of rest and then demanded something more. It needed food. I climbed out of bed, looking nearly the same as I did when I left the night before, only dirtier and more wrinkled. Mamma Rutha and Father Heron were nowhere in sight. I rummaged through the cabinets, searching for something quick to eat. But all I found was flour, cornmeal, some canned beans, and molasses.

I walked outside, to Father Heron's garden. I grabbed a handful of beans and popped them in my mouth. Sweet and crisp, they only made me more hungry. I needed something to bite and chew. A raw potato wouldn't do. I inspected his tomato plants, and found them lacking too.

Green, and orangey red at best, they were mere shadows of the ruby gems that hung in Mamma Rutha's garden. I glanced at them, but I didn't dare taste one.

I had done that once. At age twelve, after Mamma Rutha had forgotten to pack my lunch for school, my stomach had growled with the thought of them. How their sweet and tangy flesh would make my cheeks pucker and my mouth sing. *I am a creature too,* I told myself. *I am from this mountain too,* I said to her garden. I stood there in the middle of it and checked to see if I was being watched. I inhaled the fermented smell of an overly ripe, unharvested garden. My fingers burned with lust while my eyes searched for the perfect fruit. At the bottom, low to the ground, there it was. About the size of an apple, shaped to fit perfectly in the palm of my hand. I touched it. Timidly at first. Then my hand closed around it and I pulled. My teeth pierced its skin and its juice trickled down my chin.

But without ever asking me she knew. And for weeks she didn't bless me. Finally, I broke down, confessed and repented. *Why won't you bless me anymore?* I cried. *What must I do?* And that's when she told me that I must hunger. I had stolen the mountain's blessing, and so I had to give it mine. For two days I laid all of my food, my biscuits, my peanut butter sandwiches, my fried chicken beneath the June apple tree.

It was bad. Even though it was for just two days. I was so tempted to take a bite. Just one bite, one chew, one swallow of my food. But somehow, she would have known. So I hungered. Hungered so bad I crept out at night and ate dirt. Filled my mouth with the soft brown earth that smelled so good in her garden. *It's not food*, I told myself. *It doesn't count*, I whispered through my dirt-filled mouth.

The strangest thing is that the taste of dirt never left me. There were times when I still craved it. Working in the garden on a Sunday night. When there was no food in the house. When I wanted to feel low and hidden from the world. I would crawl into the wild closet of Mamma Rutha's garden, and fill my mouth with dirt. I stood there, the morning after leading the dogs away, and eyed that rich brown dirt. Thinking about its musky taste and crunchy grit. I wanted to eat it. *But eighteen-year-olds don't eat dirt.* So I hungered instead. Wishing I was still twelve.

"Coon! Here Coon! Hey Fox! Here Fox!" Father Heron's voice pierced the woods. I walked to the back porch, listening to him call those dogs. Secretly laughing at him. He walked out of the woods after about an hour and noticed me there.

"Mercy, you seen my dogs?" he asked.

"Last night when I came home from work I saw 'em running around out here, after you set 'em loose."

"No, after that, today, you seen 'em today?" he asked anxiously.

"No sir, I haven't seen 'em today. They run off some-place?"

"March out into them woods and call them dogs, while I head down the mountain to see if they've wandered down thataways," he said.

"Yes sir," I replied as I walked to the edge of the woods,

choked back my laughter, and called "Coon! Wolf! Bear!" until Father Heron left.

Suddenly I shivered with fear. The red ropes, still attached to the dog collars. Where were they? Mamma Rutha had wisely left hers with the dogs. But I brought mine back home, and I couldn't remember hiding them or throwing them away. I ran through the woods, circling the trees. Looking by rocks and in briars.

It was almost time to leave for work. I gave up, hoping Mamma Rutha had gotten rid of them. I showered and walked into my bedroom, where on the floor, curled like scarlet snakes, lay two lengths of thick red rope. I stuffed them in my closet, next to the jelly jar, to wait for a safe time to get rid of them.

It was Tuesday, and Tuesdays were always slow at work. Friday, Saturday, and Sunday guaranteed a crowd. Monday was spent recovering and cleaning up from the weekend. Wednesday and Thursday were spent getting ready for it by finding the right pigs, having them killed, and getting them ready to smoke. But Tuesday was the lull. We served only a smoked pork shoulder. Never a whole pig.

Rusty had tried to pep business up on Tuesdays with his Terrific Tuesday Specials. *Buy one pork sandwich, get barbecue beans for free!* But that didn't work. So he tried music. He paid for some of Crooktop's best "pickers" to come and play. They picked the banjo and the guitar. Outsiders called it bluegrass or country, but up on Crooktop there were only two types of live music—gospel and picking. At first it had worked. People left their Tuesday casseroles at home for the music. But Rusty eventually realized that they weren't eating enough to cover the cost, so Picking Tuesday became ordinary Tuesday again. I never made any money on Tuesdays. I never really had to work on Tuesday, though I was scheduled to. I would spend my time cleaning, reorganizing the silverware, or taking smoke breaks with Rusty. But on that Tuesday, I spent my time thinking about Trout. Wondering how much more time was left in the growing season. Whether I would see him again.

"Let's smoke," Rusty called from the kitchen.

I nodded, even though I dreaded spending time with him. It was strange that I was so drawn to a man that Crooktop despised, while Rusty, one of its most respected young men, made my stomach turn. Rusty made a decent living, came from a good family, and he went to church. Check, check, check—it was almost a complete list.

"How's your family?" he asked as he lit his cigarette.

"Pretty good. Yours?"

"Same as always, I reckon. Listen, I've been thinking about making a little visit to your place. Maybe taking your grandparents some pig. I know what a time your grandpa must have outta your grandma."

"I don't know about that. I mean, it's awfully nice of you, but Father Heron's awfully busy, and he just lost his dogs, so now is probably not the best time."

"But I worry about y'all. I worry that your grandpa needs a helping hand," he said, with smoke pouring out of his nostrils. "You couldn't even come into work the other day 'cause of something going on with your crazy grandma. I'd like to ask your grandpa if I could, well, if I could help take care of you a little. So that he won't have to worry about you too."

"I take care of myself. Always have," I replied, wondering if Della could get me hired at the Ben Franklin.

"Just the same, you reflect a spell on it. I've got a lot to offer," he said as he walked back inside.

I needed that diner job. There were so few jobs available for girls in the valley. I was too young to be hired by the bank, I refused to be a cafeteria lady at the school. But how could I refuse a man, without making him feel rejected? Only Della could answer. At the end of my shift I started walking toward the Ben Franklin.

I felt him coming even before I heard his truck round the top of the hill. That clanky roar and sputter. I knew that he was coming for me.

"Hey," he said smiling. "Where you headed?"

"Ben Franklin. How about you?"

"I was hopin' you could give me a bite of some of that pig you serve up," he said. "But now I'm thinkin' Mexican sounds better."

"Like tacos?" I asked.

"Somethin' like that. Hop in," he said, never asking me if I wanted to, just knowing that I did. He leaned over and opened the door. His arm stretched out long, and my eyes met the curve of his shoulder and the smooth tan skin that was covered with bristly hairs. I sat inside his truck. There in the middle of town, knowing that I was making May Flours' day.

The windows were rolled down and the wind whipped my ponytail around and pulled loose hairs across my face.

The air smelled fresh and pulled away the smoke that clung to me. I breathed deeply and felt happy. In that moment, I was exactly where I wanted to be.

"You doin' all right?" he asked.

"Fine. You?"

"Worn out," he said. "Boss raised the quota to thirty crates of maters today. Got stung by a hornet, and now the sting's dried up I can't quit scratchin' it. I'm thankful too. Had a good lunch of stewed maters with cornbread. My truck's still kickin' along, and then I found you walkin' down the same road that I was comin' up. That's a lot of things, but it sure ain't fine. How 'bout you?"

How about me? He was right. I was more than fine. "Fine" was the answer that I had always given. It was the answer I expected back. Hiding what made my feet ache or my heart sing, was all I'd ever known.

"I was up real late last night," I said. "With my Mamma Rutha. So I'm sleepy. And I didn't have supper last night, or breakfast today except for some raw beans, so I'm hungry. My boss makes me nervous. My job is dull on Tuesdays. But right now, I feel really good."

He drove down the mountain, toward the low river-bottom land. It was a place where most white people would go only to buy fresh vegetables or to hire people for odd jobs. White women certainly never went down there, where *Lord knows what might be done to them*. The land was a deeper, richer green than on the mountain. Filled with trees and grasses that were never thirsty. The air was thicker too, and moister. It smelled like unearthed potatoes. Or a mud puddle after a heavy rain.

There were more clouds and blue in the sky than up on Crooktop. It still looked like a puzzle, but down there the blue and white pieces were almost equal with the green and brown. And there were vegetables. Not like a garden. Or even like a crop. We were in a sea of green and red, with rows of tomatoes stretching far and wide. And mixed in between the rows were little clusters of gray tents. He had brought me home.

"So this is where you work?" I asked, wanting him to tell me about his life.

"See those rows over there?" he asked. "Those were mine today." I nodded and tried to imagine him there, his day filled with the fruits of my temptation. I thought it was a wonderful job, to lose yourself amidst rows of fuzzy plants.

There were small campfires built in the middle of the tent clusters, with huddles of brown men and women standing around them. They were laughing and smiling. And though they spoke Spanish, it was easy to tell when they spoke of happy things and funny things. They were beautiful. With caramel skin and black shiny eyes, not dull as coal dust like mine and Father Heron's. I surprised them. A white woman down in mater migrant land. And for the first time in my life, I felt white.

Crooktop was a mountain made of many colors, settled only by one. In school I was surrounded only by white children. At church, only whites. In the diner, only whites. And though most of us had distant Cherokee relatives, we were still "white." I had occasionally seen the Mexicans, when they dared make a trip to town. And once an old black man, a biologist, moved to Crooktop to study its wildlife. But he didn't stay long, and most of Crooktop was glad. My world was filled with people that looked just like me, and only occasionally was I aware of anything else.

As I followed Trout through them, they looked at me and I felt what lay between us. And it was new to me. Not that they were brown, I knew that. But I hadn't known how much my whiteness meant to them. It had never been anything more to me than a paleness that stared back in the mirror. But it meant something to them. It separated me from their happy laughter. From their warm caramel skin. It lay between us. Wider than the river.

"*¡Mi Trucha!*" an old man said in a thick accent, as he embraced Trout.

"This is my friend Mercy," Trout said. "Mercy, I'd like you to meet Mr. Miguel."

"Welcome to our home," he said, smiling an almost toothless smile.

Trout led me to a blanket laid across the ground. I sat down and stared. I felt like I was in a different time and a different country. I wondered if it had been there all along. That little world, so different from the rest of Crooktop. And so close to it. I had always known they lived there. That they spoke Spanish and lived in tents. But that they were a community? A family even? That they loved and were loved? I had been raised to believe that their way of life was miserable. So I believed the people always were too. But joy could be found in the tentworld. Pain too. Stooped backs, blistered hands, and homesick children.

But there was family there. More family than I had ever known.

Trout saw the look on my face, and he understood.

"Never seen the likes of it, have you?" he asked. "First time I saw 'em, I was just a fourteen-year-old boy fishin'. I heard 'em first. Singin' in their tongue. Never heard nothin' like that. I couldn't make out any of the words. It's like they was callin' me."

"Is that when you joined them?" I asked.

"I started spyin' on 'em. Through the briars and weeds, I laid on my belly and watched 'em. One day Mr. Miguel found me. The way I am with trout, he's with the maters. He knows when to plant 'em and when to pick 'em. He knows what bugs will hurt 'em and what won't. I felt linked to that old Mexican right then and there. He felt about maters like I felt about trout. I reckon he could tell by lookin' at me that I didn't have any sort of home to go back to. So he let me join 'em. He may be a Mexican, and I ain't. But he's been more daddy to me than ol' Earnie ever was. He's a wise man. Even the bosses listen to him. Still dreams of Mexico. Reckon he always will. It'd be about like us leavin' the mountains for the flatland. Couldn't ever get it out of our blood."

"I could leave the mountains," I said. "I've always wanted to see the ocean."

"But they wouldn't leave you. They're in you. Same as trout's in me," he said.

He was right, the mountain was in me. And parts of it would be hard to leave. Like the view of my living sky. But there were other parts, that soaked up Heron blood, that I would do anything to shed.

"You come here every summer?" I asked.

"We go where the biggest crops are. One mountain valley or another. When it gets cold we head to Florida to work other crops. We don't stay the same, either. There's new people every year. Some leave to settle down, others go back to Mexico. But a few of us don't. We just keep on movin' around."

"Don't you ever just want to stay put?" I asked, my mind thinking about the coming winter. About him leaving and never returning. He sighed, and I sensed that he had asked himself the same question before.

"Teacher told me once that the earth is just a ball that's always spinnin'. Round and round. Spinnin' the people that stand on it. But I walk with it. I ain't gonna wait for it to spin me. I spin myself."

"That's a lot of moving. Ever get tired?" I asked.

He shrugged his shoulders. "You ever get tired of standin'?" he replied.

Yes. *I grew tired.* Tired of standing in the middle of a lying house. Of standing by Mamma Rutha. Standing before Father Heron. Standing with smoked pork in my hands, and nickels and dimes in my pocket.

"Where you standin', Mercy?" he asked.

Hadn't he heard? About the silent old man and the crazy old woman? About the random peonies, the unharvested garden, the sun yellow house, the sun yellow body. My life wasn't like his pretty fairy tale, of a little boy lost in the woods rescued by a loving family. I was still lost in the woods.

"*¡Vengan, es tiempo de comer!!*" called a plump woman with glossy, inky hair.

"Grub time," he said, as he stood up and walked toward the woman. I looked around and noticed that the tents were organized in clusters, with central campfires and meals.

He returned with a heaping plate of food that smelled like summer. There were corn, beans, and tomatoes mixing in a little river of broth on the plate. And a pile of warm tortillas covering the top. We ate with our hands. Scraping the vegetables onto the tortillas with the fork we shared, sopping up the broth, and then stuffing them into our mouths. This was my second meal with him, and I was learning that using my hands to eat always made the food taste better.

"You eat like this every day?" I asked, when I slowed down enough to talk.

He looked at me and smiled. "Messy, ain't it."

"Yes." I laughed and held up my broth-covered hands.

"Let's wash up at the river," he said, guiding me toward the bank.

The river was wide. Like ten mountain streams mingling together. And it was dark. The color of the earth. It was warmer than the streams on Crooktop. And muddier. I could feel my shoes sinking as I crouched to wash my hands. I looked up and saw Trout sitting on the bank watching me. I grew conscious of how I walked, how my body moved under his gaze.

"Here," he said as his hand showed me where to sit.

I sat next to him and we watched the river, the sound of it gentle and cleansing. I looked at his worn shoes, the ones that I had noticed that night on the docks. Mine looked nearly the same, the mud from the river beginning to dry on them. I knew that he was poor. He couldn't offer me money or security, or even a life with him if he had to spin with the earth. But there was still something about him that made me glad to be me. I had never felt that way before.

"You fished any lately?" he asked.

"Not since the other day with you. Not like I was really fishing then either. I guess I'd have to catch something before I could say that."

"You fished just fine," he said. "Specially in that fancy fishin' outfit."

"Don't tease me about that," I said, wishing my face would blush again, just so he would touch it.

"I ain't," he said. "You was like a mornin' glory, all white and purple. You ever seen one?"

I had. People would plant them around their fences or mailboxes. The hardware store sold the seeds. But sometimes they would grow wild in the strangest places. Like weeds that didn't know they were beautiful.

"My momma used to grow 'em up the side of the porch. More like vines than flowers, ain't they? Twistin' and curlin' all around the posts, clean up to our roof. It's like she was hangin' little white and purple flags off our house. And then there was you. A fishin' mornin' glory."

We were close. I could feel the rise and fall of his breath.

"There wasn't much glory in my fishing, Trout. Not much at all," I said.

"That's crazy talk. You got glory all around you. Saw

it on you at the docks. I had a light. I just wanted to see glory."

Glory. It was a strange word for someone to use to describe me. *I wasn't conceived in glory.* I filled my momma's belly with shame and embarrassed my grandfather. *I wasn't born in glory either.* Father Heron was so angry with my momma's swollen belly that he ordered her to take her sin out of his house. So she went to find my daddy. She was going to marry him, she said. But he wasn't there. He wasn't anywhere. *He was gone.* She got so upset she went into labor right there. And as pain gripped her body, she didn't know where to go. Except home. To her momma, my Mamma Rutha. To her daddy, my Father Heron. She ran as best she could up the mountain. Blood spilling down her legs as I tore her apart from inside. She ran to that little square white house with the dingy green shingles. *It was her home too.* She put her hand on the back doorknob and tried to turn it. She pulled. She twisted. She screamed. She cursed. But the door wouldn't open.

I was locked inside her belly, trying to rip my way out, and I'm sure that I heard her scream. Heard her beg. *Daddy, please. Please! Oh God, please! Just let me have my bed, Daddy! Daddy, it's killing me! It's killing me, Daddy! Please, God! Oh please open the door! Please let me have my bed!*

That doorknob never turned. It would never turn for her again. While Father Heron sat silent, locked inside his house, Mamma Rutha pulled me from within her daughter. My momma lay sprawled and naked on the ground, her blood, our blood, soaking the grass and the dirt as I entered the world. I was born in blood and dirt and a dying girl's screams. There was no glory there.

"Where you standin'?" he asked gently.

I was quiet for a long time. I listened to the river, the sound of water, cleansing water.

"I don't know if I am. I'm sinking. Or floating. But there's not much ground for me to stand on. You don't see me really. You see somebody standing in glory. What was it you said, a different kind of woman? Maybe I am. But not in a good way. Not the way you think."

"We ain't from the same place," he said. "Ain't no use in pretendin' we are. But just 'cause I pick maters don't make me a blind man."

"I wasn't saying that. I wasn't saying it's because of your work. I'm just saying you don't really know me. You just see me as part of the rest of Crooktop, but you don't see how I can never be that. You don't see the things that have been done that will keep me from ever knowing glory."

"I saw how you believed in the fire trout. And how you looked at me the same way after seein' my hands. Nobody like you has ever done that before. And that's a different kind, Mercy. That's glory."

"Well, I like how you see me," I whispered, my face feeling flushed again.

"You're standin' on a bad mirror. Starin' at somethin' that ain't really you. We oughta go on and break it."

I wouldn't tell him about the mirror I was standing on. About my daddy leaving, for God knows where. About the doorknob that wouldn't turn. Long ago I had locked my secrets away, safe as the jelly jar. But every time I walked through the back door, I was surprised that it opened for me. And sometimes I felt sure I could smell the hot blood of my birth in the backyard.

Chapter X

The next morning, a car pulled up to the house. One that didn't rattle or sputter. A sheriff's car. Always clean and always fast. Father Heron walked out of the woods and shook Sheriff Barnes' hand. I walked over to the back porch to string and break beans, so that I could listen.

"Four dogs. Champion line too," I heard Father Heron say. "And I paid good money for those dogs. No telling what they'd be worth now that I've trained 'em."

Sheriff Barnes was listening. Shaking his head. Stroking his beard. He looked like the law.

"Way I figure, it's a pretty big crime," Father Heron continued. "And somebody's got to pay. Can't have that kind of stuff going on up here on Crooktop. Never happened when we was growing up."

"Glad you called the law," Sheriff Barnes said. "I'm gonna do my best to get your dogs back, or catch the bastard that took 'em. But I don't want to inspire false hope in you. Four dogs are hard to track. I'll do my best."

Father Heron had called in the police. Over four missing dogs. And it wasn't because he loved them, or craved their wagging tails. It was because he wouldn't be beaten. At his own home, on his own land, with his own dogs. I laughed right into my bean bowl. Because I knew there was no dog bandit. Just a wife and a granddaughter. And we wouldn't be caught. Father Heron wouldn't allow it. The Herons had a whore, craziness, and a bastard baby already. No need to add criminals to that.

The two men stood in the driveway and discussed their strategy.

"I'll ask some questions around town. Meanwhile you keep looking. Take care now, Wallace. Tell Rutha I said hello. And Mercy," Sheriff Barnes said as he drove away.

"Coon! Here boy! Come on Coon! Fox!" Father Heron began to shout. But his voice lacked hope. His shoulders were slumped and his hair mussed. But he wouldn't stop calling those dogs. The hate called from within him. He didn't need the hope.

But my heart held enough hope for the both of us, as I entered the first happy time of my life. I started meeting Trout nearly every day, even if it was just for a few minutes of conversation in his truck, before heading to work. Della liked to gossip about love. Girls at school had declared it. But this was different. It wasn't something that was scribbled across a locker or passed in a note.

"Tell me," Della begged. "Give me all the details!"

But it wasn't "magic" that Trout and I shared. It was love. And the difference between the two made me realize that I had something too special to talk about.

"But I tell you everything!" she said, pouting. "You love him, Mercy? You do. A girl always loves her first boy. Just remember, save room in your heart for others. You don't know what else is out there yet, something better always comes along."

"No," I whispered.

"You can't say that yet. You ain't never spoken to another boy besides Rusty. Don't quit looking around."

"And how about you? You're looking in someone else's garden."

"Yeah, I can't wait 'til he divorces his wife. Imagine it, Mercy, I'm gonna be the wife of the manager, *the manager*, of Ben Franklin. I know it'll just burn up all those priss misses from high school. I'll wear pretty clothes and cook nice dinners, and we'll have a big house. And maybe one day, once my figure's starting to fade, we'll have babies. I'll have real class. Real respect. Folks will forget about my old dirt floor."

"When is he going to divorce her?" I asked.

"Soon. He's afraid of what she'll do when he leaves her. She's a real nutcase. Even though he hasn't said it, I know he's really worried that she'll try and hurt me. Which he shouldn't be. Della DeMar can handle any kooky cat woman. I was raised on kookiness, I know every trick it can pull. But it really stresses him out to talk about it, so I don't bring it up much. You know, he's different than most men. The other night we were looking up at the stars. I said the stars over these mountains shined brighter than anywhere else in the world because of the coal here. When the miners stripped it all out, the only place it had to run to was the sky, and the moon and the clouds pressed against the coal so much that it all turned into diamonds. And you know what he said to me? He didn't tell me I was full of nonsense, or hurting his head with all of my stupid ideas, he said he liked to listen to me. That I had pretty talk. Not that I was pretty, lots of people have told me that, but that my ideas were. Who knows, Mercy, what if you're right after all? *This may be it.* One day when we're forty we may look back and laugh at us, sitting here now talking about the men we love. We may be married to those men, and sick of 'em by then. This summer may have been the start of it all. Does Father Heron know about Trout?"

"He'd kill me. Or Trout," I said.

"But he'll find out eventually, you know that, right?"

"Why?" I asked, feeling panicked.

"Well when the mater migrants pack up and Trout stays, talk will probably spread. You know how Crooktop is when there's a newcomer. Trout will have to find a job. A place to live. People will notice. People will talk," she replied. "Where will he stay?"

Staying. It was a detail we hadn't thought to cover. We were loving as though there were no October.

I shrugged my shoulders.

"Oh Mercy. *Pull your heart back in.* Don't give it all to a man that may take it and run. You've got to get some control."

I lied and said I would, then asked her about Rusty to change the subject. "I haven't encouraged him. Honestly,

I don't know where he got it into his head that I would be interested."

"Some men just live in lies. They ain't like women. Women see *too much* of the truth in themselves. They see too many dimples in their thighs and too much sag in their breasts. But some men are just the opposite. They lie and tell themselves that they aren't really fat. Or bald. Or that tight white jeans actually look good on them. And they've lied so long they think it's the truth. Rusty's just told himself that sweet little Mercy adores him, aches for him, needs him."

"How do I fix it?" I asked.

"Gently," she said. "We need to make him think that if you could have any man, you'd have him, but there's just some reason why you can't."

"And what would that reason be?" I asked.

"It's gotta be something that he can't try and fix. Something he won't want to chat with Father Heron about. Maybe ... maybe I'll tell him you're sick. With female trouble. Men always hate to talk about that. He won't even ask questions. I'll just say you have female trouble real bad and that the doctors have told you to stay away from men for at least a year, 'til you're better."

"I don't know. You're gonna tell him I got a disease? Like the kind girls get from the docks? What if that spreads around to Father Heron?"

"It won't. He won't want to admit to knowing something like that. If he blabs to the deacons, won't they wonder how he knows? Besides, I'll tell him that you're waiting only for him. That way, he's not been refused, just delayed," she said.

"And what happens this time next year?"

"Why you'll be Mrs. Mater Migrant of course, silly!" She laughed.

I laughed too. Della thought of everything in beginnings and endings. Her only concern was the once upon a time, and the happily ever after. But I was losing myself in the middle chapters. And discovering that's where all the love is held.

There were no romantic getaways or kisses beneath fireworks. No feuds or jealousies. There was just a hot thick love that shook me, but not the earth.

Our only struggle came from my refusal to take him home. I had promised him the red ropes from my closet, to better secure his tent. And he asked if he could swing by to pick them up.

"I'll bring them to you," I insisted. "'Cause you can't ever come to my home. Ever. It's just the way things have to be."

"Just get on home then," he said angrily. "Why'd you say you chose me, when all along you was still gonna live for them?"

"It's not that I want to live for them. It's that I'm scared of what'll happen if I don't."

"I don't know what your home is like or how bad it gets up there for you. But I'd rather be dead than scared all the time. Ain't no freedom in that. Ain't no sense in not being able to love who you want," he said, his eyes flashing trouble.

"I don't know what you want from me. You think going to my home, meeting my grandparents, will change everything?"

"It's time you learned that sometimes a three-legged dog was meant to be a three-legged dog. And maybe you was meant to love a man with red hands. You want me to make 'em smooth and white again? You wouldn't love me if I did," he said, walking back down the riverbottom with a look of disgust on his face. "You just go on home, and dream about a perfect life that ain't got no trouble in it. Think about how maybe you wouldn't be you, here with me now, if you hadn't been raised by your grandparents. Maybe what you think is all messed up is the reason why I saw glory all over you. Maybe the things you're always runnin' from are what you oughta be runnin' to."

I did run. But only to him. And it was perfect enough. Not completely perfect, because it was love and fear. The fear of being discovered. The fear of what we would do when the harvest ended. Like our love, September was a subtle month on the mountain. The wind became a little cooler, day by day. Gardens began to pant, winded and out of breath. Yellow schoolbuses dotted the roads again. All of them baby steps toward winter. A thieving winter, that would steal the sun, the crops, and the tentworld.

I stared at the rows of tomatoes and prayed that they would last another week. Another month. The rows gave us precious time. To fish and gather around the fires of the tentworld. To water the sunflower field that was growing in my heart.

Chapter XI

*T*here was supposed to be beauty. But there was just heat. Ripening the fruit. Withering the men. And sweat. Of more than water, of the minerals that filled their bones. And pain. As the bees stung them. As their backs humbled themselves. As their flesh was burned by the leaves that I had imagined tickled. And it was ugly. Maybe even low. With the spitting. The cursing. The peeing on the plants. And he was a part of it all.

"Hey Trout! Pick up that crate, boy! You got eight more to fill before you rest!" a white man yelled.

My eyes sought the source of the voice and tracked down the row where the man had yelled. Until I saw Trout. His shirt was off. And I thought back to the first time I saw him that way. How my eyes had traced the lines of his skin. How beautiful it had all been. Naked shoulders. Naked back. But as I stood on the bank, I saw that he was just a man. Whose shoulders looked like all other men's. A man whose naked back was just as humbled as the one next to him.

And I pitied him. Wondering, why did he choose this? And as I watched him curse and sweat, I wanted to pull him away and polish him. To make him shine the way he had before I learned what it meant to be a mater migrant.

When they stopped I met him at his tent. I really saw him then. I saw how he held his body, a little to the right, because he had picked the maters on the right of the rows that day. I saw how the red on his palms wasn't just the juice of red stain, but was the blister of his skin too. From jerking the frayed ropes that held the plants to their stakes. Rope after rope, tighter and tighter. I smelled his sweat. Not for the earthy scent that I had originally thought it. But for the scent of misery. I saw how hungry he was, but how he dreaded the taste of those tomatoes. I saw how hard he worked to keep it all from me. Teasing me about smelling like pork. Joking about how he'd like to smoke but was scared to ask me for a light.

"Why do you do it?" I asked.

"Do what?"

"This work. This life. Why?"

"Don't know no other way," he said, encircling me in his arms. "Got my own tent. And free food. Them coal boys always runnin' outta work. Not me. Not with this rich mountain dirt. Oughta plant gold here, ain't nothin' it can't grow."

"I saw you," I said.

"What?"

"I came after lunch. I watched you all afternoon."

His arms fell loose and to his side.

"And I just don't get why you would choose that. It's such a hard life. I know you can do better," I said. His eyes left mine and fell to a place I couldn't follow. "You spoke of freedom before. And of spinning. And that all made sense and was pretty. But it can't cover the hard life you have to chase to have it."

"I ain't got a pretty answer," he said. "Maybe to a fourteen-year-old boy, breakin' a body is better than goin' home. Or maybe I just ain't never been able to see nothin' but them rows. Everywhere I turn I see them rows. Nothin's certain for me, 'cept rows. Man can't just walk away from that, without somethin' else to go to."

If I could have nestled him beneath my skin and made my body his living shrine, just so those rows could never find him again, I would have. But all that I could do was look at his palms. Not see past them anymore, but really look at them.

I picked up his hand. I kissed the top, where the thick veins hid. I kissed the little row of hairs at his joints. I turned his hand over and kissed the calluses that rose just beneath his fingers. I knew the truth. He was a mater migrant. And it was miserable. Maybe even low. I kissed his palm. Full in the center. I tasted his flesh. I loved all of him. All that was beautiful. And everything that wasn't, and would never be.

Chapter XII

When a glass falls to the floor, whether it shatters or just chips depends on how thick it is. If it's a fancy goblet, one made for celebrations, it will break into a thousand pieces. But if it's a sturdy jar, the kind made for storing things, it will hit the ground with a thud. It may chip, but the body of the jar will not break. It's not as pretty, but it's ready for the fall. It was built with the fall in mind.

"What are you so happy about?" I asked him.

"You. Them eyes of yours are the color of this earth. Every time I pick my maters, I see that brown dirt and could swear you're lookin' back at me."

We laid there lazy and warm in his tent until dinnertime when Trout went outside to find us some food. I stayed inside the tent, staring up at the top, at the blue and yellow of the sky that couldn't be masked by that thin fabric. I heard his voice. Happy and light, joking about something in Spanish. And then English. Stiffer, more formal. I sat up to listen more closely.

"No sir, I ain't seen four dogs. Huntin' dogs you said? Hmmm. No I ain't. Sorry I wasn't much help, but I sure will keep an eye out for 'em. Two red 'uns and two black 'uns, huh? Yeah, I've lived down here all summer and ain't seen 'em. You been up on the mountain yet? Folks up there might of seen 'em. If they're huntin' dogs they'd probably head for the thick of it. How 'bout I ask my girl Mercy, she's from up on the mountain, see if she's seen 'em."

I was trapped. Inside a tiny tent with only one exit, and Trout and Father Heron on the other side. *He knew!* Suddenly I saw what the ending would be. Father Heron would see me. Red palm prints stained across my heart. His hate would kill me. Or Trout. *Just like it had killed my momma.*

"Awright then. I'll keep a lookout for 'em. Take care now," Trout said.

I needed a dark closet. I needed to be low and hidden. I crouched in his tent, pulling my knees to my chest, covering my face with trembling hands. *Where was my dark closet?*

"What's wrong?" he asked in a frightened voice. I wasn't just scared, *I was scary.* I couldn't speak. I could only shake my head as tears began to spill.

"Mercy! You're scarin' me. Somebody come in here?" he cried.

"No. No. NO!" I moaned. "He knows. It was him. I heard him. He knows. No. No. NO!"

"What the hell is wrong with you?"

"Father Heron. It was him. It was him!" I cried, choking on my panic.

He folded me into his arms and rocked me like a baby. I was a weak infant whose head had to be cradled to keep it from snapping off.

"Mercy. Mercy. Mercy."

"You should be scared," I whispered. "You should be so scared."

"I ain't scared of no old man. Don't you be neither. I ain't gonna let him do nothin' to you."

"He has power. It's in his hate. He killed my momma. Not with a gun or a knife, but with his hate. And he'll do it to us. If we want to live we need to go. Anywhere away from Crooktop. We can take your tent, and we'll find work somewhere else."

"Why should we let some old grandpa run us off?"

"It's the only way there is!" I cried. "It's the only way I can live. It's the only way you can save me."

He grew quiet. Searching out all the things I had never told him. All of my pain, all of my secrets lay stamped across my face and trembling in my voice.

"All my life I ain't never had nothin' worth standin' for. Hell, my momma didn't even give me a name to stand for. So I just spinned round and round. Walkin' with the earth. And it brought me to you. Now I've got somethin'. And I ain't gonna lose you."

"We've got to leave. Crooktop ain't the only place. There's a whole world out there."

"There's only one place for me," he said softly, his hand tracing the lines of my neck.

"Here? With him chasing us down?"

"Wherever you are. I'm tired of lettin' the earth spin me wherever it wants. I'm with you."

I sobbed with relief. "I'm not sure I'm worth all that."

"You're more than you know," he whispered. "I get what the preacher meant about feasts now. 'Cause I found you. Be my feast, Mercy. Everything's gonna work out just fine. I'll go wherever you want me to, if you'll just be my feast."

I picked our glass up off the floor and stared at it. Amazed by its thickness. A tiny chip, but no shatters. I was still scared. But I was a feast. And it's hard to feel desperate when you're somebody's feast.

Chapter XIII

*T*rout was unbinding me again. And not with the whisper of a word, or the embrace of his arms. It was the speed of his truck. The determined look in his eyes. We were fleeing. Heading straight into six and twenty mile holler, until we could think of a better plan. And as he drove, I could feel the mountain's fist unclenching. He was prying Crooktop's fingers off my neck.

"We'll hide out here for a couple days," he said. "He won't be thinkin' to look for you here."

"Then where?"

"Wherever." He shrugged. "If you want we can move down to middle Tennessee flatland, finish up the crops there and earn some travelin' money. Then we can roll on down to Florida and work in the oranges."

"The ocean's in Florida, isn't it?"

"Sure is."

"We'll go to Florida, then." I smiled. I had Trout. I was escaping Father Heron. And I would see the ocean. There was nothing else to wish for. Except maybe one thing. I remembered fourteen-year-old Della, trembling and clutching my hands. *Promise we'll always take care of each other, Mercy. Girls like us have to love each other. Ain't no one else around to do it.*

"Before we go to Florida, I'd like to see Della. Get her to come too."

"Too risky," he said, shaking his head. "Once we leave, we gotta stay gone. If they caught you sneakin' back, we'd both have hell to pay."

"I'd be careful. Besides, I don't got much choice."

"Last time I saw Della she was doin' fine on her own. Seemed awful happy to me too, lovin' up on some man in a necktie."

"But I promised her I'd take her with me, years ago, long before I met you." It happened my freshman year. Della'd sneak me out of study hall and over to the football stands where we'd practice trying to smoke without coughing or our eyes watering. But then the week came when she didn't show. Every morning I'd stand by her locker until long after the tardy bell rang. When Friday came and still no Della, I walked out of school to find her. I hadn't ever been to her house before, but I knew where she lived. Couple of rich girls, always jealous of the way boys leered after Della, liked to sniff their noses when they passed her. *Sniff sniff, I smell trailer trash. Della DeMar must be close.* Then they'd laugh and Della's face would flush as red as her hair, all while she mumbled cuss words so nasty I knew the only place a young girl could learn them was if she really did live in the trailer park.

I was on my way there when I heard the rumble of an El Camino and the squeal of its tires coming to a stop. Even in all the dust it kicked up, I could see her red hair. And hear her scream as the door flew open and out she rolled. Then the car took off, and there she was. Cussing, sobbing, and still laying in the dirt. I helped her up, her looking at me with no surprise. Just like she expected to find me there picking her up out of the road, instead of being in school like I was supposed to.

"You wanna tell me what's going on?" I asked her, hands on my hips, sounding like a momma.

"Lies," she said, shaking her head. "Same thing every time."

"Who was that in the car?"

"Cecil."

"Y'all fighting?"

"We was leaving this hellhole," she said.

"Leaving?" I whispered.

"Yep," she said. "Been in Kentucky these past four days. Said he was going to take me to New York, or even Hollywood. Put my picture in the magazines. Made me pose for him just for practice, working on different looks. *Look sexy*, he'd yell, then click click with his camera. *Look sassy!* Click, click. *Look pouty!* Click, click. And then, *Look happy!* That was the one that messed everything up. When he'd shout, *Look happy*, I'd just smile same way I always do. Maybe toss my hair, or stick out a hip. He'd study pictures and bring 'em to me, of girls rolling around in bikinis grinning like they was having the time of their lives. *Look at their happy eyes!* he'd yell. *And how easy their smiles seem!* It was no use, though. Smiles don't come easy to me. I told him as much, and I said maybe once we got to New York he'd make me so happy that it'd shine through in my pictures. But he said if I couldn't smile right, without looking like my face was gonna break with the strain of it, there was nothing he could do for me. *You could love me*, I says to him. Next thing I know we were headed back south and he was pushing me out of his car."

I took her home. And I could tell she was impressed with the house. With its square shape, instead of the thin rectangle of her trailer. I tried to look at it through her wide eyes. The wooden walls, instead of tin ones. The heart of pine floors, instead of vinyl. I ran her a bath. *We just got a stand-up shower*, she whispered. *It's got real fine water pressure, though*, she added quickly. I nodded my head, and added two more capfuls of the bubble bath I was usually so stingy with. Only half a capful for myself. But for a girl that never got a hot bath, four capfuls of Lavender Bliss was nothing. While she bathed I searched the kitchen for some food. I found some leftover chicken and heated up some molasses to pour over cornbread. I had her lay in my bed and propped her up with my pillow so she could eat. I was treating her the way I had imagined a momma would. Cleaning her up, filling her belly, and making sure she was warm.

"You're spoiling me," she said with a laugh when she

finished. "I hadn't eaten in almost two days. Money ran out in Kentucky. Cecil spent it all on film."

"Aw, it's nothing," I said, shrugging my shoulders. "Just leftovers and a warm bath." But what I wanted to say is, *I swear to you, Della DeMar, if you just won't leave me again I'll serve you like this all of my days.*

"Mercy?" Father Heron called out.

"Stay here," I told Della as I walked out to meet him.

I knew the minute I looked at him, I'd found trouble.

"Need something?" I whispered.

"Teacher called here today says you missed a test. Says she saw you walking straight out of the schoolhouse before the day even got started."

"Felt sick," I said.

"Well, you didn't come straight home. And you look well enough to me. Maybe I oughta give you something to feel sick about."

I looked up and saw his face, and knew that before I could blink my eyes he was gonna make me feel sick and hurt all over.

But then the room lit up so bright I wondered if he had already hit me, and maybe my eyes were injured. Or my head. Then I heard her yell.

"You touch her, you so much as leave one damned mark on that girl, and I swear this picture's gonna go straight to the police, the newspaper, and the church too!"

We both turned, me and Father Heron, our mouths hanging open in surprise, his hand still raised to hit me. Della stood there in my pajamas swinging a camera by her side.

Father Heron didn't say a word. He just gave me his *I'll deal with you later* look and bolted from the house. We laughed about it all night. How she burned two men with that camera. Cecil, once he discovers it's gone. And Father Heron, simply by taking his picture. She laid next to me, us sharing my one pillow. It was the closest thing to a slumber party I'd ever had. And right before dawn it hit me, how close I'd come to having none of that.

"You tried to leave," I whispered. "And if you hadn't come back, I'd be laying here black and blue, all alone on this mountain."

"And if you hadn't left school to find me I'd be laying in the road, hungry and dirty, and trying to figure out how to smile the right way."

That's when her hand found mine and she whispered her promise to always look out for me, and made me promise the same. I wanted to say something special. Wanted to tell her that that was the first time I could remember enjoying a night in that house. Wanted to tell her that school was a scary place without her to walk the halls with me. And that I couldn't remember how to smoke and keep my eyes from tearing up without her to show me. But it was a slumber party, and that meant we were supposed to gossip and giggle. So I just shrugged my shoulders and whispered, "Della, tell me the truth. Did I really look inside that El Camino and see an old man with gray hair? You dating a grandpappy?" Her squeals of laughter answered everything.

I laughed softly inside Trout's truck, remembering the sound of her giggles. "I gotta go back for her," I whispered.

"'Cause of some promise you made as a kid?"

"Wasn't a kid's promise," I said lowly. "It was a love promise. Same as the ones I've made to you. I can't break this one any easier than I could those."

He sighed.

"I know my mountain. I know that valley. And more than anything, I know how to hide. I've done it my whole life."

He shook his head. "At least give it a few weeks for our trail to go cold."

I nodded. It was a fair deal.

"Where we gonna stay up in here?"

"Pick a spot." He laughed. "Ain't no motels."

He drove further than we had earlier in the summer. We passed the spot where the naked boy in boots had stood, holding his dead squirrel. Then we passed the place where we had parked to go fishing. I remembered how he had called me a part of the "y'all" that hated people like him and the six and twenty milers. Now we were both exiles.

Soon it was dark, and the road was no longer dotted with shacks and old trailers. We were further in the holler than the six and twenty milers themselves.

"Where's this road lead?" I asked.

"Goes over the mountain. Rough way too. Never paved."

"I never knew there was another way off this mountain. I just always thought there was the main road and that's it. You sure he can't get us here?" I asked.

"Well, how's this spot look?"

It looked like all the rest. Wild. Trees so thick I

wondered how we could set the tent up. Or if we would even bother to.

"I guess fine," I said. "Long as it's hidden."

"The ditch ends there. I can pull the truck up into the woods a little. He won't come lookin' in here. And if he did, he'd have a hard time spottin' us. Besides, there's a stream nearby that'll serve us well."

We started walking into the woods, searching for a spot clear enough to pitch the tent.

"The locals'll come callin' any minute," Trout said.

"How come?"

"This is their holler. Nothin' hides from 'em. They've been on this land long 'fore the valley began. They know when every old tree falls. So they sure as hell will know we're here."

"Think they'll tell anybody?"

"Who'd listen to 'em?" He shrugged.

We found a small clearing near the stream and pitched the tent. Trout built a fire and started fishing. Then we ate together, picking bites off the same smoked fish. There was a crate of tomatoes in the bed of his truck, so we roasted a couple and ate them as well.

"We'll never be hungry," he said proudly. "This mountain feeds me better'n my momma ever did."

"My Mamma Rutha wasn't too good at feeding me either. Wonder if I'll ever see her again."

"You never can know. When I joined the migrants I didn't think I'd ever see my momma again. Did though, just a couple years ago after some cowboy cops did a big sweep of the mater camp. They was aimin' to scare off the Mexicans, but didn't mind gettin' to round a white boy up neither."

"You go to jail?"

"Yep. Longest two months of my life."

"Because you were all caged up?"

"That was bad." He nodded. "But the worst of it was how I'd miss little things. Like rain. I didn't have a window, but I could smell it on the guards. They'd walk by, and I'd know that outside was a rain I'd never get the chance to see. It was like pieces of the mountain were dyin' all around me."

"Was your momma in jail too?"

"No. Fella from over near home was in there with me. He got out, went and told her 'bout me. 'Hello son,' she said. Don't think she ever called me by a name. And when I got to thinkin' 'bout it, I couldn't remember her name neither. For a long time we just sat there and looked at each other. 'Know what I thought about the other day?' she asked. ' 'Bout that time you et a whole sweet potatuh pie.' "

He shook his head slowly. "Of all the days we shared, we couldn't remember the same ones. She remembered pie. And I couldn't remember a day she ever fed me. 'You scared in here, son?' she asked, her mouth puckerin' a little, like she bit an early persimmon. She was grown. It was the first time I ever seen her growed up. Little lines around her eyes. Little lines around her mouth. 'I ain't,' I lied."

"How come you lied?" I asked.

"She needed to hear it." He shrugged his shoulders.

"She died a little while ago. Got word from a girl she used to run 'round with. Said in her last moments she called for her baby boy." He shook his head. "Wished I was there."

"Why? You couldn't have done anything."

"I would've known what it was like for her to want me. And I would've told her it was awright. That I was awright." He laughed softly. "My momma wasn't near the woman yours is."

I shook my head. "She's dead. Father Heron killed her."

"No, not that one. The one that's raised you up."

"Mamma Rutha," I said, feeling tense. "How do you know her?"

"Followed you home one night. Paced behind you, watchin' the way you walked. Like the mountain pulled you up it. Watchin' the way you crept up to the house, like you was scared of it."

"Why'd you do that? I told you not to," I said, as color flooded my face.

"I was jealous. There was a part of you hid up on that mountain. And I wanted that part too. You went inside, through the back door. And then I saw her. Naked in the moonlight. Skin shinin' like dew. Hair swingin' down to her waist. Like you, all growed up. 'Chop down the apple tree,' she sang to me. I looked to where she pointed but I couldn't see a tree. The night was too black. 'Chop down the apple tree,' she sang again. The only thing I could think to say is, 'Yes ma'am, bring me an axe.' Then she smiled. Lord that woman took my breath. Beautiful. Like you are, like you will be."

He circled me in his arms. "Yes, Mercy, you are that woman's daughter. No denyin' it. Never could figure what she meant about the apple tree, though."

"This," I whispered. "Saving me from him. That apple tree wants my blood."

Chapter XIV

*T*hey're here, Mercy. They done found us."

I sat up quickly and listened. We'd only set up our tent a couple hours before. I heard a bird singing in the distance, and the sound of the stream running past us. I heard Trout's breath, slow and even.

"Don't hear nobody," I said.

"Shhh. There," he said, pointing toward the road.

"Him?" I asked, beginning to shake with fear.

He shook his head. "Huh-uh. The boys that run this place." He stood up and turned in their direction.

"What do they want?"

"To know why we're trespassin'."

They moved quietly, but quickly. I was surprised by how fast they reached us. There were six of them, four young men and two old.

"Mornin', Trout," one of them spoke.

"Mornin'. This is Mercy," Trout said.

I smiled and tried to appear friendly, though I felt threatened. I looked from face to face, seeing if anyone would return my smile. And then I saw him. Jericho Chapman.

"Hey Jericho," I said. "We was in school together, eight grades, and then even some at Valley High." He looked at me, and I couldn't tell whether he knew me or not. All I could see was the piercing blue of his eyes. They made the sky seem dull.

"You from the valley, ain't you?" he asked. "That red-head girl, Della, you's the one always runnin' 'round with her?"

"Yep. That was me," I said, wishing I had a memory of him to prove that I had noticed him too. "Been runnin' around with the mater migrants lately, though," I said, pointing to Trout. It was the first time I had ever used that word with pride. In that holler, being a mater migrant was so much better than being a Heron.

"What you doin' up in here, Mercy?" Jericho asked. "These ain't your parts."

"She's here with me," Trout said. "I brought her here."

"Bet your valley folk wouldn't like that none," one of the men said with a smirk. "No point in bringin' your troubles on us. We don't mean no disrespect, Trout, we never did mind you fishin' our streams or worshipin' in our church, but we don't want no valley trouble."

"Jericho," I said lowly. "You and I spent eight years of school together, and we never spoke 'til this day. But it wasn't 'cause I wanted to stick with my own kind. I ain't got my own kind."

"What is it you're wantin' from us?"

"Just a couple days to catch our breath," Trout said. "I'm takin' her off this mountain. Maybe into Tennessee or Kentucky."

"Who's comin' fer you?" the old one asked.

"My grandfather," I said. "'Cause he'd see me dead 'fore he'd see me love a boy that ain't from his valley." It was the right thing to say. I could sense their approval as I glanced from face to face, gazing with shock at each new set of piercing eyes. The deepest blues. The most striking greens. If I hadn't been working so hard to gain their trust, I would have thought them all beautiful. In an unearthly sense. Like I was standing before little mountain gods.

"Ever been up Thorny Ridge?" Jericho asked Trout.

"Been to it," Trout nodded. "Downstream a ways, then north, up the mountain, right?"

"Yep. There's a gatherin' there tonight. Youns come by, 'round sundown."

Trout nodded. "We'd be obliged to."

The men walked away as quietly and as quickly as they had come. But they left a deep impression on me. From more than their eyes. It was their cleanliness too. They were wretchedly poor. Soles of boots were split. And on some of them, a couple of toes without socks peeked through. But this was the land of their fathers. And they cleaned up to prove it to us.

And they were dark, with dusky skin, and black hair. A sharp contrast to their glowing eyes.

"Are they Indian?" I asked.

"Everybody's got Indian in 'em in these mountains."

"But they're different. They're something else. Not white, or Mexican, or black. Nothing seems to fit 'em."

"They're the mountains' own race. You can find people the world over that look like us. But you gotta peel back these mountains to find people that look like them."

"What are they called?"

"Some call it melungeon," he said. "Means abandoned by God, but they ain't. These mountains are a holy ground, they're a chosen people."

"I been around six and twenty milers all my life, but I've never noticed how different they are."

"Every six and twenty miler ain't melungeon. But all them men were. And besides, you've always looked at 'em through valley eyes. They look different here in their homeland. Good thing you knew Jericho."

"When we went on to high school and everything got bigger, I didn't see much of him. He dropped out after the first year. You know him?"

"I seen him 'round. You notice his left hand?"

"Huh-uh."

"Missin' two fingers. His daddy's the preacher at the snake church."

"And he got bit and lost his fingers?"

"Bunch of 'em have. I reckon tonight we'll see quite a few people missin' fingers, or with crippled hands. But it's a special sorrow to Jericho."

"How come?"

"This church don't convert people. Nobody just wakes up and says they're gonna handle snakes at church. It's the families that keep it goin'. Bringin' new children into it every year. Jericho can't quit, but he can't hardly handle them snakes neither."

"But you said a bunch of people have been bit. Why's it so bad for Jericho?"

"He's the preacher's boy."

"Well I don't see why any of 'em keep doing it if they get bit."

"They say the Bible tells 'em to take up snakes. It don't say they won't ever get bit. If they do, it's meant to test 'em or purge some sin. But Jericho gets purged more'n any of the others. He's been bit so many times I reckon it's a wonder he has any fingers at all. Everybody takes it real hard, too. They're all prayin' for Jericho's redemption. He was next in line to be the preacher. But them snakes won't quit bitin' him."

"Do they bite his daddy?"

"Oh sure. He's been bit before. But not as much as everybody else. That's one way he knows he's called to preach."

"Will snakes be at this gathering?" I asked him.

"No. If I'm countin' my days off right, tonight is gonna be a moon night for them people."

"Never heard of moon nights," I said, thinking about Mamma Rutha, naked in her garden and singing to the moon.

"Melungeons live by the moon. Tells 'em when to plant. When to harvest. What to expect out of a comin' season. It's their window into God's mind."

As we walked through the dark woods that night, climbing further and further up the mountain, I could hear them singing. Clear voices, in several pitches. Weaving together, and calling us toward them. They were assembled at the top of Thorny Ridge, beneath a black sky burning with a full moon. We stood in the woods, watching them.

"That's the last call to harvest," Trout whispered, pointing at the orange moon. "It's the mountain's way of givin' another day to work, even though it's still night."

I looked down and saw that he was right. It was as though I was standing beneath a dim sun. I could see all of my details. The shabbiness of my clothes. My stringy hair.

A fiddle whined over the voices. One long note held, until everyone hushed with expectancy. People began stomping their feet. And as the music began, they started dancing.

"What are they doing?" I asked.

"Flatfootin'."

Della used to drag me to high school dances where kids slowdanced and groped each other. But I had never seen anything like the moon dancers of Thorny Ridge. With their arms swinging loose by their sides. And their hips held still, while their feet pounded out rhythms. There were no couples. There was just a single pulsing mass.

We were spotted. Jericho and his wife came toward us.

"Hey, Mercy. Trout." He nodded. "This is my bride, Elsa."

I looked at Elsa and felt myself wince with envy. She was made of the mountain's best colors, with black wavy hair down to her hips, blue eyes to match her husband's, and warm dusky skin.

Trout and Jericho started talking about the harvest. And how the mater migrants were clearing out and getting ready to move to other sites or head south. I stood and stared at Elsa, and tried to think of something to say.

"This dancing sure is something," I said, knowing that I sounded like a tourist. But Elsa didn't seem to mind.

"I know," she said proudly. "When my momma was alive, she could dance it like no other. Her name was Mabel. Everybody called her Dancin' Mabbie. That woman had a song in her feet. She'd be drawin' water from the well, and her feet would be a tappin' out a dance. No one's as good as her."

"Well, your people sure know how to have a party," I said.

"Oh it ain't a party," she said seriously. "It's a prayer. We always come to this ridge on the harvest moon. We come to show we're thankful for the summer. For the warmth and the food we scraped out of the ground. An' we come to pray for mercy on us through winter. Preacher'll have a meetin' soon."

I looked at the moon dancers, a bouncing mass. It was a strange prayer.

"Watch the moon," Elsa said. "If it don't disappear at dawn, if it just melts into a hot and high sun that never had to rise, that means our harvest is strong. But if that moon goes away, and like any other ol' day we have a sunrise, then it don't look so good for us. Means our harvest moon went cold. Means our harvest might not be enough to withstand a long hard winter."

"You believe it?"

"Some young folk don't. They say its just the ramblin's of old-timers. But I've been fat and happy through winters when the harvest moon turned into a hot sun. And then I've seen my starvin' days too, when that moon goes cold."

It was a story Mamma Rutha would believe in. I wished that I could see the moon become the sun. Just so that one day, I could tell her about it.

"You wanna learn to dance?" she asked, smiling.

"If you think you can teach someone like me." I laughed.

She did her best. She began by showing me the way to stand. With relaxed arms and feet. Tense knees. And hips locked in place. I felt silly. Shaking my feet in a directionless shuffle. I blushed when I noticed Trout watching me. I let Elsa pull me into the crowd. And surrounded by dozens of expert flatfooters, I absorbed their rhythm. In my mind at least, I became a good dancer. I had never felt so free in the middle of a crowd of people. I felt the Heron in me slipping away. I felt my eyes become a piercing blue. For a second, I nearly believed—I was one of the mountain's chosen.

Then I saw her. From the corner of my eye, dancing as though she were a young girl. Mamma Rutha. I started running toward her. "Mamma Rutha!" I cried out. But my voice was smothered in the crowd. "Mamma Rutha!"

I came to the spot where she was dancing. She was gone. I looked in every direction, and realized that she didn't want me to find her. Maybe she didn't want to be Mamma Rutha there, any more than I wanted to be Mercy Heron.

Elsa led me over to a blanket on the grass and brought me a cup of what she called "corn."

I took a sip. It was bitter fire. I coughed and gagged.

"What's this?" I asked.

"Homemade corn. Your people might call it shine."

I sipped my corn slowly and soon found myself talking to Elsa about things I never told anyone. I told her about my dreams of the ocean. And how sometimes I wondered if God had messed up.

"Maybe I was supposed to be born by the ocean. Not on this mountain," I said.

"Why'd you say a thing like that?"

"'Cause why would God plan it out like this? Put me on a mountain, without a momma or a daddy. Give me to a grandfather that I won't ever be holy enough to belong to. And then fill my head with dreams about a land I've never seen."

"Maybe he put you here so that he could call you to him there," she whispered. "He can't call a person if there's no place for them to go."

I nodded. "Like your Jericho. I hear he has a burdensome call."

She smiled sadly. "My poor Jericho. He was born a prince in these parts. That's what being the preacher's boy means up in here. An' everybody always expects him to have dreams and visions and prophecies. They want him to lead them to a higher place. But even this mountain's got a top on it. Jericho can't get 'em past that."

"I know what he's feeling," I said. "I don't handle snakes. But I know what's it's like to not live up to expectations."

"Nobody understands that he's just a man," she said. "Nobody but me and the snakes. With every fang in their little mouths, they show him how earthly he really is."

"He should just quit the snake church."

Elsa sighed. "He is the church, Mercy. He's its baby. He never had one momma and daddy. He had dozens of 'em. Watchin' him. Makin' sure he was doin' what's most holy. He'll die tryin' to win their love." She shook her head slowly and held up her hands before her. "He used to have beautiful hands. But they bite my Jericho more'n anybody else. 'Elsie,' he cried once. 'I've got a blackness in my heart that I can't find. It's in there, the snakes see it. But I swear to you, Elsie, I don't know what it is. What have I done? What blackness sits in my soul?' So I set out to that church and freed every single one of them snakes."

"I don't blame you," I said.

She sighed again. "But it just made him think I might be the blackness. I won't hold them snakes. Now folks is always talkin' 'bout how them snakes wouldn't be bitin' him if it weren't for me. And you know somethin'? If I thought my leavin' him would free him up for his callin', I'd do it."

I finished my glass of corn, and Elsa brought us some more. The sounds around me were starting to blur. The stomping, the laughing, the fiddles.

"I can help Jericho," I whispered, with numb lips. "You gotta feed him a snake. A whole one. Everything but the choking bones. The head, the heart, the rattles. Everything."

"Why?" she asked, with wide eyes. "Is it like a spell or somethin'?"

"It's how a man becomes animal. Your Jericho needs to think like them snakes. And he needs them snakes to know that he is a part of them. You feed him one. And them snakes will never touch him again."

Elsa nodded slowly, and started telling me the details

about the last time Jericho was bit. I nodded my head and pretended to listen. But my mind was buzzing with my own thoughts. I realized I didn't hate the mountain anymore. I had escaped Father Heron. I had escaped the June apple tree. I let that wild mountain embrace me and claim me as its daughter.

It would be the first night in my life that I hadn't slept under Father Heron's roof. And as chill bumps crept up my arms I realized it would be the first night that I would spend with Trout. It was real. I was free.

Trout pulled me to him, and we walked to the singing, dancing crowd. I let him kiss me, in the middle of the crowd, and never once felt afraid of being seen.

Jericho's daddy went to the middle of the circle and started praying about the coming winter. He called for people to testify to the blessings the harvest had brought them. There were stories of new babies born and old people healed. Stories of food that lasted when it shouldn't have. Of rain that came, just when it was most needed.

"It's our harvest night, Mercy," Trout whispered lowly. "We're startin' a whole new life."

I nodded and reached for his hand.

"Jericho," Trout said. "You called to preach, ain't you?"

Jericho looked down at the ground and shrugged his shoulders.

"Don't worry, we ain't in need of snakes," Trout said.

He led me to the center of the circle, the moon shining down on my head like a crown of glory. And with Jericho's prompting, we made our promises real. *Wherever you go, I'll go. Your people are my people. And your God is my God.*

I was trembling while I said it, and while I listened. Trembling when he took my hand and led me deeper into the woods. Trembling when I heard the sound of water, the sound of a pure mountain stream nearby. The whole time we walked, his eyes stayed on me, looking in me. I let his eyes search me out, until my body felt no surprise when it felt his touch. Not like the sweet kisses in the tentworld or on our fishing dates. But a touch simply because he knew that my skin, my very being, was now his.

His callused fingers gently, *so gently*, touched the side of my face. Softly pushing back my wind-tangled hair. His red palm lifted my chin. *Another touch*. The prickle of his beard was like tomato leaves rubbing against my skin. Was he holding me down in the water? Is that why my skin burned so? Was he whispering love? Or was that just the wind in the trees? *Another touch*. Red palms on cool pale skin. A gentle invitation. *And still another*. His eyes, eyes that no longer asked, held mine. I was drowning. Drowning in deep green river pools. And there were sunflowers everywhere. Floating past me. Floating on me. Within me.

Chapter XV

*L*ife coursed through me with every pulse.
I ran my fingers through that black mountain dirt and held
on. It was what my momma laid on when she gave birth to
me, when she died. And it was what I had laid on the night
before, when I first knew love. All of my hunger, sorrow,
and new joy, I shared with the earth of that mountain.

Elsa visited our tent later that day. "I did it," she said. "I
made him a rattler stew. An' I says to him, 'Jericho, this here
is a rattler stew. An' it might kill you. But it might save you
too. I leave it to you whether you want to try.' He set himself
down and ate the whole kettle. He even said he liked it."

"Did it work? Has he been to church?"

"Ain't been a meetin' yet. But we've tried it on our
own. We snuck down there and he held them snakes like
they was nothin' but fuzzy pups."

"He's part snake now," I said.

"He is. Never seen nothin' like it in all my days. He even shook 'em to try and rile 'em up, and they never even hissed. But the best part is now he knows I ain't the blackness in his soul."

She hugged me close. "You know we're kin," she said lightly, giving me her full smile.

"Yes. We'll always be friends."

"No," she said, laughing. "I mean you're my people. Your Mamma Rutha, she's my people too."

"How?" I whispered, in shock.

"Ruthie Clyde was her birth name. She still comes up in here sometimes. Often one of our men will stumble up on her in the woods. Ain't all there in the head now, is she?"

"No. But how is she your people?"

"She's from this holler. Fell in love with a valley boy, though. Moved out to his part of the mountain. That was all before my time, but folks say this whole holler was in an uproar about it. She was a beauty in her day. An' everybody hated to see her waste it on a good-fer-nothin' valley boy. 'How can you leave your homeland?' folks asked her, before she ran off to marry him. 'It's easier to leave my home than it is my heart,' she cried. She loved him somethin' fierce. Funny when you think about it."

"What's funny?"

"How you're doin' the same thing she did. Leavin' your home for a boy. But Ruthie Clyde makes us kin. She was my grandmammy's sister."

When Elsa left, I realized I was proud of her beauty. I was a part of that. I felt a sense of ownership in the wilderness too. It belonged to some of my ancestors. I even wondered if that made me part melungeon. Maybe there was more to me after all, than a dull paleness that stared back in the mirror.

I was washing up in the stream when I heard a branch break. It was close. Maybe thirty feet away. Leaves rustled without any wind to blow them. *Danger, danger, danger,* my heart whispered.

Trout was supposed to be loading up the truck. If I had been sure of the way and it were just up to me, we would have left long ago. But with darkness approaching, all of the woods looked the same.

There was another movement. The sound of underbrush being pushed back. It could be a bear, I thought. *Or it could be Father Heron.* I hoped it was a bear. Whatever it was, as I sat and listened to its movements, I grew sure that it was tracking me down. Its path never darted to the side. It was following one clean straight line to where I sat, shaking.

Go, go, go. That was my only thought as I felt my legs pull into a blind run. Something crashed behind me, responding to my flight. It wasn't tracking me anymore. It was chasing me. A tree root reached out and grabbed my foot, sending me tumbling to the ground. I looked behind me. Moonlight bounced from limb to limb, lighting up pockets of the woods. A scream swelled in my throat. Every glowing pocket held a pair of black eyes. I picked myself up and ran as hard as my body could. Into branches. Through briars.

I saw the truck in the distance.

"Trout!" I screamed. "Trout!" It was a familiar sound. The scream of dreams, just like Mamma Rutha when her chicken was killed. Soon Trout was with me. I pulled him, dragged him, to the truck.

"GO!" I screamed. "GO!"

After a couple tries the truck started, and soon we were moving. I turned and looked through the rear window. My eyes searching for any trace of moonlight to show my danger. A shadow moved. A darkness low to the ground. And then another, close to the first. And though I knew better, with all my heart I knew better, I couldn't help but think I saw them. His great hunters. Fox, Wolf, Coon, and Bear.

"What in the hell is goin' on?" Trout cried. "Who's after us?"

"Don't know." I didn't know if I was being hunted or going crazy. "I just need to get off this mountain," I sobbed. "I won't really be free 'til I know he can't find me."

"It's awright now," he said, grabbing my hand. "Woods can be a scary place at night."

"I don't know what it was," I said. "It was like the minute the sun set I felt danger everywhere. And it was more than a feeling. I saw things too, in the moonlight."

"Maybe it was a melungeon moon givin' you a sign that danger was comin'," he said. "Ran into Jericho today. Told me he's seen some strange cars drivin' up in here past couple days. Said if it was him, he'd be headin' off the mountain soon."

"I'm part melungeon," I whispered. "I'm kin to Elsa."

"Maybe it's that part of you that saved us tonight."

We drove through the night and Crooktop hid itself in the dark. I looked in the rearview mirror and imagined I could see it, towering over our truck with its broken top.

I felt the need to say goodbye. That mountain held more than my Father Heron. Mamma Rutha and Della were up there somewhere. So were my momma's bones.

By morning, though, my mountains had disappeared for good and everything else seemed too big. The sky went on forever. Green hills rolled as far as I could see. And the air was thick and heavy.

"Where are we?" I asked.

"Middle of Tennessee. We're further south here, there's a little bit left to pick before the chill sets in."

"Where'd the mountains go?"

"Eight hours northeast," he said, smiling. "Big world, ain't it?"

Crooktop had loomed over me all my life. But eight short hours proved it was never as big as it wanted me to believe. We slowed to a stop, and I looked around at a new camp. It seemed familiar, with a river nearby, and little tent clusters dotting the fields. The last of the tomatoes were still hanging heavy on the vines. And rows of peppers were planted next to them. *I'm home*, I thought.

"Well, let's see if we can work," he said.

I had never imagined that we might be refused. Instead I had been preparing myself for an ugly life. The life of a mater migrant.

"You mean they might not want us?" I asked. Suddenly, even the ugly life seemed precious. Without that work, we had no jobs. No food. And no money to get us to the ocean.

"Well, camp's windin' down. Boss might not be lookin' to hire just when he's gettin' ready to close the fields down."

We went looking for the camp boss. Trout had worked

for him before, and told me that he could be harsh. "You pick your maters, and he'll treat you good. You joke around and have an empty crate at the end of the day, he'll make you pay."

We found him by the trucks, watching crates being loaded. He was a big man, with thick layers of muscle over an even thicker layer of fat. He was young too. Not much older than Trout.

"How'd he get to be boss?"

"Born for it. His uncle owns this farm."

"Do I call him Richard?" I asked, seeing the name stitched on his shirt pocket, right below "A.C. Cropping Incorporated."

"Never," Trout said. "If you're doin' good, you call him Boss. If he's yellin' at you, you call him Sir. And behind his back you call him whatever you want."

When the trucks pulled away, Trout took me to him.

"Hey Boss. Crooktop camp's dried up. We was wonderin' if you need some help finishin' up here."

"Who's she?" he asked.

"Mercy Price."

"Where y'all from?"

"Up in the mountains. We're on our way to Florida, need to earn some travelin' money."

"Well I'll be damned," he said, before spitting on the ground. He crossed his arms over his chest and studied me. My eyes fell to the ground, and I tried my best to seem capable of hard work.

"Ain't never bossed a white girl before. I've hollered my head off at them Mexican girls. But this here's a new thing for me."

"She's worked in gardens all her life, Boss. She'll work good, you got my word."

"Gardens." He laughed. "This ain't no pretty garden party. This work ain't fitting for you. Hell, it ain't hardly fitting for you, Trout. You need to head back up in them mountains."

"My hands can pick them maters as good as any Mexican girl's," I said.

"But are your hands as willing to blister? Is your back as willing to hurt? Them Mexicans swim over here and beg to blister and hurt. They don't got other options. You do. You was born for a better life than this."

"I was born for a life with him," I said, looking at Trout.

"I won't cut you any breaks," he said. "I don't care how soft and pale your skin is."

I nodded. "We're real grateful, Boss," Trout said.

"You see that corner field over there. Y'all can start there today. Show her how it goes, Trout. Make sure she don't bang the maters up too much. Don't stop 'til you got twenty crates."

"Sure thing, Boss," Trout muttered as I followed him away.

Already I felt like a mater migrant. I hated that white boss so much I felt my skin turn brown beneath his stare. Trout handed me a crate. And I was surprised at how big it seemed. Full of tomatoes it looked like a small box. But empty, I saw how deep and wide it really was.

"How long will it take to fill this?" I asked.

"Not as long as it would earlier in the summer. During the early season we have to be real careful 'bout which ones we pick. We have to leave most behind until they hit their peak. But now the season's almost over, and what we don't pick will rot. So pick anything that ain't near rot. Look for mushy skin or black spots, that's how it starts."

I squatted down in front of a plant and began to eye it for rot.

"An' watch out for them mater worms. Fuzzy green things, 'bout as long as your little finger. They give a nasty bite. Watch out for bees too. They love a rotten mater."

"When's our first break?" I asked.

He smiled at me, and I knew my question was silly. "Depends on how the day goes. Just start here, at the row next to mine."

I put my crate down and cupped my hand around a tomato. After two tugs, it broke loose, and I laid it in my crate. It looked so small. It would take a hundred rows, I thought, to meet our daily quota.

"Pull it like this," Trout called. I watched him grab the stem of the tomato, right where it connects to the vine. With a quick jerk the tomato snapped loose. He stripped an entire plant like that, before I had even spotted all the tomatoes on my plant.

"Takes time," he said. "You'll figure it out."

Soon he was far ahead of me. I was still squatting in front of my first plant, trying to figure out which tomatoes were rotten. After squishing two in my hands, I wondered if they all were. I saw Trout get himself a new crate. Mine was only a third full.

Hours passed. Trout brought me new crates. I didn't know how many I had filled. Was it really only eight? I heard the boss yelling in Spanish, and was glad I couldn't understand.

"Trout," I whispered as he passed by. "Do they serve lunch?"

"Not unless you've met your half quota by noon."

"You think I will?"

"That was an hour ago, Mercy. You only had six. When you find a mater that ain't quite perfect, but ain't all bad either, eat that."

I ate two flawed tomatoes for lunch, and began to pick up my pace so that I wouldn't miss dinner. I cursed myself for complaining about my diner job. Carrying pork platters was nothing compared to dragging twenty crates of tomatoes to the loading dock. As the afternoon dragged on, I knew Boss was right. I was too weak for this type of work. And if the Mexicans could've told the truth, they would've said they were too. I started dreaming about baths filled with ice chips. And tried not to holler too loud when a yellowjacket stung me.

Evening came. Trout met his quota and I was four crates behind. He bundled tomatoes from other rows in his shirt and snuck them into my crates. By nightfall, I was finished. Twenty crates, all approved by Boss.

"Don't look like you'll make it back tomorrow." Boss laughed. "Them maters beat you down."

I collapsed in Trout's tent, forgetting to eat supper.

"It won't always be like this," Trout whispered, rubbing my aching muscles. "We get to Florida there'll be other work for a girl like you. There's restaurants there, and shoppin' malls. I hear they even have little huts that sell ice cream by the ocean. I could see you workin' a job like that, couldn't you?"

Before I found the strength to answer, it was a new day. With a new quota.

"At least twenty-two per man today. Gotta finish this field up 'fore frost comes. And there'll be crate-and-a-half bonus pay for every crate over. And beer too for any man that hits twenty-five."

The migrants cheered and ran to get their crates, eager for the extra pay and beer.

"I won't get twenty-two," I told Trout. "You go for the bonus, that's good money we need. Don't waste your maters on me."

Trout and some others headed for a far field, where the tomatoes were the heaviest. I stopped at the first row I came to, and started picking. It was hotter that day than before. And I didn't worry much about whether the tomatoes were rotten or not. I passed the time thinking about a little hut by the ocean, where I could spend my days selling ice cream.

"You're picking rot," Boss yelled. He picked a tomato out of my crate and threw it at me. As I wiped the rotten juice off my face, he picked up my entire crate and dumped it beside me.

"Would you eat that?" he yelled. "Here, take a bite of this one! You think that's fit for eating?" He shoved a black tomato in my face. I turned my head away and forced myself to hold back my tears. "Don't put nothing rotten in that crate or I'll make you eat it next time."

I sat down on the ground and began sorting the dumped tomatoes.

"It's the skin," a girl whispered to me. I could see her

staring at me through the leaves, from the other side of my row.

"Pinch the skin to see if it gives. If it sinks in deep and doesn't press back at all, it's too ripe. You want the skin to push back some."

"Thanks," I whispered.

"Here," she said, pushing several tomatoes on the ground over to me. "Boss don't want you to make your quota. He likes it when new girls don't."

I started picking again, determined to meet my quota. I no longer thought about my body. Or the bees. I was too busy worrying over Boss. I dragged crate after crate to the docks. All full of pinched tomatoes. And when I collapsed in Trout's tent that night, I couldn't help but wonder at how the world was still the same. The mountains might have disappeared. But enemies hadn't. Neither had fear.

Chapter XVI

*T*he days passed slowly, like my rows of tomatoes. My body learned to struggle through the work.
And my heart learned how to love Trout freely. There was
no need to be careful anymore. He kissed me hard in the
middle of the tentworld. And at night he led me to the
fields and laid me down among the rows. Our love was as
ripe as the harvest.

"It's always gonna be like this," Trout whispered one
night. The smell of tomatoes curled around us, and I
wished that was all there was. No white bosses. No quotas.

"I mean, you won't work like this always," he said. "I'll
do better by you in Florida. But the rest of it, the holdin'
you in my arms and the havin' you as my own, none of
that's gonna change."

"That's all I want," I whispered. "If I can have that, I'll pick these maters forever."

"Look there," he said, pointing to the full moon. "That was made for people like you."

"I can't see nothing in it. Mamma Rutha could've."

"C'mon," he said, smiling. "Just try."

I laid back on the dirt, my face turned up to the sky, and stared hard into the moon. I noticed for the first time the shades of gray swirling in with the light. And how even those dark spots glowed.

"I see us by the ocean," I whispered. "And when we kiss we can taste the salt in the air. Nobody knows that you're a mater migrant. Or that I'm the deacon's granddaughter. Nobody cares that we're in love."

"Any babies in that moon?" He laughed.

I laughed too.

"It's a big moon, Mercy. Too big for just us," he teased.

"Don't know about babies, but right there," I said, pointing to the moon, "that dark spot there, you see it? That's you catching a big ocean fish and making up some story about how you set its belly on fire."

Sometimes we stayed in the rows until we fell asleep, like Adam and Eve lost in the garden. But we found happiness back in the tentworld too. It was a place where everyone tried to make up for hard days by being as jolly as possible. Most of the migrants understood some English, and I was quickly learning the most necessary Spanish phrases. Like, *Maldiga el diablo blanco al infierno* for "Damn the White Devil to hell." White Devil, that's what we called Boss.

Many of the migrants had known Trout for years. Trout

would sit and talk with them about old times—the fields they used to work, the bosses they loved or hated. I listened and learned more of his secrets. Like how he cried the first time he left the mountains. He was a young boy frightened to learn that his world didn't go on forever. *Trucha que llora*, they called him, the Weeping Trout. I learned about his first love too, Marta. *She made you weep again, Trucha*, the migrants teased. He had been sixteen when he loved her. Neither one understood the other's language. They spent hours sitting by each other, smiling and staring. When her family went back to Mexico and took her with them, Trout's heart was broken.

I listened to these stories about Marta, and tried to smother my questions. *Was she beautiful? What if she came back from Mexico one day?*

"He loves you more," an old woman leaned over to whisper to me. They called her Madre. She had worked the fields for decades, and earned the respect of everyone. If the rows at this camp had a leader, it was her. "I saw him with Marta," she said. "And after her, there was no other 'til you. You are the great one for him."

"Thank you, Madre," I whispered, as my face flushed with emotion. It didn't matter if Marta was beautiful. I was the great one.

I found other mothers in the tentworld too. Women that were happy to teach me things that no other woman ever had. Like how to season foods. How to take simple, earthy ingredients like beans and tomatoes and give them full interesting flavors with some fresh peppers and a little salt. Or how to wash my clothes by hand, using only river water and a smooth rock. They taught me how to make a man comfortable, with a good meal and a cozy tent. They even tried to dress me up. They braided my hair with red ribbons, and called me their Mercia. I wasn't white to them anymore. I was their daughter, their sister. The blisters in my palms proved it.

There were even a handful of children. Always giggling and begging Trout to teach them to fish. They were lost to any world outside of the fields. They never went to school. Or to a doctor. Most were born among the rows, their mommas' labor assisted by Madre's capable hands. They spent their days under a shade tree, where Lila, a fourteen-year-old girl, watched them and taught them how to draw letters in the dirt.

Our world was one of order. Where women tended to meals, while men fished, brought firewood, and carried water. It was a safety I had never known. The only thing that made me uneasy was Boss. I hadn't told Trout about what happened with him. I just made sure I pinched all of my tomatoes. I passed over the ones that even hinted of not pressing back. And I met my quotas. No matter how hard it was. I didn't eat, not even a bite of overripe tomato, until I met that quota. My body was suffering for it too. My hunger left me. When morning came I would smell those tomatoes, the same scent that I loved at night, and vomit.

"Too skinny," Madre told me. "Bring a tortilla to the rows."

"It's my stomach," I said. "Boss has got me tied up in knots."

She nodded her head. "Camp almost over. Big Boss in Florida is nice. You like him. You be safe there."

I'm safe, I thought. For the first time in my life, it was clear how to avoid the danger. Just meet my quota.

But one day, my stomach wouldn't settle. I crouched between tomato plants and heaved. I tried to force myself to eat a tomato. But as soon as I pressed its skin to my mouth, I would gag. I couldn't stop heaving. I looked at the dirt, and when no one was looking, I tasted it. Just a few grains pressed between my teeth. Salty grit. I stopped shaking. My body grew calm.

"Been out here two hours already, don't have a crate yet," Boss hollered down the row. I nodded at him and started pinching tomatoes.

But I was weak. My body worked too hard to lose the little food I gave it. I dragged crate after crate to the loading docks. But by evening, I only had fourteen. The quota had been twenty-one.

"What's wrong?" Trout asked when he saw my quota sheet. "You sick or somethin'?"

"No. Yes. I mean I was this morning. And then I just couldn't do it anymore. What's Boss gonna do?"

"Nothin' too bad. Just look down at the ground and say Sir to him."

He was coming toward me. Marching with straight shoulders, his gut pushed out. "What'd I tell you, Mercy? First day I hired you, what'd I say? I said I wouldn't cut you no breaks. And now you're a full third short of what you were ordered to pick."

"Sorry sir."

"Well, it may be nighttime, but you ain't finished. You get back out there, and you pick seven more crates. And don't come back 'til you're done."

"Sir," Trout said. "It's dark, she can't tell what's rotten and what ain't."

"She can once she brings 'em to me. You pick 'em, bring 'em here, and I'll throw out the bad and you can go get more to replace 'em. Now go. And you, Trout, I don't want to see you sneaking into them fields to help. You do and I'll send you both on your way and keep your week's wages for trespassing."

"It's all right," I said to Trout. "I ain't that tired, I can do this. I'll just be a few hours."

He looked at me, unsure of whether to believe me. "Really," I said. "It's fine."

But when the campfires went out and the tentworld fell asleep, everything looked different. The rows no longer seemed like my love garden. I couldn't see the worms that bit me. And the only thing I could smell was rot. Hours dragged by and I filled my crates slowly. I thought about Trout asleep back in the tent. I thought about Della, looking for me, wondering where I was. And then I thought about Crooktop.

I stood up and looked around. Though I couldn't see it, I knew the land stretched out far and wide. For one moment, I missed my mountain. It was high above those rotten tomatoes. And it hid me from the greatness of that sky. I remembered Father Heron's house, jutting off the land. And lost in those dark rows, the bitter thought occurred to me that everything there hadn't been bad. The work had been easy. Now, my body was breaking. And I had always had a warm bed at night. Now, I was standing in the rows, being bitten by green worms.

"You like to work hard, don't you," a voice called out through the darkness. It was him. Boss.

"Used to it," I answered, wondering which row he was in.

"How many crates you filled now?"

"Three."

"They back at the docks?"

"Yep."

"I'll check 'em over, see how you've done."

"I've pinched them all, they're good. Even if I can't see rot, I've learned how to feel it." I could hear the plants moving. He was coming toward me.

"Never had a white woman in trouble before."

"I was sick," I said lowly. "You never had people get sick before?"

"Them Mexicans are made of steel."

"Well, I'm finished with the fourth. Gonna take it back now," I said, even though my crate wasn't full. I hurried my pace until I reached the docks, hoping Trout would still be there. He wasn't, and I turned to see Boss behind me.

"Let me see here," he said as he started thumbing through the tomatoes. He began grabbing them and tossing them away, without really looking at them. He didn't care about rot, he just wanted to torture me.

"You're throwing good tomatoes away," I said.

"You think you know better? This your family's field?"

"No sir."

"Well, let's see here, I believe you've got two full crates now, instead of four. That means you still owe me five."

I returned to the rows. I didn't bother pinching the

tomatoes. I tossed anything I could find into the crates. But at the docks, he played his game again. He tossed out half of my tomatoes. I now had four full crates. I still owed him three.

I couldn't stop shaking. I had been awake and working hard for nearly twenty-four hours. And I hadn't eaten. My heart started to beat funny. I even began to see things. Father Heron's shadow. The chicken whose head he chopped off. I needed water. I considered eating a tomato, or sucking it for its juice. But my hands were covered with rot, and I had been bitten by so many green worms. I couldn't bring myself to taste them. I walked down to the river. The water looked like black glass. I waded in, and shivered with its pleasant coolness. I thought about swimming away.

"One more, then you're done," he said after I brought him three more crates. "I'm going home, you can just set it up here."

I don't remember picking that last crate, or setting it up by the docks. All I could see was the light spreading across the sky. The sky seemed to smirk with it. And all I could feel was amazement, as I found myself standing in the rows again. Facing a new day's quota.

Nina, the woman that first warned me about Boss, came to me and looked in my crate.

"No good, Mercy," she whispered. "You must meet today's quota. You will never come back to us at night. He will make you pick every night 'til you meet your quota."

Why is she talking to me like this? I wondered. *I met my quota. I picked seven crates. How many more do I need?*

I started picking tomatoes. But before I had finished

stripping one plant, Nina returned. Without speaking she quickly swapped her full crate for my nearly empty one.

"To the loaders," she whispered. "Go!"

I stared down at that full crate of tomatoes. It was like she handed me a box of gold. It didn't seem real, and I wasn't sure what to do with it. She picked up the crate and shoved it into my hands.

"Carry this to the loaders and tell them to mark it on your quota sheet."

I did as she told me, only half understanding what was going on. But soon it all became real. Women were taking care of me. Not just my emotions, like Mamma Rutha would do. But my body. Bringing me their full crates, over and over. Sneaking me bits of food and drink. They saved me. No woman had ever done that for me before. And as I carried my twentieth crate to the docks, full of tomatoes that I hadn't picked, I thought about my momma. And wondered if the way I felt that day, so protected, was the way my whole life was supposed to have been.

The next morning, as Trout and I waited to hear our quota for the day, Boss glared at me over the crates. But I felt good. I had escaped spending another night in the fields. And now, with plenty of rest and food in me, I could meet my own quota.

"Them Mexicans must've snuck you their work," Boss growled.

"No sir. I just did what you asked. You wanted twenty crates, you got 'em."

"Don't know if it's good enough."

"But I met the quota!"

"I know about girls like you. You run off from a good

family, with some low-class boy. Bet somebody's looking for you back in them mountains, ain't they? Bet they'd pay money to get you back."

"What are you talkin' about?" Trout asked.

"About taking your girl back," Boss said flatly. "About making me some extra money." He stepped toward me and tried to grab my arm. Trout pushed himself between us.

"Watch it, Boss," Trout said lowly. "She's mine."

"Buddy of mine made five hundred bucks running a white girl out of migrant land."

"We're done married," Trout growled.

Boss pulled a pistol from his pocket and let it dangle casually by his side. "Who says?"

"I'll go," I whispered. Trout would've taken on a dozen pistols before he'd let Boss take me. "Put your gun away. You wanna take me back, I'll go. Nobody wants me there, they ain't gonna pay you nothing."

"Get behind me, Mercy," Trout said firmly.

"I can run again," I insisted. "Once I get back, I'll just run away again." It was a lie. Even as I said it, I knew that Father Heron would kill me before he'd let me go back to the migrants. Trout knew it too.

I stepped toward Boss. I even let him grab my arm.

"Don't take her," Trout said. I could see the panic on his face. It was reflected off of mine.

"Buddies say I could make good money off her. Pretty girl like her, somebody's gonna be missing her."

Trout pulled the keys from his pocket. "Here's my truck. It's worth 'bout five hundred."

"Got me a good truck already."

"How 'bout an Orvis fishin' rod. Ain't no better made. Just leave the girl."

It was his greatest treasure, that gun-barrel blue fishing rod. It had traveled all around the Southeast with him. Fished in all kinds of streams. It was a part of who he was.

"Nice rod, but it don't beat cool cash," Boss said, shrugging his shoulders.

Trout nodded slowly. "Reckon, if I picked triple quotas for a week that would. Be the same as havin' three workers for the price of one. Plus that Orvis rod. That beats anything you'd get paid back in the mountains."

Boss nodded slowly, adding sums of crates and money in his mind. It was a good deal.

"You'll die trying to pick all that. That what you want?"

"I just want her."

Trout walked into the fields and didn't return for a week. He slept in the rows and only bathed in the rain that fell. He ate tomatoes or drank the juice. He spent days on his hands and knees shuffling from plant to plant in the farthest field. From that distance, he seemed strong. Picking with speed. Running to the loading docks with his crates.

But my eyes were lying. He wasn't strong. He was crazy. Sixty crates a day was impossible. Boss's words echoed in my head. *You'll die trying to pick all that.* And there was nothing I could do. Boss was always watching to make sure nobody helped him. He even stood guard at night, the shadow of his pistol swinging by his side. Every morning I ran to the fields, waiting for the sun to rise so that I could make sure he was still there. When light would hit the far field, there he'd be, stooped back shuffling from plant to plant.

Back in the tentworld, people whispered around me and gave me sad looks. Like I was already a widow. I walked around, mumbling a prayer with every breath. *Strong back*, I would whisper, when I would think about how he had to lift heavy crates. *Full belly*, when I would think about how he didn't eat.

But there was more to him than his back or his belly. There was our love. And that week, it was bigger than the fields. Stronger than the rows. He finally collapsed, but he had met his triple quota. I mothered him like he was a small child. Feeding him broth and milk. Shushing children outside the tent, so that they wouldn't wake him. I bandaged his bleeding hands and rubbed his muscles. His body became more than flesh to me. It was the price he bought me with.

When a new week began, I returned to the rows humbled. If Trout could pick sixty crates a day for me, then I could pick twenty for him. My hands turned red with stains and blisters. I became more than a worker, I was a mater migrant. Dependable with my quota. Careful with the plants. And wise about rot and worms.

I began a life of sharp contrast. But the good was *so good*, I learned to swallow the ugly. I broke my body during the day, but I received the care of a dozen mothers at night. I buried my anger when Boss called me the palest wetback he'd ever seen. And I kept my mouth shut when he cheated me of full crates I had picked. Because at night, Trout called me his feast and rewarded me richly.

And when it all ended one morning, when I awoke to

the sound of tractors turning the earth under, I felt proud.
The rows had made me ugly. Bones jutting out from my
body. Wild hair spilling in tangles down my back. But
Boss hadn't beaten me. Neither had the heat, the rot, or
the bees. I stood in the middle of an empty field. A red-
handed skeleton of Mercy. I had never been stronger.

"No work today," Trout said when he joined me in the
field. "Camp's over."

"We made it," I whispered. "Remember that first day,
me asking about breaks and lunches?"

Trout laughed. "You sure changed. You're as good out
there as any of us old-timers."

"Don't hold up as well," I said, looking down at my
body, at my ugly blistered hands.

"You're prettier than you ever were. Look more like
her, the way she was that night I followed you home." He
was right. I looked like Mamma Rutha. Nature had tanned
me, scratched me, weathered me.

"What do we do now?" I asked.

"Say our goodbyes. Then I guess you have to get Della?"

I met his worried eyes and nodded.

Every fire roared with a kettle of food. Fried fish, tortillas, stewed peppers. But no tomatoes. It was the only day
that nobody ate any tomatoes. We played games for the
beer Boss had left behind on the loading dock. All of us
racing through the fields in search of a green tomato. Trout
found one, and shared his beer with me. After weeks of
boiled river water, I thought it was delicious.

Everyone was happy. We had received our last wages. I
listened as they sang songs in their language, and felt like
I understood. I looked at my body, the one that matched

theirs, and decided maybe it wasn't so ugly after all. It marked me as one of them. And they were beautiful.

When the sun set, the mood grew calm and quiet. People were packing up their tents and whispering good-byes. Women began to come to me. Pressing things in my hands.

"For your pretty hair," Nina said. I looked in my hand and saw the ribbons she had loved to braid in my hair.

"But they're your best ribbons . . ." I began, before she hugged me and walked away.

"For your garden," Susa said, as she handed me a bag of dried pepper seeds.

"For new starts," Lara said, holding out a green tomato.

"From old Mexico," Madre whispered, as she handed me a scrap of paper. I read the scribbled title. *Tortilla.* "Family secret," she said. "Don't share with outsiders."

And then it hit me, as I clutched that scrap of paper to my chest. I knew why Trout stayed. Why he never wanted to leave. I lost my body in the rows, but I found something more precious. My fairy-tale family.

Chapter XVII

*E*verything back at the Crooktop camp was dead. The plants were tilled back into the ground. Even the rot was gone. Only a few migrants were left. The ones that had stayed behind to prepare for next spring.

"We'll meet back at the fire trout stream," Trout said. "Nobody should be expectin' us back now. Stay off the mountain. Don't go near your grandpa, or any place he likes to be."

I promised to stay hidden, and started walking through the ditch that ran by the road. Cars would pass me and I'd duck low, hiding myself in the brush. I was thankful Della lived on the outskirts of the valley, in a trailer park where none of Father Heron's people would ever go. She lived in a single-wide, the lowest of all trailers. But it was a mansion in the eyes of her mom, because Della had spent much of her childhood playing on the dirt floor of a garage. Before Della's dad died, they had all lived in a home owned by the coal company. It was a cute little home with blue shutters and a front porch that they could live in as long as her dad worked the mines. Della couldn't remember living there, though when we passed it she always waved to it. *My real home*, she called it. After her dad died, her momma and all five children were homeless. They didn't have any family on Crooktop to take them in. So the church did.

For a little while they lived in the sanctuary, earning Della the nickname Church Mouse, at least until she grew up and went wild. Eventually the preacher convinced a rich man to move his lawn mower and give Della's mom an old garage. The garage had originally been attached to the rich man's home, but he had built a new garage, and cut and moved the old one to the far end of his property to store his lawn mower in it. Everybody pitched in to divide it into two rooms. One bedroom and a general room. The rich man agreed to allow electricity to be connected to the garage from his house. So they were able to hook up an old stove for Della's mom to cook on. And the folks on Crooktop donated items they no longer wanted—a rusty bed, a dresser without knobs or handles, a broken radio that would only work when it stormed, an old washtub for bathing. So there were six people, piled in a bed and on the floor. A dirt floor with two braided rugs. There was no running water, but the rich man allowed Della's mom to carry water back from the wash-up sink in his basement. But only if he or his wife was there.

Over the years things had gotten better. Especially after the other four children escaped. They could remem-

ber the little house with the blue shutters. And they had
to outrun the garage that stole them away. The three boys
found work and started sending a little money home. It
wasn't enough to change Della and her momma's life,
but they didn't have to beg for as many handouts. Della's
momma got a job too. And a boyfriend. And then another
boyfriend. And another.

Somewhere between all the boyfriends, the garage was
abandoned and Della and her momma moved up in the
world, to a single-wide trailer. They even managed to get
a car. But the trailer never fully replaced the little white
house with blue shutters.

As I neared the trailer, I noticed a girl sitting on the
cinderblocks that were stacked up like steps to the front
door. I walked up and recognized her as Della's co-worker
from the Ben Franklin.

"Hey," I said. "You here to see Della?"

"Ooohhh," she said, her eyes growing wide. "I don't
know where she is. Nobody answering the door here, but
Boss says I can't leave 'til I see her."

"You need something?"

"Her apron. She left with it and it's store property. If
she's trying to keep it, why that's the same as stealing.
Boss said I ain't to come back without it, but there ain't
no telling where that crazy girl could be. Probably runned
off somewhere by now. I would if I was her."

"What happened?"

"It ain't polite to gossip," she said, ready to explode
with her eagerness to tell me.

"Well, it's not gossip, since we're Della's friends. We
ain't trying to hurt her."

"Okay. Since you're a friend I guess it won't hurt nothing. All I really know is that her and the boss were hankying around, you know? And then one day, the boss's wife comes in and asks to see him. And Della looked at her and said that he wasn't taking any visitors that day. And his wife says, 'Well, I reckon I ain't a visitor if I'm his wife.' *And the look on Della's face!* Why she looked like a ghost! I swear she did! Plum scary, it was. And the wife says, 'Is something wrong?' And Della says, 'Shouldn't you be shopping for cat food?' And we all started giggling because that was just a crazy thing to say to the boss's wife, now wasn't it?

"And the wife, she was a real sweet little woman, just looked so confused. She said, 'I'm sorry, honey, I don't know what you're talking about, I just want to see my husband. Besides, I can't have any cats anyway because the doctor says they're dangerous if you're expecting.' And Della, *why I thought she was gonna die right there.* Her eyes fell to that lady's tummy, and sure enough it was as round and hard as a watermelon, ready to pop with a Boss Junior.

"So the lady says to Della, 'Are you sure you're okay, honey, you look like you might have a fever, is my husband working you too hard? If he is you just tell him that I said to give you a break, okay, honey? Don't let Randy push you around, because it's all an act anyway, he's just a cuddly teddy bear inside.'

"Well, Della started screaming at her. She pointed at that nice lady and screamed, 'You ain't fooling me! He told me all about you! And your cats! The ones that you feed steak! And you won't let him touch you! So you ain't fooling me. I know you! I know you!' Della's face, it was so red it made her hair look pale. She was having an honest-to-God fit, right there in the store. I felt plum embarrassed for her, I really did.

"And oh, I just felt so sorry for that lady. She didn't know the boss was hankying around. And there she stood, in her husband's own store, with her belly ripe with his baby, and this red-faced crazy girl screaming at her about cats. That lady's eyes, why they just grew wider and wider. And her neck became all blotchy, like she was getting hives. 'RANDY!' She started screaming. 'RANDY!' Not an angry scream. But Lordy, it was a scream for help. 'RANDY!'

"And the boss came running out of his office. And boy oh boy, the look on his face when he saw the two of them standing there face to face. 'Laurel?' he said. 'Laurel, you should be at home! You are in no condition to be out shopping. I told you I'd take care of all those errands, you need to take care of yourself and the baby.' 'But Randy,' the lady said. 'Who is this girl? What's going on?'

"Well, the boss looked at Della. And I could almost see Della shrinking down right then and there. 'Randy?' Della whispered, like somebody had slashed her voice box. Then the boss said to his wife, 'She's just some stupid high school dropout that can't work a register to save her life. She'd try and seduce a fence post, too. Anything that comes around her with pants on is fair game. And I've told her, Laurel. I've told her time and again that I have a wife, a perfect little wife who's gonna have my baby. But she just don't get it, and every day she'd think she could flirt me into forgetting about you. That's how I knew she was crazy. 'Cause I could never forget about you. I almost fired her. Then I thought about how you're always saying people deserve another chance. But this is the last straw. I can't have her upsetting you with her crazy talk.'

"Then he turned to Della. 'Della!' he screamed. 'THIS IS IT! Turn in your apron, and go on home.' And then everybody hushed. And we all just looked at Della. But, I swear, it gives me chills just thinking about it. It was like there was no Della there! It's like she was already gone. She just stood there with a thin little smile on her face. And those eyes, why they were as blank as a clean sheet of paper. I guess she does have some mental problems after all, to look like that. Why you'd have to, to be able to look like that.

"And the lady, well she just said, 'No, Randy! You don't have to take her job away, it was just a misunderstanding.' She was just the sweetest lady. Especially after the way Della had treated her, screaming at her like that! You know, Della should have really been more careful. Why my momma said Della could have sent that poor lady into labor right then and there! But anyway, Della just walked out with her apron still on. None of us have seen her again. And Lordy has the boss been in one bad mood! Shew! It's got me thinking Della's the lucky one to be gone!"

Her face was red when she finished talking, and her eyes glowing. She was loving the scandal of it all. A young May Flours.

"Get on outta here," I whispered lowly.

"Can't leave 'til I see her. Boss says so."

"Tell him she's done gone to the ocean."

She gasped. "The ocean? Lordy me! Well, she is the lucky one, ain't she?"

She shook her head in amazement and then hurried away, eager to tell everyone that crazy Della had run off to the ocean. I knocked gently on the door. There was no answer.

"Della?" I called out. "I'm back home!"

There was still no answer, but when I laid my head against the trailer I could hear movement inside. There wasn't much those thin metal walls could hide.

"I know you're in there. C'mon, let me in. You mad at me for leaving? You know I'd never leave you for good. We promised, remember?"

She didn't answer.

"I'm coming in!" I opened the door. Slowly.

The trailer smelled like stale bread. There were beer cans scattered on the floor and old ashtrays piled high. My eyes kept falling to clumps of red-brown that dotted the floor. It rose in little piles around the trailer. And it was everywhere. Scattered across the floor. On the counters. The old orange couch. I felt dread, sinking like a weight in my stomach. Something was wrong. *Bad wrong.*

"Della?" I called out again, my voice half whispering.

I could hear bedsprings squeaking. *Creak, creak.* I peered around the corner into her room. And I saw her. My beautiful, pitiful Della. Curled into a little ball on her bed rocking back and forth. With empty eyes staring wide open. Her hair was completely gone.

"Hey," I whispered.

There was no answer. Just the squeak of bedsprings as she rocked back and forth.

"Oh Della," I whispered as I walked over and sat on the edge of her bed. She hadn't heard me. I wasn't even sure she saw me. So I just sat helpless and watched her. There was real pain in that room. It was hanging thick on the walls, dripping from the ceiling. The pain of a little girl who could never wear a white dress because she would ruin it on her dirt floor. The pain of a girl who only remembered her daddy in dreams. The pain of a woman who handed her love-glass to a man and watched him stomp it.

I thought about Mamma Rutha. How she touched and blessed to heal my wounds. I touched Della's hand. The hand that had instinctively searched out mine when she had a new secret to tell. I pulled her fingers open, un-clenching her fist, and touched her open palm.

I touched her arm. Caressing from her shoulder to her palm. I began to sing the verse Mamma Rutha sang to me as a child whenever the dark scared me.

"You will abide under the shadow of the Almighty, and He will cover you with His feathers. Under His wings you will take refuge, and no longer be afraid of the terror by night."

As a little girl, that verse sent me running to the oaks to look for God. Made me defend birds from Father Heron's dogs, just in case they were trying to kill God. I longed to find the bird that would hide me from the terror of night.

And now it was Della's terror of night. I traced her spine. The little knobs raising from her skin. I touched her shoulders. Pressed the muscles over the blade. And then I touched her head. She flinched as though the touch were painful. The rocking stopped. And she lay still.

Out with the old, in with the new! she used to say with a laugh as she changed her hair after a breakup. And this was the new. Her head felt so smooth. Silkier than her hair. And cold. I stroked her head, singing to her as she lay still, with shocked eyes. And then she lifted her hand, trembling and thin, to her head. She touched the naked scalp and let her hand fall limp by her side.

"You're still beautiful," I told her. "Always beautiful. Nothing could change that."

She lifted both hands and cradled her head. A shudder ran through her body. She was weeping. Without a moan or a sob escaping her lips. Without tears escaping her eyes. I folded her in my arms. And I sang until she grew still. Until my voice grew hoarse and my throat dry. When she finally slept, I pulled the blanket around her and left the room.

I walked through the trailer and picked up the hair. There was so much of her long, thick hair that had been sexy and teasing, tossed over round shoulders. And now it was dead. I wanted to get it out of the house before she saw it, so I tied the bag off and threw it in the yard. I washed the dishes and swept the floor. And opened the windows to let in some fresh air. I looked in the fridge to see what I could fix her to eat. There was beer. And wine coolers. A small bag of pot. Some dog food. Nothing for Della except a pack of old bologna. There was never anything for Della in that trailer. I had a few dollars in my pocket, so I walked down to a little market nearby.

"How's Della doing?" an old man behind the counter asked.

"What?" I didn't know him. And I didn't know how he knew Della.

"Well, I seen you go into the trailer. Della's mom done

took off. Says she couldn't handle her and was scared of her, waving a pair of scissors around. So she took off to stay with somebody else for a few days, because she said Della done gone crazy. Crazy over some man too. Imagine that, Della DeMar, heartbroken. After all the hearts she's done broke, seems odd, don't it?"

"Where did Della's momma go?" I asked.

"Dunno. Probably to a boyfriend's. But I dunno who that'd be these days. She's real torn up about it all, though. Just a weeping. Saying somebody hurt her baby. She loves Della. Just some things a momma can't take, I reckon."

"Well, if you see her, tell her Della's calm now."

"Hmpph. Yep, I'll tell her. Good thing you're here. Crazy Rutha's your grandma, ain't she? Craziness probably don't scare you none, now does it?"

"Don't know who you're talking about," I mumbled. "Don't know nobody named Crazy Rutha."

I ducked behind the aisle and hoped that he believed me. Prayed that he didn't know Father Heron. I picked out a loaf of bread, some milk, cheese, and butter. A couple cans of tomato soup. Some oatmeal pies. And I thought about how wrong he was. *Craziness scared me.* When I saw Mamma Rutha naked and wild in her garden, or a shaven Della curled in her bed, it took my breath. These people were a part of me. And that made me wonder if *it* was too. If the thing that made them stand naked or shave their head was just waiting for the trigger moment.

A Mexican man walked in the store, and I recognized him from camp.

"Hey," I called out to the clerk. "You got some paper and a pencil I can use?"

"Sure," he said. "You writing a note for Della's mom?"

I shook my head, and wrote Trout a note telling him that something had come up with Della and that he was to meet me by the fire trout stream Monday. Instead of tomorrow. I told him that everything would be okay, and that I loved him. I took the note to the Mexican man, and asked him to give it to Trout. He shook his head in confusion.

"*¡Trucha!*" I said, hoping his Spanish name would trigger a memory.

"*Oh. Trucha. Si,*" he said as he pocketed the note.

I paid for the groceries and carried them back to the trailer. With the dishes washed and the windows opened it already smelled better inside. As I put away the groceries, I could hear Della starting to stir. I warmed the tomato soup, made a couple of grilled cheeses, and carried them back to her room.

She was sitting up in bed when I walked in. Her eyes were a little less vacant.

"Hey. Hungry?"

"Mercy," she whispered, and gave me a weak smile.

"Yeah, I'm here. You need to eat."

I tore a corner of the grilled cheese off and held it up to her lips. Her mouth parted slightly, and I pushed the food in. We sat like that, me feeding her bit by bit, spoon by spoon, until I was satisfied that she had eaten enough.

"You sleepy?" I asked her.

She nodded.

"Well, you sleep. I'll be right outside. And when you wake up, we'll have oatmeal pies."

"Is my momma here?" she whispered, her lips trembling.

"She had to step out for just a little while. But she'll be right back. She told me to tell you she was coming right back."

Della nodded and curled back under her covers.

"I'll be right outside," I said as I gently closed her door.

She still wanted her momma. I could feed her. Sing to her. Rock her. But she still wanted her momma. That never stops. Even when they die. Even when they leave you.

I laid down on the ragged orange couch and fell asleep. Soon I was at the ocean. I was *on* the ocean, standing on the water. And it was smooth and calm. Trout was standing across from me. *Look*, I said. *We're standing on mirrors.* And he gave me that smile. The one that didn't hold back. I took a step toward him and the water rippled, sending waves all around us. *Easy now*, Trout said. *Don't break the mirror.* I took another step. Bigger waves came. *Just hurry up and get there*, I told myself as I took another step. My foot sank and soon I was beneath the mirror, staring up at Trout. He was all alone and the waves were growing high. *Mercy!* he was calling. *Mercy!* And all around him the waves were growing higher and higher. Until they crashed over him. He disappeared.

I startled awake and hurried outside.

It's gonna be okay. He's okay, I whispered. I couldn't stop shaking. A surging heat filled my body as my knees pulled me to the ground. My hands groped the grass as I retched and gagged. Hot foam spilled from my mouth. *Was it bitter seawater?*

I stretched out long and straight on the ground, until my body grew calm. Della began to move around inside. I walked back in and found her on the couch. A good sign.

"Hey sleepy," I said.

"Hey," she said softly. "Where you been lately?"

"Long story. You hungry? I got some oatmeal pies. And milk."

"No. I don't reckon I want anything just yet," she said.

"Wanna watch some TV, then? Weather's clear so your reception should be pretty good."

"No. I don't really wanna watch TV. You can if you want, though."

I sat down on the couch next to her. "I just wanna be here with you," I said. "That's all."

She nodded.

"I saw you had some new nail polish. Spicy Peach. Real pretty. Want me to paint your nails?"

I went and got the nail polish. More for me than her. I needed the distraction. I picked up her hand and began to polish her nails. She had such pretty hands.

"Be careful with that hand now. It ain't dry yet," I told her as I picked up her other hand.

"Mercy?" she said.

"Yeah?"

"My momma. She ain't coming back tonight, is she? She ain't been around for a while now."

"I don't know, she may be coming back tonight," I said, trying to sound hopeful.

"It's okay. You can tell me. I ain't gonna do nothing crazy if you say the truth. I already know it anyway. She ran away from me, didn't she?"

"Yeah. I guess she did. I found you here alone. The man at the market said your momma took off a few days ago. Said she's staying with a boyfriend. But I left a message for her that you're okay. I'm sorry she ain't here with you now."

"Oh it's all right. I'd probably scare anybody half to death. Except you. Don't reckon nothing scares you much. You're so strong."

"Nah, I ain't stronger than you or anybody else."

"You are, Mercy. I wish I was you sometimes. I don't want to make you mad or nothing. I don't want you to think I'm jealous green, but sometimes, I just wish I was you."

"You don't. I mean maybe now, while you're hurting so bad, maybe now you think it'd be better to be somebody else. But not really. Not deep down."

"You just don't see it, do you?" she asked dryly.

"Why you would want to be me? No, I guess I don't. You're more than pretty. You're beautiful. When we walk into a room together, I'm invisible next to you. And that's okay with me, I'm used to that. But I can't understand why you would ever want to trade places with me. You'd never be comfortable being invisible."

"I may get the first looks when we walk in a room. I may turn heads. Hell, I may even get the second looks too. But you, Mercy. You didn't just get a look or a turned head. You got eyes that love you. And I ain't ever had that. And that's worse than invisible. Thought I had it. But I didn't. I just had another turned head. Nothing like what you got with Trout."

"But just because things didn't work out with Randy, that don't mean that you won't ever find real love. It just means you ain't found it yet," I said.

"No. It means a lot more than that. It means I don't

even know real love from the fake. I couldn't see. I just couldn't see," she sobbed.

"Shhh. You don't wanna be me. I had to hide my love for a mater migrant."

"I'd hide forever. I'd never leave this trailer if Randy would have just loved me," she cried.

"You just keep on waiting. Soon you'll turn a head that'll stay turned. It's impossible not to love you."

"But it's easy for you to love me. I guess because we found each other when we were scared and lonely. But that's just you. Nobody else is like that with me. I mean, even you, with your momma dead and your daddy runned off, got more love than me. You got your Mamma Rutha and Trout and me. We all love you. I ain't got nobody but you," she cried.

"Your momma loves you. You got me and your momma and one of these days you'll have your own Trout too."

"My momma, huh? Well if love runs, then my momma loves me. I ain't never run, Mercy. That time her boy-friend Al stole all our food money, Momma just sat down in that corner and didn't move. Just sat there and cried. And I never told her I was hungry. When I got so hungry I ate all the dog food I never told her. I didn't want her to know I was hurting. I loved her. *And I didn't run.* And then that time when she got so stoned she slept for three days straight. Remember that? What did I say to her when she woke up? I said, 'Good morning, Momma, what do you want for breakfast?' I never yelled at her. I never told her what it was like to look at her and think she was dead. Or to lay my head on her chest to see if she was breathing. I never even told her she had been asleep for three days. I just went on like nothing ever happened. Because I loved her. And love don't run."

"But there's all different kinds of love. Mamma Rutha's taught me that love is like this mountain. Outsiders say it just looks the same ol' green all over. But we live here, and we know it's not. We know that the oak is a different green than the pine. Love's the same way. It's got differences too. Like your momma and my Mamma Rutha. They don't love us the way we think they should. Their love ain't the oak. But it just may be the pine."

"But what do you do when you need it to be something it's not?" she asked.

"I don't know. Maybe you look in other places, but stay thankful for what you do have. It's better than nothing."

I went to the kitchen and poured a couple glasses of milk.

"Here's an oatmeal pie. I know they're your favorite, so no sense in acting like you don't want one," I teased.

She took the pie and the milk and laid them on the couch.

"Mercy?" she asked. "That song that you sung to me. Back in my bedroom. What was that song?"

"It's from the Bible somewhere. It's one that Mamma Rutha used to sing to me when I was scared of the dark."

"I like it," she said.

"I do too," I said. "Used to make me fall right to sleep. I'd dream of a big bird, and the next morning I'd go looking for God in the oaks."

"You know I still remember living in that church," she whispered. "Being the little church mouse and sleeping on that pew. How I stacked two hymn books together for a pillow. Everybody told me I was staying in God's house, and I was so curious as to why he hadn't said hello. So I went looking for him. I peered under the pews and peeked into the choir loft. Then I saw this picture of a man with brown hair down to his shoulders and a beard. And he was wearing a fancy red robe. My brother, Ben, found me and asked me what I was doing. *I found God,* I told him. But he told me the picture was just God's son. *Well, what's God look like?* I asked him. Ben shrugged his shoulders and said, *Like the man in the picture, I guess, just older.* I looked at the picture and imagined that man a little older, with his fancy red robe, a white beard, and long white hair. And I knew then, that God was really Santa! I started to pray. I told him what I wanted for Christmas and asked him to bring my daddy back because Momma said God had taken him away. But that Christmas, our first Christmas in the garage, Santa didn't come at all. No daddy. No tree. No presents. Nothing. Momma said it was because he forgot about me. And I decided then and there that I didn't like my Santa-God anymore. But you know, Mercy, I still get the weirdest feeling every time I see Santa in the miners' parade at Christmas. He's back there in the bed of that pickup truck, and I always feel like it's God marching right toward me, staring at my heart to see if I've been naughty or nice."

Della laughed a moment, but then she grew quiet and stared at the empty walls. "It's not him I'm really scared of, though," she said lowly. "What scares me is that if he's real, then dying's just a doorway to someplace else for me to hurt."

"But if you go to heaven, the preacher says there's no sorrow there."

"That may be true for other people, but you and me? It's like when the McDonald's came in over the mountain when we were just little kids. And it had that playground. One day when my momma took off and hollered, *I ain't no momma no more!* to us crying kids, a neighbor came by and took us there. And I knew that at that playground there could be no sorrow. But when I got there and I slid down that purple slide, I could still hear the echo of my momma's words. *I ain't no momma no more. I ain't no momma no more.* And that's how I'm afraid heaven would be for me. It'd be a beautiful place, but all the bad stuff I've done and all the bad stuff that's been done to me would stick to me."

She picked up the nail polish and began to polish my nails. The night had grown a deep black and the room was lit up by a lamp without a shade. I watched her paint my nails and marveled at how pretty she still was. Even without her hair, her skull was so well shaped in rounded curves and perfect circles. The naked skin of her head so silky and glistening. And without her hair to hide behind, the features of her face were enjoying the center of attention. *Look at us*, the golden spokes of her eyes seemed to say. *See how perfect we are*, her lips called. There was no red-brown cover to shield or distract. And her face was loving it.

But the shadows would still cross. Dimming her golden spokes. Pursing her lips. Trembling her fingers. Smearing the polish.

"Della," I said softly, "you're gonna be okay."

A tear washed its way down her face and clung to her chin.

"I still love him. Not Randy, I hate him. But I love the man I thought he was, I love the shadow. What I crave was never even flesh and blood. *And I can't shut it off!* I keep reaching for him when I sleep. I keep whispering his name. I've tried to get rid of him. Hell, I even shaved my head. But my shadow love won't leave me. It still comes to me at night and asks me to talk my pretty talk, about the stars and the clouds. It wakes me in the morning to ask me what I dreamed about. Wherever I hide it finds me. *How can I ever be okay again?*" she cried.

"You will be. I've got a plan for us. I'll tell you when you're stronger," I said.

"Everything is so scary now. Loving the shadow is all I am, and I can't shut it off. I'm so scared," she said as she began to curl into a little ball on the couch. Her face was down, against my knee.

"Shhh Della. I know you're scared. We'll find a way. We'll shut it off."

Chapter XVIII

*T*he next morning, Della's momma woke us.

"Well Lord help! Did you girls party so hard you couldn't even make it to bed? You know you need your beauty rest, Della! Can't lure in the men if you got puffy eyes, my little kitten!"

"I don't want a man, Momma," Della said lowly.

"What? Now Mercy Heron, what kind of holy ideas you gone and pumped into my Della's head? Course you want a man, sugar! Hell you don't just want one, you want a bunch! And we're gonna get you one too, precious. Why, you know Bill? My man? He's gotta brother that'd suit you just perfect, love! I mean he may be a little older, he's around my age, but that's what you need, baby, a real man. Not a little pantywaist from the Ben Franklin!"

"I *don't* want a man, Momma," Della said through gritted teeth.

"Well I wish you'd just hush up all this whining and moping. You and I both know you want a man. We DeMar women, we need our men. It's just that simple."

"Wanting a man is how I got into this mess! A man ain't gonna fix nothing for me! A man ain't gonna do nothing but make it all worse! I just want to be me, by myself, Della DeMar without a man!"

"You're in this mess because you didn't listen to your momma. I warned you. Over and over, when you were little, what did I tell you, Della? I told you to never, ever hand over your heart. Give 'em your body, your mind, your sense of humor, your Friday night. But don't you ever give 'em something you can't walk away with when they turn their backs on you. Or when they die. And you went out and did exactly what I told you not to! Damn it, Della! If you'd just have the sense to listen! I don't tell you these things because I feel better by saying them. I tell you because I want to protect you. Because I've handed out my heart. And when the man turns his back on me, I've had to walk away and leave my heart right there with him. And I didn't want that for you!"

"But I wanted to, Momma. I wanted to give my heart away. To somebody I thought would never turn his back on me," Della sobbed.

"But you gotta listen to your momma. Watch how I treat men. I don't ever give 'em my heart no more. It makes the hurting they try and put on me so much easier, because they can hurt my body, or steal my money, but they ain't ever even seen my heart. So it don't matter so much when they walk away. Just watch your momma. I'll show you how to protect yourself. And listen to me, the best thing to cure your ache is to remind yourself that that one pantywaist at the Ben Franklin wasn't the only man that you could have a good time with!"

"But I don't wanna be like you. You run around with younger guys and older guys and married guys and single guys. And you don't ever really know them. And they don't ever really know you. They use you, Momma. They *use* you. And I'm not saying I didn't ever have a good time doing things the way you taught me. But don't you ever just want something more? More than to use and be used? Even before Randy, I knew I did. I'd look at that picture, the one you threw away when I was little and I dug out of the trash. The one of you and Daddy. His arms around your waist. And you're leaning on him. Your head resting over his heart. And the look in your eyes. And his eyes. I've never seen that look on you, except in that picture. And I wanted that look in my eyes. I wanted that look in Randy's. I didn't wanna be like you are now. I wanted to be like you were then."

"You know *nothing*, Della DeMar. You think you know everything just because you dug some picture out of the trash? Well, who would you rather be now, missy? Look at us! You say you don't want to be like me, huh? Well, I'm fine. I just had a great time with my man. And you have *nobody* but poor old Mercy Heron. I feel great. And you're curled up like a dead weed on the couch. I just had my roots done. *And you look like a circus freak.* Eighteen years old and as bald as a baby. So who would you rather be now, if being like me is such a bad thing?"

"Still, Momma, I'd still rather be like you in that picture."

"That's because you're just crazy. Waving around scissors. Ranting about some shadow that's chasing you through the house," she said with a cruel laugh.

Della curled back up on the couch with her back to her momma. Her hands covered her head, like she was hiding.

Her momma stared at her back, and her ears listened to the silence. She listened to the sound of Della leaving her. Keys dropped from her fingers as her mouth parted into an unheard gasp.

"Oh. Baby Della. I'm sorry. Momma's sorry," she whispered. She dropped to her knees by Della and laid her chest and arms over her.

"Momma's here. And it's gonna be okay. Stay here, Della. Don't you go away from Momma. Don't you leave me too, Della."

As they laid together like that I got up to go make some toast.

"See that?" her momma said when I handed her a piece of toast. "Mercy's done made breakfast. You'll feel better when you eat. Come on, just a few bites for Momma."

Della sat up and ate the toast.

"Momma?" Della said weakly.

"Yes baby?"

"All my pretty hair."

"Now don't you worry about that. Momma's gonna fix you right up. I've got some new lipstick—Secret Crimson Crush, and some new eyeshadow—Mountain Moss Green. By the time I get you fixed up, your eyes and mouth will be so gorgeous nobody will notice your hair. Besides, I had been thinking you needed to try something new and short. All the magazines say short is what's sexy now. And all the movie stars got their heads nearly shaved. So you just give it a couple weeks, and I swear, Della, you'll be in style with the hottest, sexiest little hairdo."

There was a knock at the door.

"Who is it?" her momma called out.

"Uh, ma'am? My name is Randy."

Della's hands started to shake.

"Who the hell is Randy?" Della's momma whispered.

"C'mon, Della, let's go back to your bedroom," I said. "Don't open the door."

"You mean it's that jerk from the Franklin?" her momma asked. I nodded my head as I grabbed Della's hands and tried to pull her up from the couch.

"I've got a thing or two to say to him," her momma said, springing for the door.

"No!" I called out. But it was too late. The door was open and Della's momma was a screaming, cursing, spitting woman. Randy just stood there looking past her.

"Della," he called. He hadn't seen her yet.

"It's okay, Momma," Della said. "Why don't you go out for a while."

Her momma grabbed her keys and fled. Thankful for the chance to escape.

"Come in," Della said. He stepped in, and stopped. He saw her, the gleam of her head. She took his breath.

"Della, what in the hell have you . . ." he began, but stopped. He stood there with a mouthful of words that wouldn't be spoken. Not to the bald woman that sat on the couch.

"Why are you here?" Della asked him.

"I just wanted to make sure you were okay."

"I am."

"You don't look it."

"Why did you come here? 'Cause you were afraid you'd killed me?"

"What? Of course not. Don't talk like that, Della."

"Then why are you here?" she said, her voice raising.

"I don't know. I guess I wanted to apologize for ever . . . if I ever . . . led you to think that you and I . . . or that me and my wife was . . ."

"That's not why you came," Della said, folding her hands to keep them from trembling.

"Soon as you're feeling stronger I'd like to talk this out. Right now I just wanted to say that I'm sorry for ever making you think—" he began.

"No," she said, her voice angry. "You're only sorry I wanted more than sex. And now you came here to make yourself seem right. To make me understand why you did what you did. You came here to justify."

"You think you're blameless?" he said lowly. "I'm not saying I am. I know I'm not. But I'm just a man, and you know what you are. You with your low-cut blouses and tight jeans. You come into my store and you prance around and offer it to me. And you expect me to say no? 'Cause I got a wife at home? 'Cause I got a baby on the way? Truth is, you didn't care whether I had a wife or not. You gave it up without ever asking. You know what you do to men. And you like it. You do it on purpose, Della. So don't you sit there and act like it was all me. 'Cause we both know it wasn't. We both know you wanted it and wouldn't stop 'til you got it, wife or not."

"I guess it was the crazy whore in me," Della whispered softly.

"You can't help it," he said, his voice softening a little. "You can't stop it because you don't know better. You ain't ever been taught right. I couldn't resist your temptation and you couldn't stop giving yourself away. You can't help what you are, I guess."

"Go."

"I'd like to talk to you sometime when you're feeling stronger. I don't want you to think I don't care, I do."

"Go," she said.

"Maybe in the future we could talk this out and then you could see."

"Leave," she said. "Leave." He walked out, shaking his head. I sat with her on the couch until her momma returned, and then I went to her room to finally get some sleep. When I woke up, Della was watching TV while her momma and two men sat in the kitchen passing around a joint.

"Let's go outside," I said to Della. "It's nice out there tonight."

She smiled and joined me at the door.

"That's fine, girls. Me and the boys gonna stay inside where the fun's at!" Her momma laughed.

We sat on the hood of her momma's car. A car so dinged up it was hard to tell what its original body shape had been. She still seemed sad, but calm.

"I see you gotta date," I teased her.

She laughed. "Yep, it appears I do. A stoned forty-five-year-old man that can't keep his eyes off my momma. Some date."

"You look real good. I like your eyeshadow."

"Thanks. You know he keeps looking at my head. Like when we talk or something. Most guys just stare at my boobs, but not him. He just looks at my head, and I can see the disgust in his eyes. But you know what's really funny? I kind of get a charge out of it. Here this gross man came to my trailer looking for some loving for himself, and he don't want it because of my bald head. *He doesn't want me!* All I have to do is just look at him, or touch it, just stick my hand up and start rubbing the baldness, and he looks like he's gonna get sick. Why, if I had my hair, I'd be beating him off with a stick! It's a different feeling altogether, to be unsexy. It almost feels powerful. I'm just Della. I ain't a woman really, or a sex magician. Don't know if I've ever been just me. I had boobs by the time I was ten. And hips by the time I was eight. Men have always been after me. And now they ain't. I may keep it this way."

"You've always been the standard for what's sexy here in Crooktop. You wait, all the girls at the high school are gonna start shaving their heads if you keep yours bald." I laughed.

"You think they will?" She laughed too. "Wouldn't that be wild? Men would have to learn to like it then, I guess. You gonna go to church tomorrow?"

"I can't go into town. Can't risk seeing Father Heron."

"Where you been? I looked for you at the diner and couldn't find you."

"Off with Trout," I said, smiling. "We're running off again on Monday."

"What? Where to?"

"We been working the tomatoes at another camp. Now we're leaving for the ocean. That's why I come back to get you. I can't leave you behind."

"So you're leaving for good?"

"I have to. Father Heron found out about me and Trout. And I won't let Father Heron kill him or me neither. So we're running."

"Maybe if you gave him a chance, Mercy. Maybe he'd come around to Trout."

"He ever come around to you? You been my best friend for years now. He let you come to the house? Can I ever be honest and tell him when we're gonna hang out? No. I have to lie and say I'm working just to get to see you. And you ain't a mater migrant."

Della nodded her head slowly. "He's a damn fool," she whispered. "An old hateful bastard."

I laughed. "If there's one thing Father Heron would hate to be, it's a bastard."

"I can't imagine you off this mountain," she said. "It's all you know."

"I love him more than this mountain," I whispered, remembering Mamma Rutha. *How can you leave your homeland?* her people had asked. *Because it's easier to leave my home than it is my heart.*

"I love you more than this mountain too, Della. And I want to take you with me."

She smiled, with tears in her eyes. "There ain't nothing for me here anymore. If you'd asked me a few days ago,

I wouldn't have been able to leave Randy. But I can now. I want to leave everything behind. That dirty trailer. My momma. That awful shadow that chases me. I don't want none of it anymore."

"So you'll come?" I asked.

"Yeah. I'll come with you. When we leaving?"

"Early Monday morning. I'm meeting Trout by a stream. You can meet us by the river, in the old migrant camp."

"I can't believe we're really gonna do it. We're gonna leave this hellhole. After all our talk about one day escaping, we're gonna do it."

"You bet we are."

"What do you think Trout's gonna say about my hair?"

"Same thing he always says about you," I said, laughing. "'That Della DeMar is one wild woman.'"

Chapter XIX

*T*he hour before sunrise is an hour of tricks on the mountain. It may appear to be a cool October morning, filled with the whispers of a coming winter, and turn out to be a hot Indian summer day. The black of night may fade into a cool purplish navy before bursting into a warm butterscotch sky. It's an hour of indecision. The first yawn and stretch of a new day, a Monday.

A bobwhite was awake. Singing his simple song to a sleepy world. Just three notes. Two the same, and then one a little higher. Mamma Rutha said they were singing their names. Bob-by-White. I whistled it back to him. He answered, and waited for me to repeat. Bob-by-White!

We played our game, singing to each other, as I walked down the valley. I looked up Crooktop, Mamma Rutha was out there somewhere. Probably sleeping beneath a poplar tree. "Shhh," she would have whispered to me if she had heard me singing 'Bob-by-White.' "Give the mountain some peace, some peace to draw its strength for a new day." But I had too much strength myself to walk quietly. I was taller than the mountain. Hotter than the coming sun. Happier than the song of the bobwhite. Because it was Monday, the day of love.

I thought about him, walking up the mountain as I walked down. How he might already be there. Sitting on the rocks, looking into the fire trout stream. "Don't show nobody this place," he had said. "It's our secret place. Where the fire trout was born."

I had whispered vows of forever that night up on Thorny Ridge. And as I walked down the valley I was living them out. *Wherever you go, I'll go.*

When I was little, I never dreamed of my wedding the way that Della had. Della would cut clippings from magazines of flowers and cakes and dresses. She had a whole shoe box stuffed with ideas. She wanted a princess dress. With lots of lace and pearls. A long train that swept behind her. Flowers and flowers and flowers. Flowers everywhere. And her hair. Now that would be the challenge. Highlighted, crimped, curled and fluffed, it would definitely be bridal hair. There would be an organist. A handbell choir. A limo with champagne. Maybe even a honeymoon to the coast. I would be in the wedding of course. Wearing dusty rose, the color she said I looked the best in. Her groom would be in a tux, looking like something out of a soap opera. With shiny shoes and slicked-back hair. Della's mom would be teary but composed. And everyone that didn't like her would envy her, and everyone that loved her would be *so proud.*

My wedding had been different. A harvest midnight. A mountaintop for an altar. Moonlight for a veil. A gray tent with red ropes for a honeymoon. *Oh, but the groom!* Just the thought of him had put white lilies in my hands, a wreath of baby's breath in my hair, and white satin over my body.

I was close. My heart began to beat a searching rhythm, seeking its mate. My hands began to tremble, ever so slightly, knowing that they would soon be covered by his. I pushed back the thick leaves. Breathing in the wet steam of the morning. I stumbled over briars and pushed them back with my bare hands, never feeling the pain. I could see the rocks in the distance. The ones that he had first held me on. My pace quickened, pushing me toward the stream.

"Trout?" I called out.

I was early. I had left while the mountain still slept, and he was still on his way. I sat down on the rocks and waited. I smoothed my clothes and pulled my fingers through my messy hair. I used a small pebble to try and push back my cuticles. When I had fixed myself as good as I was going to get, I looked around. Arched hickory and oak branches created a green cathedral ceiling. The ground was covered by a lush moss carpet. All of it framed by stained glass as the first yellow rays of sun spilled down on the silver stream. But where was my groom?

I waited until the dew was dry and the morning's frisky creatures grew slow and lazy in the heat. Until my stomach began to complain with hunger. Until the sun reached its peak. I kept my eye on the path that he would walk up. *Any minute.* When my feet grew numb from being dangled off rocks, I let them dangle as dead limbs. When my back knotted from a lack of support, I just let the muscles twist and harden. I wasn't moving without him. I told myself if I just waited long enough. If I hoped hard enough. If I focused all of my energy, my very breath, on willing him there, it would happen.

As night fell, our secret place became nowhere. I was alone in the middle of nowhere.

But I was still waiting. Finally standing, my legs struggled to support new weight. Pacing. Back and forth in the moonlight. *I will wait forever*, I told myself. *Until I die from hunger, or sorrow. I will wait until he comes.*

"Please come, Trout," I whispered to the bit of moon peeking through the woods. "Please hurry. Please. Please. Please. Please come now." The moon didn't answer me. And Trout didn't come.

It was a noisy night. Branches creaked from the squirrels that scampered across them. Something large and unknown rustled in the brush. My ears strained for the sounds of the path. Any minute they might hear footsteps. I dozed in and out of consciousness. Sleeping until a noise would wake me. The snap of a branch. "Trout?" I would call out into the darkness. My voice sounding small and hollow. No answer. And no more noise. So I would doze again. Until another snap. "Trout? Is that you?" No answer. Sleep finally pulled me from my misery.

I was walking through a field. And soon I was standing by a pool of water. Looking into it. There was baby's breath in my hair. And a light. At the very bottom. And it was swimming toward me. Closer and closer. A shimmering light, growing brighter.

So bright it woke me. Even through sleepy eyes I could still see the fading light. I sprang to my knees. Was it the fire trout? A last sparkle. Then nothing. Had I imagined it all?

I knelt by the stream until dawn. Through hours so dark I couldn't even see the water, but could only hear it. I was keeping watch for the fire trout. When dawn returned, I knew I had to go to him.

Maybe he didn't get the note. Maybe the Mexican man had only pretended to understand who Trout was. Maybe he was sick or hurt. My mind held all the maybes, but it clung to what it knew. Wherever he was and regardless of why he didn't come, he loved me.

I traced my way back toward the valley. I wondered what happened to Della. If she waited by the river, just like I had at the stream. I would make it all up to her. After I found Trout.

A car passed me and the driver waved. Was it someone I knew? Someone from First Baptist? Did they know I was on my way to love the mater migrant? Would they call Father Heron? As panic began to take control, I told myself it didn't even matter. Because I couldn't turn around. Even if Father Heron himself stood in my path.

I stood in the flatland and caught my breath. I started looking for his tent. I saw tents with gray rope. White rope. Brown rope. Yellow rope. But no red rope.

"Trout?" I called outside the tents. "Where are you, Trout?"

He never answered. I began to feel sick. Everything seemed to be moving too slowly, like I was walking through molasses. Like my mouth was filled with peanut butter. "Trrrrooooouuuttt," it called thickly.

But then my eyes saw it. And my heart quickened so that I felt dizzy. The old brown truck. Worn and beaten, it was the most beautiful thing I had ever seen. I ran to it. He wasn't in it, but it meant he was still there somewhere. He had probably just gone for a morning walk. Maybe he was headed toward our secret place at that moment. I sat down in the bed of the truck. It was my anchor. My one solid link with Trout.

I sat there for a couple of hours. Until the other people in the tents began to stir. I imagined that Father Heron had heard by now. I was back, and I was with the mater migrant. It was a thought that I decided to deal with later. I told myself I'd suffer anything for Trout. *Anything*, if he would just come.

The migrants began to build small fires and brew coffee. My eyes darted from one face to another. Until I saw the Mexican man that I had given the note to. Stirring his coffee, laughing over a joke with his friend.

I walked over to him. He looked at me curiously.

"¿*Trucha*?" I asked him.

He shook his head.

"Trout! ¡*Trucha*!" I insisted.

He shook his head again.

I pointed to the brown truck.

"¡*Trucha*!" I said again, my voice grating with frustration.

He stared at me with calm eyes, and nodded.

"Gone."

"You don't understand. I need to see *Trucha*. I was just here with him a few days ago."

"Gone."

"For how long? A morning walk?"

He shook his head, and turned to walk away. I grabbed his arm. I would have held him forever to get my answers.

"No come back!" he insisted, his face very serious.

"There must be a mistake. His truck is here. Did you give him the note?"

"Gone. No come back," he yelled as he reached in his pocket and pulled out my note. I stared at it, and I believed I would die from the pain it brought.

I had seen death before. Once, I found a dead groundhog stretched stiff and cold beneath a peony bush. Like a stuffed animal, or a cheap carnival prize. I stared at it and wondered what death would do to me. Would I become a plastic doll?

I had my answer. When he said that word. *Gone.* When he showed me that note. I looked up to see the peony branches. To smell their sweet flowers hanging over me. And all of the things a doll can't do fell upon me. A doll can't stand on its own. So my legs gave way, pulling me to the ground. Dolls can't have blood coursing through their veins. So thick red love spilled out of me. Dolls can't cry. So my wet eyes were replaced with empty ones, that couldn't even blink. Trout was gone. And so was Mercy.

Chapter XX

*S*o there I lay, beneath the peonies. With eyes that only saw glimpses. Of the rough weathered hands that carried me. With ears that only heard prayers. Pleading for mercy. *Mercy for the Mercy doll.*

I had a doll once when I was little. A plastic baby doll with fuzzy yellow hair. How I loved her. I named her Sally, after a beautiful lady at church. I would rock her. Sing to her. Pretend to feed her. I took her everywhere with me. Even to church. And that's why Father Heron killed her too. He said she was an idol. That I loved her more than Jesus. *Maybe I did.* I was only eight, and at least I could see Sally. It was hard to see Jesus, with Father Heron always standing in front of him.

He burned her. In the backyard after church. He built

a big hot fire and made me throw her into it. "No!" I cried. "Don't make me burn Sally!" We ran away. Me and Sally. We hid behind the tiller in the shed. "Don't cry, Sally," I whispered to her. "We'll stay here forever so you won't get burned up." But he sniffed us out, his nose smelling our fear. And when he found us, he made me wish that my limbs were unfeeling plastic things like Sally's. I cradled her in my arms. One last time. I smelled her fuzzy hair. It smelled like baby powder. I kissed my baby.

"I love you, Sally," I whispered.

"Throw her," he said.

"No!" I screamed. "I'm not gonna let you kill her!" And then he took my arm, the arm that clutched my Sally, and held it over the fire.

"Let go or burn with her."

It felt cold at first. Like he was holding my arm down in icy water. Then the pain came, and I knew that I was burning. The tiny hairs on my arm singed and withered. He watched in silence as I cried. I looked at Sally, her pink skin blackened by smoke. And then I let go.

She fell down into the hot red flames. I turned to run, but he held me there and made me watch my baby burn. Her fuzzy yellow hair turned black, and then gray, and then fell off. Her eyes were open staring straight at me. "Close your eyes," I begged her. But she just looked at me, asking why must Sally burn? Her eyes sagged and drooped until they were little colored pools of melted plastic. Her twisting body made a shrill hiss as it withered into ash. My baby was screaming for its momma.

And now I was somebody's doll. *Don't love me more than Jesus*, I wanted to tell her. *Or he might burn me too!*

Then I'd be a melted pool of plastic. My stringy hair would turn black, then gray, then fall off. And my eyes would droop and sag. If only my plastic lips could move, I would tell those rough hands, *Please don't love me more than Jesus.*

PART TWO

Eternal Peace
in Glory

Chapter XXI

*S*omeone was singing my song. "*I awakened you under an apple tree, la la la . . . There your mother brought you forth, la la di di la . . . Now set her as a seal upon your heart, for love is as strong as death.*" As strong as. Why didn't it say stronger? Wasn't it love that was making my plastic hands begin to tingle and move?

Just as Crooktop had its hour of tricks, I had one too. And I had been stuck in mine. Waffling somewhere between life and death. Plastic and flesh. I couldn't make the decision the way the mountain did every morning, choosing sunny or cloudy, dead or alive. All I could do was lay there beneath the peonies, feeling plastic.

Someone else decided, though. Rough hands and bitter herbs pulled me from beneath the peonies. My limbs were bent and stretched until they could feel the blood pumping through them. Colors were flashed before my eyes, making them blink. I stopped gagging and began to swallow. All of it, proof that I wasn't plastic. When my eyes began to see again, I couldn't help but wonder. Look at it all, I thought. Legs. Arms. Chest. Belly. I had felt it disappear, but it was all still there.

I didn't know where I was. Treetops swayed over me, and clouds peeked through the leaves. I could hear the rustling of animals nearby. And birds were singing all around me. *I'm in heaven*, I thought at first. *Heaven is a mountain with no pain.* But soon my back began to ache from laying on the hard ground, and my skin shivered from the chill in the air. I knew then, I was still on Crooktop.

I sat up and saw Mamma Rutha kneeling by a tree, whispering softly. I watched as her lips mouthed my name, and wondered what she prayed for.

"Mamma Rutha," I said, my voice breaking from lack of use. I watched as she inhaled slowly, and then sighed.

"Oh Mercy baby."

"What is this place?"

"Where wounded things go to heal."

I looked around more carefully, searching for the healing. I noticed that I was in a nearly perfect circle of emptiness. Just dried leaves on hard mountain ground. While large old trees pressed together to frame me, like they were holding hands.

"How'd you find me?" I whispered.

"Heard you."

"You weren't close enough."

She shrugged her shoulders gently. "I'm very old, Mercy

baby. My ears don't work so good anymore. I've learned to listen other ways."

"And what about him? Can you hear him?" I begged. She shook her head, and I could see the pity on her face. It was like looking in a mirror. I was the picture of misery.

I rolled over, a weak effort to hide myself. I was angry with her for no reason. Except maybe that she didn't leave me to die. Or maybe that she was able to find me with her crazy ways, but couldn't tell me where Trout was.

"I know you met him," I whispered. "That night in the garden. He told me all about it."

"I remember."

"He thought you were beautiful. He said he hoped I'd look just like you one day." I started sobbing.

"Shhh. Don't fight the healing."

I looked down at my hands. I had to stare a long time before I could see any red. "I've been here a long time, haven't I?"

"Can't measure grief in weeks."

"No," I whispered. "I've got a whole life's worth."

"That's why I brought you here."

"But we're still on the mountain," I said defiantly. "Don't know exactly where, but I can feel it, Crooktop sucking away my breath. This mountain will strangle me one day."

"It's different here. Found it when I was a little girl. I'd come across a doe with buckshot through its hind leg. And I followed her up the mountain, dragging her useless leg, a trail of blood dripping to the ground. I wished she would stop fighting her death. *I'll ease the death pain,* I promised her. But up the mountain she drug herself. 'Til she came to this clearing. She laid down in the middle, her breathing slowed, and I thought she died. But I walked to her and saw the soft rise of her belly. She was alive. I watched her through the evening. And into the dawn of the next day. I went home, gathered some bandages, some salve for her. But when I got back, she was gone. All that was left of her was the dried blood on the fallen leaves."

Mamma Rutha picked up a handful of leaves and scattered them around us.

"I knew then she didn't drag herself here to die," she continued. "She came here to heal. To hide in the tree circle, and lay on the soft bed of leaves. Wasn't a month later, I became that doe. My momma had just pulled a pone of cornbread from the oven. I was hungry, and too little to know the danger of a hot iron skillet. When I wrapped my fist around the handle I heard my flesh melt before I felt it. The singe and sizzle. And when I dropped the skillet, the skin of my palm stayed on the handle. See that?" she asked, holding up her left palm, which even after all the years was several shades darker than the other. "Weren't no doctors to come by. Didn't know of any healers then. *Poor Ruthie*, I heard folks whisper. *That hand won't never heal.* I asked my momma to fix it, when the pain nearly drove me crazy. *Ain't nothing can fix that kind of burn*, she said. Then I remembered that doe. And I pulled myself up the mountain, and laid down in my crazy pain on this soft bed of leaves."

"What happened?"

"Still got my hand, don't I?" she said, laughing. "When I come back home, the fire had left me. My hand had scarred up nicely and was ready to heal. Over the years I've tracked many a wounded animal to this place. They don't always live. But this is the ground for last battles."

"No mountain ground can put out my fire," I whispered.

I spent the next few days sleeping, and eating the food and herbs that Mamma Rutha brought. My body was recovering from the hard work of the rows. But my heart wasn't healing. And I didn't even hope it would. Mamma Rutha was always singing around me. Touching me and blessing me. It was like we were holding church. Only I didn't want to be saved.

"Come here," she told me. "There's one more thing to try." She was losing hope too. She led me outside the clearing, to a great oak tree. I could have hugged it three times over and still not measured it's width.

"Terebinth tree," she said, as she touched it gently.

"It's an oak," I said. "Biggest one on the mountain, probably."

She shook her head. "It's a terebinth tree."

"Never heard of it." I double-checked the leaves. Broad ovals with scalloped edges. Definitely an oak.

"You know, Mercy baby, from the holy scriptures."

"I don't know 'em like you do."

" *'I will make an altar to God who answered me in the day of my distress,'* " she whispered lowly. " *'And Jacob took his foreign gods and buried them under the terebinth tree.'* " She knelt to the ground and began clawing the dirt. She motioned for me to join her. "Terebinth trees are made for burying."

I noticed a spot that seemed groomed, almost like a

grave. And then I made out the shape of a cross, formed from a pile of pebbles.

"What's buried there?" I whispered.

"Your momma's killing," she said without looking at me.

When the hole was about a foot deep, she stopped digging. "Now speak it," she said.

"Speak what?"

"The things you need to bury."

"I won't bury him," I said. "I won't."

"Mercy's grief," she called out loudly, her eyes focused on the hole in the ground. "Mercy's momma being killed. Her granddaddy's cruel heart. Her love gone missing. All of it, we bury here. Amen."

Then she covered up the hole quickly, like she could trap her words in the ground. She took a handful of pebbles and formed the letter M over the spot. I shuddered. I was staring at my own gravesite, freshly dug and marked with my initial.

Later that night, I woke up to see the woods on fire. Every tree glowed. Bright and strong.

"Mamma Rutha!" I called. "Foxfire!"

She was sitting next to me, watching me. I could see her smile clearly, from the light of the trees.

"It's done this every night since I brought you here." She laughed.

"What is it? What is it really?" I asked, springing to my feet. "Is it just fungus?" Deep down I wanted her to say no. I wanted her to tell me again that it was the mountain's soul. And that I was part of the chosen few.

"The mountain's trying to make you strong again."

"Every night it's like this?"

"Since you've been here. It's not just for you, though," she said slowly.

"I know," I answered. "The mountain loves you."

"No. It's not for me."

"There something else wounded here?"

"Yes."

"A deer or something? Where?"

"It's choking on grief," she said solemnly. "And it lives here." Her pale skin glowed with the burn of foxfire, and my eyes easily followed the direction of her hand. I gasped and shook my head in disbelief. Her hand cradled my stomach.

Chapter XXII

I woke up alone. Mamma Rutha had done all she could, and she saw no reason to stay. *What am I gonna do now?* I thought. I couldn't stay there. I wasn't like my grandmother or Trout. I didn't know how to live off the land. *I'll go back to the migrants,* I thought. *They'll take care of me.* I liked that idea. I even let myself wonder if I would find him there. But then it flashed through my mind. Mamma Rutha's hand holding my belly. *What if she was right?* I had been sick, vomiting in the rows. And then sick outside Della's trailer. I tried to remember the date of my last period, and couldn't. I ran my hands over my breasts. They were much too heavy. *I'm gonna have his baby.*

I sat down and hugged my knees close to my chest and sobbed. I wished she hadn't left me. I wanted someone to tell me what to do. *There's nothing I can do,* I thought.

I didn't know how to find the new rows without Trout. And even if I could have, everything was different. I had barely survived them before. How could I survive, large and clumsy? And later, how would my baby survive that life? I shoved my hand in my pocket and pulled out all the money I had. Seven dollars and forty-seven cents. Trout had the rest of my wages from the rows.

As daylight faded, everything settled into two choices for me. I could leave Crooktop. Or I could go home. *I wanted to leave.* But I couldn't figure out how without a car or money. Or a place to go. Or Trout to lead me. I thought about myself, broke, hungry, and pregnant in some strange land.

Soon it was dark. And as the night grew cold, I learned the same lesson my momma had. An abandoned pregnant woman craves the familiar. Even if it's dangerous. Even if it kills her. *I knew Father Heron.* And the only thing I could think to do was choose the danger I knew best. And run from the ones I didn't.

It was a long walk home. It was my momma's walk. I traced her steps, the same ones she took after my daddy went missing. I took one step after the other, not thinking about how far the distance was, or how my feet ached. I looked up the mountain. He was up there. And deep within me, I believed he knew that I was coming. That he had always known I would be back.

I knew what I had to do. *Deny my Trout.* Look Father Heron in the eye and tell him it's over. Tell him that Trout left me. I didn't know at first that he was a mater migrant, I would lie. *He tricked me,* I would say. And then I wondered if at least that much was true. Was it all a trick?

My hand touched the back doorknob. And fear froze it. *What if it is locked?* I remembered the story his silence screamed. Of blood, murder, and *locked doors*. I couldn't turn the handle.

"Come in, Mercy," his voice called through the door.

It only made sense to run. That's what my legs screamed at me as I forced them to walk through the door.

"Hello, Father Heron." His back was to me. There weren't any lights on in the house. It was a dark shadowy place, filled by his lumpy silhouette as he sat in his chair, facing the window.

"What do you need to tell me?" he asked. It was one of his favorite games. Confession. My judge would sit on high and force me to confess the sins he already knew.

"Nothing you would be interested in."

He rose from his chair and turned toward me.

I was trembling. Angry at that man, that old gray man, who was eyeing my love, toying with it, tossing it to the devil.

"I didn't think you would be interested in love. Real, honest-to-God love!" I screamed.

I was shaking with rage. Rendered foolish by my anger. Dancing everywhere but around him. The silence began to scream. Wailing, screeching silence. *Blood, murder, locked doors. BLOOD MURDER LOCKED DOORS!*

I didn't feel the blow. I just heard it. Like a tree, dead and dry, being broke in two. And then I heard the ringing. The sharp ringing in my ears, as though a thousand mosquitoes swarmed above my head. I disappeared. Swallowed by a forest of dead and dry trees. Swarming with mosquitoes. Snap. Ring. Snap. Ring. And then a grip, at the nape of my neck, jerking my knotted hair, lifting my eyebrows high.

"Please, no!" I heard myself beg as my eyes met his.

"It's over, Father Heron. He left me. Same as my daddy did. I swear to you. It's over. I'll never see him again. Please don't kill me. Don't kill me," I cried.

"You will show the world your stain. I will not let them gossip about our name anymore. You will show them that it's your sin. That I have nothing to do with the whore you are. And they will hate you. But not me. Because your sin isn't mine. You were born in sin. *It's what you are, Mercy.* You will pour it out at the altar. This Sunday."

"I will," I sobbed.

He dropped his grip and I fell loose and ragged to the floor. It was smooth and dusty, smelling of mold and dirt. It felt cool against the heat of my skin. And supportive. Lifting the weight of my body. The dead, dry, broken tree. *The feast of Trout.*

Sometime during the night, I heard my song.

"I awakened you under an apple tree, la la la . . . There your mother brought you forth, la la di di la . . . Now set her as a seal upon your heart, for love is as strong as death."

It was really the Song of Solomon, the song of the Shumalite to the Beloved. But as I lay there feeling some of the pain my momma must have felt, thinking about Trout, asleep on his back, mouth open, I knew that it was still my song.

As Mamma Rutha sang to me she rubbed balm over my bruises. Singing and rubbing, until her hands and throat must have ached. Until the sun was shining bright and full.

"Thank you," I said when I had enough strength to sit up.

"You will be okay, Mercy baby," she said, gently touching my face.

I went to bed and studied my life. *This is it*, I said to myself. I had imagined a life of love. By the ocean, with my Trout. *"A silly dream,"* I whispered. I would never escape Crooktop. I would always be caged in that house. And just so that I could go on living, so that my baby could go on living, I would confess on Sunday. It was the sacrifice the monster demanded.

Chapter XXIII

I barely stood. My feet felt unattached to the trembling body that hid behind a dingy white dress with purple trim. I was trapped between pine pews covered in scratchy brown cloth. My ears were filled with the humming buzz of a bored congregation. "I Surrender All," they sang.

"This may be your last chance, brethren. Your last chance to surrender all," the preacher said, his Bible stretched out toward us, inviting us. My feet began to move. Scuffed cream pumps shuffling down a worn center aisle. Preacher Grey's face betrayed his surprise. Everyone else was surprised too. Their singing grew louder. Carrying me to the altar. Mercy surrenders all.

"Yes Mercy, thank you for coming forward, how can the Lord help you today?" Preacher Grey whispered. He looked at me, and his eyes dimmed with concern. "Honey, what is it? What's wrong?"

"I don't know how to say this, Preacher Grey."

"You can tell me. You can trust me," he whispered softly.

"I have sinned," I said, staring at his unpolished shoes.

"Well, I've got good news. God rejoices when we ask for His forgiveness. It's a gift that He paid dearly for, and He wants us to use it. Mercy, all you have to do is use the gift."

I stared at him. The fervor in his eyes. It was more than belief, it was a knowing. And I envied him that.

"I'll kneel with you and pray. Just confess in your heart and ask for forgiveness. It's that simple."

"But I have to confess to everybody."

"Our sin just has to be between us and God. Nobody else has to know," he said, smiling.

"But Father Heron knows about my sin. And he, he wants me to confess to everybody."

"God's the only one you gotta deal with, Mercy."

"But Father Heron, he said I have to."

"He's just misunderstanding. Let's kneel here, and then when you're finished I'll tell everyone that you came forward to confess some personal sin and to make right your relationship with God. That should be enough to satisfy him."

I knelt there at the altar. My lips murmuring words my heart never heard. Everything was so still there, crouched low to the ground. I could feel Trout all around me. His eyes filled with sunflowers. His hands filled with the mountain's fish. His heart filled with foxfire. And I had lost it all.

Preacher Grey stood with me. "My friends, rejoice with

Mercy today. For she has found forgiveness and reconciled with God." I nodded my head.

"And as I dismiss in prayer, I want to remind you of the fellowship supper after church next week. Pray with me please," he began. But the prayer never came.

"Pardon me, Reverend, but these good people need to know how bad she wronged them. Tell 'em Mercy," Father Heron's voice called out.

"Deacon Heron, that isn't necessary. Mercy only has to ask God, nobody else. She is already forgiven."

"That may be true. But the Bible also says to honor thy father and mother."

"And is your way of having Mercy honor you public humiliation?" Preacher Grey asked.

"What my way is, Reverend, is none of your business. Need I remind you that Mercy is my granddaughter and you are this church's employee? I expect you should stay out of how I choose to raise her," Father Heron said flatly.

Preacher Grey's face was flushed. He looked embarrassed and confused. His wife's eyes were panicked. I was messing up their life. Their home, their income, I was messing it all up.

"It's okay, Preacher," I said.

I turned to the congregation. "What Father Heron wants me tell you all is that I've sinned real bad." *Oh God the love. Such love.* "I ran off with a man." *He had foxfire in his heart.* "And he was a mater migrant." *Thick red love.* "I am sorry, and it is over and will never happen again." *This is my life now.*

Chapter XXIV

I began my life again. An empty body breathing, eating, swallowing. I never searched or questioned. Instinctively I knew there were some places it wasn't safe to look. Like my heart. At times I wondered if it was even still there. And if it was, what would it hold?

"Let's go for a walk," Mamma Rutha said.

We walked through the woods every evening. The leader revering everything around her, while I blindly followed. Until one day we came to a stream that wasn't much more than a puddle that trickled.

"I wanted to show you something, Mercy baby, but they're all gone now. Oh well, maybe they'll come back later."

"What was it?" I asked.

"Well, it was the prettiest little patch of wild morning glories you ever saw. Right here in the middle of the woods, all twisted around this little stream. Found them last month. I was hoping they'd still be here. I should have known better since it's November. Everything starts to die now."

"What?" I whispered.

"Just morning glories," she said. *Don't look*, I told myself. "The prettiest little patch, right here." *Don't look for your heart*, I begged. "All twisted around the little stream." *There it is. There's the heart.* "Full bloom in September too." *Is it shattered?* "But dead in November." *Don't go inside.* "That's when everything dies." She sighed. *It's pulling me in. I can't stop it.*

I was inside my heart. I looked around, at all the middle chapters scribbled on the walls. I read the ending. *He's not coming back.* And I cursed my heart for finding me and making me cry. Heavy sobs until my body ached, right by the dead morning glory stream. My lips kept mumbling one word, over and over. *Why?*

Later that day, I watched Della creep through the yard, with an eye out for Father Heron. "Hey. He's not here," I said. She squealed and ran to hug me.

"Oh Lord, you're alive! The rumors in the valley are crazy. I began to think Father Heron had really killed you!"

She looked good. Her hair had grown out into a little crop of auburn fuzz and her eyes weren't as haunted. I wondered if she had shut off the shadow love. Would I be as lucky?

"You think my hair's coming back in lighter?" she asked. "Momma says it's coming back in strawberry blonde. If it is, Mercy, I swear right here and now that I won't ever color it again! But how are you? Man was I mad at you two for leaving me at the river! But I know now it ain't your fault. I thought he was better too, I guess we shouldn't have expected that much from a dirty mater migrant."

I wanted to grab and shake her until her wagging tongue fell out of her head.

"Don't call him that. If you care at all for me, Della DeMar, you will never call him that again."

"I'm sorry. It's just after everything that's happened, I thought you wouldn't want him anymore. Folks are saying you killed yourself. Some nasty folks said that Mamma Rutha had finally gone totally nuts and knifed you to death. Stupid little valley. I knew that you were just laying low after what Trout did. And that you were probably mad as hell. I mean, it's one thing to date a mater migrant, oh, I mean crop worker, but it's another to find out you're dating a criminal. Don't worry, I'm getting over Randy, and you'll get over Trout."

Had she said the word "criminal"? Or did I just imagine that?

"What did you say?" I asked her, suddenly feeling panicked.

"Who needs those men!"

"No. About Trout. And the criminal thing."

"Now don't get mad, I didn't call him a dirty mater migrant again. I just called him a crook. I reckon since he's locked up in the valley jail, I can at least call him that."

"Jail?" I heard my voice ask.

Della looked at me strangely. "You mean . . . you mean you didn't know?"

I shook my head.

"Oh Mercy. I am so sorry. *You didn't know!* How awful. You probably just thought he had run off. I bet you've been grieving your heart out. I thought you knew what the rest of us did and was raging mad over it. I figured that you had broke up with him. Washed your hands of him and said good riddance. Poor Mercy, everybody else knew where he was and you had no idea."

"Tell me," I found the strength to whisper.

"Okay. I'll tell you what they're all saying in the valley. You know how that goes, it ain't all true, but some of the bits and pieces always are. I went into Rusty's diner. By the way, he wanted me to tell you that you're fired. Not because you haven't been there, but because he heard about your little confession at church and man is he mad at us! He got all red in the face when he saw me, and said, 'Tell that mater migrant whore of yours if she prefers a red-stained man over being with me, manager of a successful diner, then she can stay down in the riverbottom for all I care!' I just had myself a good laugh at him. The look of horror on his face, to learn that women preferred poor mater migrants to him. It was a sight to behold! But anyway, I was in the diner, hopping mad at you two for leaving me at the river. Then I overheard an old woman talking about a white guy that just got arrested down in the riverbottom. And I asked her what she was talking about. And she said that Trout had been arrested for stealing four trained hunting dogs. And that they had hard evidence against him. Said they found two ropes high up on the mountain that still had the dog collars attached, and then the other two matching ropes were what he was

holding his tent up with. They had him arrested and he's
down in the jail right now. Don't know whose dogs they
were, though. The owner had searched out the mountain
and found those two ropes, and he knew the minute he
went down to the riverbottom and saw the same ropes
who had done it. But they haven't found the dogs, so
they're thinking he must have sold them. Mercy, are you
okay? You look so pale!"

I was pale. My heart had turned white with fear. I was
shaking so hard that my chair began to groan.

"What's wrong?"

"It's Father Heron. They were his dogs. He's done this,"
I cried through chattering teeth.

"No," Della said, her eyes growing wide. "He's been
homecooked. All the law serves up here is homecooking.
The old men all get together and decide who the good
guys are and who the bad guys are and the rest of us just
suffer for it. They probably planted them ropes."

"No, I gave him those ropes. Me and Mamma Rutha
took the dogs high on the mountain because they were
killing for the fun of it. We used four red ropes. She left
her two but I brought mine back. And when Trout needed
new ropes for his tent, I gave him mine. I don't know what
to do."

"Shh. We'll figure something out."

"I'll tell them it was me. Then they can send me to jail
if that's what Father Heron wants. But I won't let them
send him. I won't!" I said, rising to my feet.

"Mercy Heron, you have done lost your mind! Father
Heron don't care about them dogs! It was Trout he was
after! If you go down there and confess, it won't make any

difference. They'll keep him locked up and throw you in there too."

"I should have known," I said, pacing back and forth. "I should have known Father Heron had done something. Nothing will satisfy him except my misery."

"You have to get a hold of yourself. Calm down and we'll figure something out."

My stomach surged. The same way it had that night at Della's trailer. I bent over the porch and spilled my breakfast over the ground.

"See, you're making yourself sick," Della said.

"I've got to go."

"Where? Where are you going?"

"To see Sheriff Barnes. To tell him the truth."

Chapter XXV

I forgot about the baby. I only thought about Trout in jail. How he hadn't left me after all. And how my red ropes had slipped themselves around our necks, and hung us.

I found Sheriff Barnes' car parked outside the Credit Union. I waited by it until he walked out of the bank. He was whistling. Probably congratulating himself on being a "good guy" and catching the "bad guys." An honest day's work.

"Hey there, Miss Mercy." He smiled at me, flashing me his shiny white dentures.

"Hello, Sheriff Barnes."

"Nice day out, isn't it?" he asked.

"Yes sir."

"Reckon it's gonna rain, though."

"Seems like it will."

"How's your grandpa getting along?" he asked.

"He's doing well, thank you. So is Mamma Rutha."

"That's good. Well, I'm on duty, so I gotta run on. You know how it is, the law never rests." He laughed.

"That's why I'm here, Sheriff. I have some information for you about a crime," I said, my heart beginning to speed up. I was scared. But I also felt powerful. Father Heron thought he had won by having Trout locked up. He never expected me to confess. I was about to declare a victory, even if it meant going to jail.

"Well Mercy, now is not the best time . . ." he began, looking at his watch.

"I need to confess to a crime, Sheriff," I interrupted. "A crime for which someone else is being blamed."

"Maybe you want to talk this over with your grandpa before you come talking to me."

"No, I don't. I'm grown now, Sheriff. And I want to take responsibility for my own actions. Them dogs that were stolen. Fox, Coon, Bear, and Wolf. It wasn't the mater migrant that did it. It was me. I hiked them up to the top of the mountain late one night because they were killing our other animals. Then I gave some of the rope to the mater migrant because his ropes were going bad."

"Well, I appreciate your honesty," he said, smiling. "I have to get back to work now."

"Wait, does that mean that Trout will go free?"

"I can't comment on any official business."

"But sir, it's my business too!" I said, my voice raising. "An innocent man is being punished for something I did!"

"I really have to go now, what's done is done," he said, his voice edgy.

"What's done is done? You have an innocent man in jail. Are you no better than the criminals you catch?"

His eyes flashed danger and he stepped toward me. So close I could see the blue in his fake gums.

"Not that it's any of your damn business, you little mater migrant whore," he said through clenched teeth. "I'd like nothing better than to lock you up too. But your grandpa's already had to live down the slut for a daughter he had, a crazy wife, and now a slut for a granddaughter. And I don't want to add the shame of a criminal to him now. That's the only reason why you ain't in handcuffs. An innocent man? Is that what you call him? Well, I knew you was mixed up in this business from the beginning. And he was claiming ignorance. Said he didn't know about no dogs. So I said, 'If you don't know, then tell me where you got those red ropes from.' And he wouldn't. So I says to him, 'I know your little whore is in on this. So if you don't want that filthy bitch to be right here where you are, you better spill your guts.' He signed a confession right then and there. Said he did it all. So is that what you call innocent? Get out of my sight 'fore I arrest you just for the hell of it."

His words were a confusing mixture of hate and rage. Leaving me flinching but only half hearing. But I strung together one thing. *Trout was not going to be freed.* I had been so certain that the sheriff wouldn't let an innocent man be imprisoned. Why had I been so certain? What made Sheriff Barnes any different than Father Heron?

"Please," I begged him, my hand grabbing on to his arm

as he turned to get in his car. "Don't do this. I know you're a friend of Father Heron's. And I understand that you don't think much of me, or my momma or my grandma. But I am begging you. The man is innocent."

My touch burned him. He jerked his arm free and got into his car without even looking at me.

It had begun to rain. I sat down on the curb and let wet mirrors pile high all around me.

"I'm so sorry," I said out loud. "I'll make it right, Trout." My feet were shaking with cold I didn't feel inside. The puddle they rested on began to ripple.

I remembered our day together in the rain, when he asked me if I believed in luck. "Look like you're standin' on a mirror," he had said. And I had told him no, that I didn't believe in luck. Had I been wrong? Was all of this because of my broken mirrors? I pulled my feet out of the puddle and placed them on the curb.

Della found me sitting alone and soaked. She half carried me to her momma's car.

"What's wrong? What did Sheriff Barnes say?" she asked, her eyes wide and scared.

I groaned, loud sobs escaping from the well of my heart. "He already confessed. They told him they were going to put me in jail if he didn't. I told Sheriff Barnes it was a lie, and that Trout was innocent. But he didn't care. He didn't care because Father Heron wants Trout in jail. Father Heron knows that is the best way to kill me."

"Nobody's gonna kill you," she whispered.

"This will! And I deserve it. It's my own fault. That promise we made when we were fourteen. That's why we came back. He didn't want to, but I made him."

"I don't know what to say, Mercy."

"I need to see him. Before they ship him over the mountain."

"Okay. We can do that."

"And I may not know how to fix it yet, but somehow I've got to. I don't care what I have to do," I said.

She squeezed my hand and nodded. "Me too. Anything you need me for. I'll do it."

I knew she would too. And not just because she loved me. That was one reason. But because she hated the people who pulled all the strings on Crooktop. The same ones that set her momma up in a garage with five children and then went home to their nice warm houses to congratulate themselves on the good deed performed. She was like me, cursed and angry.

We drove down to the valley jail. It was like any jail. Shabby and dirty. With lots of concrete and poor ventilation. It smelled of urine and dirty mop water. People were never held there long. They either served their time for a minor infraction or were shipped off to the penitentiary over the mountain after final sentencing. My body sensed his presence. It didn't need my mind to tell it that he was near. He was so close to me that I felt I could smell him above the urine.

There was only one young guy behind the desk watching a small black-and-white TV. He was pimply-faced and thick. He wore a smug look, born from the uniform he wore. He ignored us when we walked up to the desk.

"Excuse me, sir?" I said.

He nodded.

"I'm here to visit Trout Price."

"Don't know nobody by that name," he mumbled, without glancing up from the TV.

"Well I'm sure he's here. His name is Trout."

"Sorry, no Trout here," he said.

"But there is. Trout Price?" I persisted.

"Look lady, this here is a jail, not some local hangout. We don't register people by their nicknames. So we ain't got no Trout in this here jail," he said, eyes meeting me for a brief second before returning back to the TV.

"But Trout's not his nickname. It's his real name."

"Well I don't know what to tell you. Sounds like a nickname to me, and unless you know his real name I can't help you."

"The mater migrant. He has red hands. Wavy hair," I said, my voice beginning to break.

"Oh, him. He won't tell us his real name and the sheriff's awfully particular about using only legal names, so he's just been assigned a number. Let me look, oh here it is, the mater migrant is Prisoner 3902 Price."

"His real name is Trout. It ain't a nickname. His name isn't 3902, or whatever you said. It's Trout Price." I choked, my voice betraying my emotion.

"Well if it sounds like a nickname, and you don't have ID, then the sheriff assigns a number. They'll probably do the same over at the pen too 'cause who ever heard of the name Trout? His momma must have been crazy or something." He laughed.

"Can I see him?"

"Can't see him," he said, turning his attention back to the TV.

"There's an hour left in visiting time."

"Sorry," he said, shaking his head.

"Why?" I asked.

He ignored me.

"Why can't I see him?" I asked again, my voice growing louder.

He still ignored me.

I reached over the desk and yanked the TV cord out of the wall.

"What the hell . . ." he began, rising to his feet.

"I just want you to give me some answers!" I yelled. "Tell me why I can't see him when visiting hours aren't over!"

"The mater migrant ain't allowed visitors," he said.

"I ain't just a visitor. I'm his family. We got married."

"Sheriff Barnes said a young girl your age might come and say anything to try and get back there. Sorry," he said, sitting back down.

I sat down on a chair across from the counter. I was numb.

"You been a cop long?" I heard Della ask.

"A year."

"Wow. A whole year? Bet you seen a lot of action." She smiled.

"I've seen my share," he said, switching his TV back on.

"Ever had to shoot anybody?"

"Not yet. But you gotta be prepared. It's a dangerous job."

Della pretended to shiver. "The way you said that just gave me goose bumps all over. You must be real brave. Bet your parents are proud of you."

"Yeah, I guess so." He smiled.

"I wish I could be that brave. I bet you ain't scared of nobody, are you? I mean, you're young and strong. You obviously work out a lot. I bet nothing scares you, huh?"

"Nope. I reckon I can handle myself against anybody."

"Wow." She giggled. "That's really cool. I bet you ain't even scared of the sheriff, huh? I mean he's just an old man, and you, you're where the real power is. I can see that. Anybody could see that in you. Why just looking at you I can tell you ain't just strong and brave, you're smart too."

He smiled.

"You've got a nice smile too."

"Thanks, you uh, you do too."

"Really? You think so? Wow. It means a lot to me that you think my smile is pretty. Nobody ever said that to me before. It means a whole lot coming from somebody like you," she said, leaning over the desk, pressing her full breasts against the counter.

His eyes slid down and enjoyed the show she offered him.

"Can I tell you a secret?" she whispered in her sexiest voice.

"Sure," he said, excitedly.

"Just being this close to you has got me all hot and bothered. Imagine what would happen if I came behind the counter."

"Oh, uh, wow," he said, his eyes starting to bulge.

"Would you like that? Would you like for me to bring all of my excitement to you behind the counter. Nobody's gonna be coming down to the jail at this hour," she whispered.

"Oh, uh, oh Lord." He giggled nervously. "Your friend is still back there."

"Hell, let her go see the mater migrant so you and I can be alone. The sheriff won't ever know, and we'll get to make each other's dreams come true."

"I don't know, the sheriff, he wouldn't like it," he began.

"Oh, I see. You're scared of the sheriff after all," she said poutily. "I guess me and my friend will just go away now, and leave you all alone with your TV."

"Well wait a minute now. I didn't say no. I just said the sheriff might not like it. I guess your friend can go back. But just for a couple minutes. That's all. Okay?" he said, starting to giggle again.

"I'll make every second count, I promise," she whispered.

"Hey you," he called. I looked up. "You got a few minutes, just until I holler for you. Go down the hall and turn left, it's the last cell on the right. You can't miss it, there's just four cells in the whole building and he's the only prisoner here. No funny business, though, or I'll lock you up too!"

I saw him before he saw me. He was sitting on the ground with his head down on his knees. Gently rocking back and forth. He was dirty. His cell was dirty. And there was no window. No place for him to look out at the mountains he loved. It was a hell worse than fire and brimstone. Trout loved his freedom. I had never even thought about whether I was free or trapped until I met him. "These red hands are freed," he had said. "But not by broke mirrors." And now he wasn't free. He wasn't spinning. Or standing.

He wasn't even lost in the rows. He was just rocking back and forth in a dirty jail cell. My captured Fire Trout.

"Hey," I whispered through the bars. He looked up slowly.

"Mercy?"

"Yes. It's me. Just got a few minutes," I sobbed.

He ran to the bars and grabbed my hands.

"I'm so sorry, Trout. It was me that stole them dogs. It was me and Mamma Rutha. I told 'em too, but they don't care, 'cause Father Heron wants you here. Maybe if you take it back too. If you'll tell them it wasn't you."

"Shhh," he whispered. "Don't you be sorry for nothin'. I ain't."

"I can't make it without you."

"You can. All you need is your glory. That's somethin' that old man won't ever be able to stamp out. Remember how I said you was your worst mirror? Well go on and break your old one, and use mine. And when you look in it, you'll see the glory."

He was crying now too. Sunflowers drowning in big tears. Deep green river pools overflowing.

I nodded my head. "Someday it'll all be okay, won't it?"

"It already is. We're okay already."

"Time's up!" the cop called from the hall.

I sobbed, my hands gripping the bars of his cell.

"Go on home, Mercy. Walk outta here, head held high."

"I said time's up," the man called out again.

"Use that new mirror of yours." He pulled his hands from mine and turned and walked away.

"Wait," I begged. I would have stayed right there forever if I could have. I would have rather stayed there with him, amidst the stench of urine, than to walk out alone.

"Please," he said, his voice breaking.

"Find me," I sobbed before walking away. "I'll go where you go, remember? Find me."

My head was held high and my hands were full and heavy. I was carrying his mirror. The heart of the Fire Trout. And it was heavy with love.

Chapter XXVI

*D*ella's young cop told her the details of Trout's case. How he had been arrested and taken before a judge. Because he was a "drifter" and a flight risk, a hefty bail was set. But I would have done anything to make that bail. I would have robbed the Miners' Credit Union if I had to. But I hadn't known. I was locked in plastic, dying over his disappearance, as he lay locked in prison. If I had met that bail, we would have stood on sandy shores, letting salty waves hide us from the eyes of the law.

But despite his guilty plea, Della's cop told her that Trout would still face a judge for his sentencing. Finally there was someone else. Someone that wasn't Father Heron or Sheriff Barnes. Trout would face that man and await his sentence. And I would meet him there and announce my guilt. So would my Mamma Rutha.

It would be four days until I freed him. It never stopped playing in my mind. How I would see him as he stood before the judge. The sound of the gavel as the judge declared Trout's innocence. The look, the fear, that would shadow across Father Heron's eyes. He would know then that some things wouldn't die when he told them to. My momma may have. But not me. And not my love.

I would rise from my seat, and I would speak the new wedding vow that hid in my heart. Not the one that I had whispered on Thorny Ridge. That was a safe vow, born of a love that ran. Everything was different now. And so the love in my heart would vow itself to him in the only way that remained. *I, Mercy Heron, am guilty.*

Imagine the feel of cold steel circling your wrists, I would tell myself as I checked the days off until his sentencing. *Imagine the feel of cold steel caging your body*, I would whisper as I lay in bed mouthing my vow. *I, Mercy Heron, am guilty.* I tied my hands together with rope just to feel the pinch against my skin. I sank low within my jelly jar closet, just to breathe the scent of caged air. I wanted the steel, the cage, the misery. Because none of it held loss for me. All of it was my vow of love.

And all of it depended on Mamma Rutha. Without her, I was just a mater migrant's whore, desperate to free her lover. Without her to confirm my confession, to admit that she helped, the judge might not believe me. For the first time in my life, Mamma Rutha was everything that I needed.

And for a moment, I worried over her. I could accept prison if it meant freeing Trout. But Mamma Rutha? Without her creatures, without her green, she would become the withered fig. And I would be the one that withered her. I decided to tell them that I took advantage of her feeble mind. I would look at the judge and I would tell him, *She is crazy.*

Della knew what I planned, and she begged me not to.

"Please don't do this," she cried. "They'll lock you away, and then I'll have no one. What if I tell them I saw someone else do it? I could tell them I saw Randy take the ropes from Ben Franklin, and then heard him bragging about stealing them dogs."

For a moment, I thought it might work. It could be proven that the ropes came from Ben Franklin. And Randy worked there, with easy access to them. But it wasn't certain. Randy was respectable. It would be hard for a judge to believe that Randy, young married manager, soon-to-be father, committed the crime instead of a drifting mater migrant.

I was the only thing certain. *And I really was guilty.*

"Couldn't you at least talk to Father Heron?" Della asked. "Tell him that you will confess. Maybe he'll change his mind."

"He won't have pity on Trout."

"But he loves the Heron name. Maybe he'll change his mind so that you and Mamma Rutha won't shame it. Give him one last chance to save you."

Chapter XXVII

*I*t was her birthday, and all of the Heron house knew it. Thirty-five years ago that day, she was new. Before anything bad or sinful. And I imagine Mamma Rutha loved her. Loved the way she curled her little toes. Or how greedily she sucked the breast. And I imagine Father Heron was proud that day. Of being a family man. Of having his seed established. Maybe he was disappointed she wasn't a boy. But she was still his.

Mamma Rutha was gone. I had never seen her there on *that* day. I'm sure she disappeared to honor her in her own wild way. The bone blessing was good enough for most dead things. But not her.

I was never sure what I was supposed to do. I didn't know how to honor the stranger that gave me life. And yet, I couldn't seem to convince myself that it was just a day like all others. So I walked a little more quietly. I stared at Mamma Rutha's picture of her. I pretended that I knew the smell of her skin. The feel of her hair. Pretended I had heard the sound of her voice. *My pretty baby girl,* she might have said.

It was late. Closer to noon than morning. I laid in bed and thought about her. Imagined saying, *Momma, save me.* I listened for Father Heron, and tried to think of a way to convince him to free Trout.

He was in the kitchen, sitting at the table. I rounded the corner and found myself staring at his back.

"Always tried," he mumbled to himself. I stopped still. "Always tried. Mary."

It was the name that was never spoken. *Mary.* He called the birthday girl by name. I grew cold inside. Thinking about him as more than my Father Heron. Thinking about him as a daddy that spoke her name. A daddy that *tried?*

He sighed. Deep and heavy. Like he carried a weight that no one had ever seen. Was it the weight of killing his daughter?

A car pulled up and honked its horn. He jumped. I ducked around the corner and back into my bedroom. I watched him walk to the car. Nothing out of the ordinary. Same ol' levelheaded Deacon Heron. Solid as a rock.

I went back to the kitchen and that's when I saw it. Laying there on his open Bible. It was her, about twelve years old. And him. Arms around each other. Standing on the back porch, just in front of the back door. *Arms around each other!* And she was smiling as though she liked him. As though she *loved* him. And he was looking at her. As she gazed straight ahead grinning at the camera. He was liking how she giggled. How she called him Daddy. He liked everything that was Mary.

It was the second picture I had ever seen of her. And I studied it, memorizing the way she stood. An arm around him. A hand on her hip. Memorizing her bare feet. The part in her hair. The boldness of her smile. It was like I was meeting her for the first time. And yet she was younger than me, but already dead.

I wanted other pictures. More of her to meet. I began flipping through his Bible, carefully marking the page he had left it at. Listening for the sound of his return. There was a folded-up piece of construction paper stuck in the middle of Psalms. I opened it and stared at the crayoned scribble.

> DEAR DADDY,
> HAPPY FATHER'S DAY! THANK YOU FOR being my DADDY. I LIKE it WHEN we fish.
> Love,
> MARY

She had drawn a picture on the front. Three stick people. Her and him and Mamma Rutha. She was in the middle, and all the stick people held hands. I looked at the words. She called him Daddy. Something much more than Father Heron.

I kept flipping. Through the Old Testament, into the New. Until I found another sheet. This time not construction paper.

Dear Dad,

I never meant to hurt you. But I love him. I really love him. Like Momma loves you. Maybe more. I know he isn't like the boys at church. And I know you think I'm too young. But Momma was married younger. Just stop being so angry about it. Just because I love him don't mean I quit loving you. I love you both. I wish you'd talk to me. Ever since you found out about us, you haven't spoken to me. And Momma's acting real nervous around you lately. I miss you. Won't you please let me love him?

Mary

There was another. Tucked in Hebrews.

Dad,

He told me what you did. How you threatened him to make him leave me alone. It won't work. I love him and he loves me. And I'm gonna marry him. Even if we have to run away. You haven't spoken to me for weeks now. So I guess I have to write you to get you to listen. I love you, Daddy. But if you want me, then you're just gonna have to learn to live with the fact that I love him too.

Mary

There were no more letters. But I knew how her story ended. I had always thought he killed her out of his shame and anger. But maybe it was jealousy too. Because she loved another. He heard her come crawling back. *Daddy, please open the door! Please, Daddy!* But would not move as everything that was Mary lay dying on the other side of his door. Now all that remained was his shame, her letters, and me.

It wasn't easy to learn that the man I hated, once loved. That someone once pleased him. I had missed something. After eighteen years of watching and waiting, his silence still managed to hide things from me.

He had never looked at me the way he looked at her. He had never taken me fishing. I had never told him that I loved him. I had never thanked him, except out of fear. I lacked something that she had had. Her sparkle, standing there grinning with her hand on her hip. Her affection, standing there touching him so easy and natural. Her fearlessness, telling him *I'm gonna marry him, even if we have to run away.* I had everything of her death, and nothing of her life.

The car started again and I stashed the letters back in their places and ducked around the corner. I heard him come back in and sit down. There were so many things I wanted to ask him about her. Mamma Rutha couldn't answer me plainly. She sang to me about my momma. But she couldn't talk about her.

I walked into the kitchen and sat across from him. I was brave, believing that as he stared at her picture he might remember some of the old love. That he might remember it, even as he stared at me, Mary's child.

"Is that a picture of Momma?"

He nodded.

"Gosh. She was pretty, huh?"

He nodded.

"Do you mind if I look?"

He placed the picture down on the table and slid it over to me. Our eyes met. One pair black and seeking. The other black and sad.

"She looks like you," I said.

He sighed again. "I . . . always." He stopped.

A dog barked and he stood up and ran outside. I smiled and laughed softly at my luck. It was her birthday, but she's the one that gave me a gift. My new weapon against him. She showed me that he was more than my Father Heron. He was her daddy too.

Chapter XXVIII

ou killed her."

I had planned my words carefully. *Father Heron, will you change your mind?* That would never work. I had to make him want to. I had to call upon more than his fear of shaming the Heron name. I had to call upon his love for Mary.

When I was a little girl, I used to play Mary. I would take my Sally doll to hide in the woods and I would imagine that I lived there, with Momma. She was more beautiful than the faded picture that Mamma Rutha kept by her bed. With honey-colored hair that tickled her shoulders and dark eyes that flashed happiness. She would set wild daisies before me. And throw clusters of ripe blackberries all around me. The daisies would change into a feast of fried eggs. The berries would smear into jam. Together we would dine, and laugh over how good it was. She would hold my Sally doll and I would wish that I was still small enough to be held. *Mary is the mother of Jesus*, my Sunday school teacher told me. But the one I craved was the Mary that would feed me. The one that would rock my Sally doll. *Mary, mother of Mercy*.

"I know you killed Mary," I told him.

He didn't move, but I sensed the internal jolt of his body. I sensed the way his breath hung still within his lungs. The way his back felt every inch of his spine straighten and stiffen.

"I know you killed my momma. Your own daughter, and you killed her."

He looked up at me, as I stood, shaking but powerful, looking down upon him. His eyes held murder in them. They were cold and unrelenting, like a metal knob that won't budge when you try to turn it.

"Get out," he said lowly.

I shook my head no, and backed up a step to place the kitchen table between us.

"You killed her. She loved you. You made her smile, and you killed her."

He stood up, and I saw how his hands trembled. I backed up another step and showed him the picture from his Bible.

"Look at Mary, Father Heron. See how she smiles standing next to you. See how her eyes loved you," I whispered.

His eyes fell to the picture, and they grew weary. With her silly grin and mocking eyes, she spoke to him. I was her baby girl. And she was his. He reached for the picture and cradled it in his palm.

"You don't know anything," he whispered. "You don't know anything about that day."

"I know you can still make it right," I said, beginning to sob. "She will forgive you if you make it right."

He knew what I was asking for. Not his approval. Not his love. Just his help. My body felt too weak to pull in air to breathe. But the prayers still came. I was speaking without breath. I was speaking without ribs, or lungs. Without a mouth, a tongue, or lips. The words called from me.

"If you will help me, it will all be right again," I whispered.

He stood in the doorway, his hand still cradling the picture that I had stolen.

"She wants you to help me," I cried. "I stole them dogs, Father Heron. Me and Mamma Rutha. Not the mater migrant. Let him go. Help me, Mary's daughter."

"You are not her daughter," he whispered.

"I am," I cried.

"You are nobody's," he said, never pulling his eyes from her picture.

"I am Mary's," I sobbed. "And you can help her, by helping me. Change your mind. Set him free. We'll disappear, we're already married. You'll never be shamed by me again. I am Mary's."

"You have nothing of her."

"I have her nose," I cried. "Look at it, Father Heron. And I think I have her hands. Look."

I turned my face toward him and held my hands before him. Praying that he would find something to love. Praying that he would see her nose, her hands, when he looked at me. I gently took the picture from his hand.

"Look," I whispered. "See the way her nose is a little too round? Now look at mine. They're the same, aren't they? And look there at her hands. Look at the one she's holding on her hip. See how little it is? With its narrow palm and slender fingers? But then look at how her thumb is wide at the knuckle. Now look at mine. Almost the exact same, aren't they? And look at my eyes, Father Heron. Look at how they're shaped like beechnuts. And the color of coal. They're yours. You're looking at your eyes. I'm from you too."

He took the picture from my hand and looked at me, looked through me. I focused all of my strength on summoning the image of her. I thought of her, barefoot in the woods, with her honey hair and eyes snapping with color. I thought of her, and I hoped that my hair looked lighter, and that my eyes flashed happiness.

"Please help Mary's child. You can make it as if that day never happened."

"Don't you pretend you know anything about her," he said, his voice breaking. "And don't ever speak of that day again. If you value your skin, don't ever. You know nothing about that day."

"Maybe," I whispered. "But I'll die without him. And then you'll have killed me too. For Mary's sake, help me."

He sighed, and I almost sensed a breaking point. There was such power in her name. There was such strength in the ability of those letters to sweep a tide of misery over us. Grief over the fact that she died. Hate over being left behind, alone. Anger, that all either of us had left of her was her name. Her name joined us together. More than our eyes ever had. More than our blood ever could.

"Please," I whispered. "Tell them it was all a big mistake."

There was nothing left to say or do. If I would ever be his child, if he would ever look at me and see her, it would be then. If he would ever do just one kind thing for her name's sake, that was the moment.

His back was to me, and still I knew that his eyes sought comfort in the weathered wood of his shed, and hid from the aching limbs of the apple tree. His eyes sought anything that wasn't Mary's nose, Mary's hands, his eyes. His back was to me, but I still heard his cage close tight again. He didn't speak a word, and yet I understood everything. Mary was dead, and I might as well be too.

"I don't need you," I sobbed. "I will tell them that I did it. And Mamma Rutha will tell them too. I may go to jail, but he won't."

"They'll never believe you."

"When Mamma Rutha confesses too they will. Mamma Rutha will agree with everything I say. That will be two people saying they stole them dogs. The judge will listen. Trout will be freed. You don't have to help me. I can go to jail to free him. All I need is Mamma Rutha."

"You can't have her," he said lowly.

"Yes I can. She loves me."

"You can't have her," he repeated.

"She isn't yours. She hasn't been since you killed her child," I cried. "She will confess."

"If you ask her to confess to the dogs, you will lose her forever."

"She isn't afraid of you. You can't hurt her," I cried.

"Ask her to confess to the dogs, and I will tell."

"Tell what?"

"The truth."

"About what?" I whispered.

"That she killed your momma."

Chapter XXIX

*T*here was another mirror. That's what happened when Father Heron spoke those words. *She killed your momma.* He held up his mirror before me. I didn't want to look, and yet I couldn't close my eyes. They locked upon her, the twisted ugly one within his mirror.

She's not real, I told myself.

"I don't believe you," I whispered to him. *Lies lies. Mary lies.* "You're lying," I said. "Because I heard her." *Daddy, please! Please let me in, Daddy!* "That day, in her belly, I heard you kill her." *Please open the door!* "And you have no proof," I whispered. "If you tell them, they won't believe you. Just like I don't. You have no proof."

"Ask her. She'll tell you. Just like she'd tell them if they asked. Ask her how she killed your momma."

I began going over everything I had always known

about my momma's death. I sang to myself the songs I had heard Mamma Rutha sing to the moon. *With Sorrow's eyes her daughter cried. With stolen blood my daughter died.*

I found Mamma Rutha by the stream where the morning glories once grew. I sat next to her and looked at her. I couldn't see murder in her, like I did in Father Heron.

"How did she die?" I asked, knowing that she would understand who I spoke of.

"Under the apple tree," she said.

"Father Heron killed her?"

"Yes," she said, her hand dropping to feel the cool water.

"Because she was having me. He says you did it."

Her hand stirred the water.

"I know," she said calmly.

"How can he say that?"

She looked at me, and for the first time I began to see the death in her eyes. Not murder, like I heard in Father Heron's silence. But a death of great anguish.

"How did she die?" I asked again. She looked back to the water and pulled her hands from it. Her fingers ran over the earth, and into it. Feeling the grit of blackness between them. She shivered, and then grew still.

"Without a soul, a body is just waiting to die. Needing to die. In misery 'til it does." She stopped and looked at me. Her hand touched my face, and she smiled.

"She loved trees," she said. "Was blessed by 'em. As soon as she could walk on her own, she headed for the trees. Watching how they stretched their limbs. Watching how they'd reach for the sun. She'd raise her tiny arms above her head. *Look, Momma, I'm a tree*. And I'd call her my little sapling. Mary, my baby sapling."

She wasn't looking at me anymore. Her head was tilted up, her eyes following the lines of the trees near us.

"All of the mountain loved her," she continued. "All of the mountain sang to her. And she would sing to you in her belly. *Rock my baby in the treetops*. Maybe you remember? She laid herself beneath a tree, you know. Ran to it when he killed her. It was her love for him that made the killing hard. When he stared at her from the other side of the door, she loved him. And prayed for him to love her enough to open it. And when prayer didn't work, she begged him. Maybe you heard her? His hate choked her soul. But she knew where she wanted to be buried, and she ran to the closest tree she could find. The apple tree. I found her body there. He chopped her down. My baby sapling. All of her was shaking. And cold. Her eyes were white all over. They never even saw me. Blood was everywhere. On the bark of the tree. On the apples that rotted on the ground. Her lips, soggy with pain. Her body cried out for its soul. And there was nothing left of my Mary. Just a body that couldn't hold in its own blood. A body that couldn't see, couldn't breathe for the hate that smothered it. I called to her soul. I sang to it. But it had been choked. All that was left was white eyes wild with agony. Eyes that didn't know me. They asked me to make it stop. They knew the soul had been killed. I pulled you from her. And I held you up to the sky. *Look Mary*, I screamed. *Your baby, Mary, reaches for the sun!*"

Mamma Rutha was standing now. Next to the stream with her arms raised toward the sky.

"The body couldn't hold the blood inside," she said. "And it was in misery to die. I cut my hand and I held it over her mouth. Trying to pour blood back in her. Won't a momma do anything, give anything, her blood even? But the body wanted to be with her soul. It wanted to stretch towards the sun. It was all I could do to help her. So I took her to her soul."

I looked into the stream and I saw the mirror again. Framed by the vision of Mamma Rutha, with arms lifted to the sky. I recognized the ugly twisted woman within. With howling white eyes and lips soggy in pain. With a body unable to hold its own blood. It was the soulless Mary, before she was carried to the sun.

Chapter XXX

*T*he courtroom surprised me. It was smaller than I had expected. With a low ceiling and an uneven shape. Smelling like a room that once held men covered in starch, but was now filled only with the dusty scent of old wood and waxed floors. With only an American flag and a plaque of the Ten Commandments for decoration. There was nothing great about the room. There was nothing that spoke of the agony it held. Or of the hope. Its walls never realized the significance of everything they framed.

I hadn't known what to wear. I wanted to look respectable enough to be believed. But not so respectable that I couldn't be a common criminal. I ended up wearing a church dress, not the dusty rose one and not the purple and white one. It was deep blue and plain. And I pulled my hair back off my face, because I didn't want to look girlish. I was afraid that if I looked young and sweet, a judge might pity me, and prefer to send Trout to jail over me. And I left my lips naked. I didn't want to look pretty. I wanted to look guilty. Believable and guilty. I glanced at my dress as I sat in the courtroom, and I felt the shabbiness of my life.

I had been nervous all morning. Remembering all the Perry Mason shows I had ever watched. The way an audience would pack the courtroom. The way the newspaper would take everyone's picture on the courthouse steps. The long speeches of the lawyers. The feverish emotion of their arguments. The looks of shock that would sweep the entire room when someone unsuspected would declare her guilt. The sound of the gavel as the judge would cry, "Order! Order in my court!" to silence all the whispers. I would cause all of Crooktop to lose order when I declared my guilt.

Two men strode in with heavy steps. One was young, and one was old. Their backs slightly bent with the weight of the briefcases they shouldered. The old one's case was worn and tattered, with papers bursting from the unzipped top and bulging sides. The young one's case was still thin and shiny, looking as if he took great pains to polish it every morning. They matched their cases. The old one looking tired and pasty. His belt had long given up the fight against his belly, which spilled over his waist as though someone had squeezed him too tightly, causing everything to overflow. But the young one was trim and eager, with a neatly groomed appearance that spoke of his importance.

I listened to them. The old one was teaching the other. He was explaining how to "nail the crook every time."

"It's all in your opening, son. That's where your whole case is won or lost. The jury makes up its mind after the first five minutes, so you got five minutes to sell yourself. If you can convince the jury to like you, they'll do what you ask. To hell with the evidence. To hell with all that nonsense about reasonable doubt. It's about us, son. It's about the suits that strut before 'em."

They were lawyers. The ones trying to take Trout's freedom. They were my enemy. And yet they hadn't seen me sitting there, and they didn't even know my name.

"And you know how to get the jury to like you, son? You be like them. Jurors are common folk. The high school dropout. The angry neighbor. The farmer that has his hidden field of marijuana. They want to be looked in the eyes and asked for help. Not preached at."

"And I suppose telling them how the law was created to protect them from people like the defendant doesn't hurt either, does it?" the young one asked.

"Ah hell. The jury is the law. Those twelve people are the power. The moment you forget that is the moment you lose your case."

"Well, at least there's no jury to worry about for this next case, since the fella pled guilty earlier. Here he comes now, let's get this boy sentenced and shipped on over the mountain where he belongs," the young one said.

It should have been a perfect moment. My body should have sensed his presence, and my heart should have sought out the beat of his. The walls should have taken on a new life, pulsing with the greatness of holding him. I should have smelled his skin, the way I had always been able to. Our eyes should have met. Mine, the color of his earth. And his, the garden of my desire, the river of my drowning.

But that very first moment blinked by so quickly I could only remember it later as I laid in bed. And in that moment, before my mind could whisper to my heart, *It is your love*, I didn't know him. And it wasn't because he was completely changed. Hair, lips, eyes, skin, everything that makes a body, it was all the same. And yet somehow so different. With cool steel circling his wrists. And the easy way, the calm peace that always hung upon him, replaced by a face that looked older and angrier. That looked less wise somehow. And for that brief moment, for that second that I did not know him, I looked at him, and I saw a man that belonged there.

Another man entered the room and walked over to Trout. He placed his hand on Trout's shoulder, and I instantly liked him. They spoke briefly, and I guessed that he was Trout's lawyer. He looked younger than Trout, in a suit that was too big. Like he had lost too much weight, too quickly, and hadn't had time to buy new clothes. He left Trout and walked over to the table on the right. The prosecutors stood up and they all shook hands and began joking about the new golf course built over in the foothills. I was filled with bitterness. How could he do that? How could any man touch Trout and then touch his enemy too? How could he be on Trout's side and joke about golf with those that wanted to hurt him?

"Oyez, oyez, oyez," the bailiff called out. The prosecutors rose to their feet. Trout's lawyer turned from where he was already standing to face the bench. Sensing the air of importance that floated in the room as the bailiff called those words, I rose to my feet too. I looked at Trout. There were three lawyers on one side of the room. And he was alone on the other.

"The Honorable Judge Moser presiding," the bailiff continued. "All people having business before this court draw nigh and you shall be heard. God save the state and this honorable court. Court is now in session." With those words, a new man walked in. Draped in black and looking like a judge. With thick white hair sharply contrasting the blackness of his robe. He had heavy eyebrows that knitted together even when his face bore no expression, giving him a look of fierceness.

"You may be seated," the judge said lowly without looking up as he shuffled through loose papers scattered about his bench. He put a pair of reading glasses on that his eyebrows defiantly peeked over, and looked up at the room. After I had been sitting there all morning, behind the lawyers, the bailiff, and Trout, the judge was the first person to notice me. In the moment our eyes greeted one another, I searched for kindness. And I willed him to have mercy. *Mercy for Mercy's love.*

"Morning, gentlemen," the judge said, telling me he was a good person. He looked at Trout, not just the lawyers, but Trout too, and called him a gentleman.

"In the matter of *State versus Price*, the defendant earlier entered a formal plea of guilty to felony larceny, is that correct?"

Trout's lawyer rose to his feet, "Yes, Your Honor."

"Counsel, are you ready to present arguments with

regard to his sentencing?" the judge asked, looking toward the prosecutors.

The young one rose, "The State is ready, your honor."

"Very well then," the judge said, looking at his papers again.

"May it please the court," the prosecutor said, "the State will be brief, Your Honor. We don't have any witnesses to call. We just want to emphasize to Your Honor that this man, this migrant drifter, entered the private property of one of our most respected community members." He began flipping the pages of his legal pad.

"Let's see, uh, Wallace Heron, who lives up on the mountain," he continued. "The defendant entered his property at night, while his wife and orphaned granddaughter slept within. He then stole four hunting dogs of great value. And not just ordinary mutts, your honor. These were purebreds, purchased from a line of champion hunters. The defendant has admitted to all of this. But he shows no remorse. He won't even tell Mr. Heron what he did with the dogs. He offers nothing to mitigate the sentence for his crime. Therefore, the State requests, Your Honor, that these facts all be weighed together, to impose the maximum sentence for felony larceny. Thank you."

He took his seat and the judge continued to shuffle papers around as I tried to absorb all that I had heard. I had carried four dogs into the mountain to help Mamma Rutha, to keep them from killing her creatures, and suddenly it was larceny. I didn't even know what that meant. *Larceny*. It sounded complicated, and bad.

"Thank you, counsel," the judge said lowly. "Counsel for the defense, are you ready?"

"Yes, Your Honor," Trout's lawyer said as he rose to his feet.

"May it please the court," he began. "The defense also will not call any witnesses, and thus will be brief, Your Honor. But we want to point out that this crime was committed without any aggravation. No one was hurt, no one even knew until the next morning. My client was not armed and the police did not find a weapon among his belongings. He may be a drifter, but perhaps he is just young and has lost his way. We ask for leniency, Your Honor, for this sin of his youth. Thank you."

"Thank you, counsel," the judge said. "Does the State have any rebuttal?"

"No, Your Honor."

"Well if there is nothing further," the judge began, and I knew. In the shiver of my legs as they pulled me to my feet. In the spinning of the room that pulled the air from my lungs and refused to put it back in. It was time.

"Wait." I was letting them know it wasn't over. I was telling them it wasn't finished. There were vows yet to be said.

"I took the dogs." I didn't whisper. I felt brave and strong, as I stared at the back of my love that wouldn't look at me.

For a moment they didn't know what to do with me. The lawyers exchanged glances with each other that changed from confusion to amusement. For the young ones, I was probably the most exciting thing to ever happen in their short careers. The judge looked at the lawyers, who all shrugged their shoulders.

"What is your name, young lady?" the judge asked, his eyebrows arching into dangerous mountains.

"Mercy Heron. I stole my grandfather's dogs," I said simply.

The young prosecutor was rising to his feet, accepting my challenge, "Your Honor, since the defendant has already pled guilty, the State would ask the court to ignore this young lady, who is obviously confused and disturbed."

"And what does the defense have to say about this? Do you know this young lady?" the judge asked Trout's lawyer.

"No, Your Honor, I was not made aware of her. But in the interest of justice, I would ask that we be allowed to examine her," he said, his interest piqued by my challenge as well.

"Any objection, counsel?" the judge asked the prosecutors.

"Yes, Your Honor. In the interest of efficiency, the State asks that this girl be excused from the courtroom. Again I stress that guilt or innocence is not an issue here today. The defendant is guilty. He has already entered his plea."

"But perhaps her testimony could present mitigation," Trout's lawyer countered.

"What'll it hurt to see what she has to say?" the judge said casually. "Allowing the State, of course, ample opportunity to cross."

I was called forward and I took an oath, swearing to tell the truth. My eyes avoided him now. They danced all around him. Noting the color of his skin. The curl of his hair. But never settling on his face. Scared to settle there and not be answered. Trout's lawyer reminded me of my oath, and asked me a simple question. *Tell us what happened.* And that's what I did. I told them about the dogs. How they were killing the mountain's creatures. How they ran wild around our house at night. How they were taken deep into the mountain and freed. How I gave Trout the ropes for his tent. I pledged my vow, and I never looked at him.

"Ms. Heron," the young prosecutor said, once Trout's lawyer sat down.

"Yes?"

"What is your relationship to the defendant?"

Trout's lawyer stood and objected.

"It is relevant, Your Honor. It goes to her credibility. If this court is going to be asked to believe her, it needs to know the exact nature of her relationship with the defendant," the prosecutor replied.

"I'll allow it," the judge said.

He asked again about the "exact nature of my relationship to the defendant." I almost lied. But I knew they could see it. It was stamped across my flesh. I was his. And if I lied about my love, they might not listen to my guilt. So I told them. *He was my love.*

"You took the dogs deep into the mountain?"

"Yes," I replied.

"And you did it by yourself?"

I nodded.

"I didn't hear you, Ms. Heron. Is it your testimony before this court that you led four large dogs weighing over a hundred pounds each, through the densest part of the woods, in the middle of the night, miles and miles from your home, by yourself? You're asking us to believe that you did that all alone?"

It was the cruelest question. The one that had been stalking me from the moment Father Heron said it. *She killed your momma.* It gave me a savage power of choosing between Trout or protecting Mamma Rutha and Mary.

Oh how I wanted to choose him. For every selfish reason in the world. Every part of my body that was mine wanted to free him. But part of me was hers too. Mary's. And it was that part that knew I couldn't. Mamma Rutha wasn't ashamed of her actions on the day my momma died. If Sheriff Barnes questioned her the way he had questioned Trout, there was no telling what paper he could get her to sign. I would become my Father Heron, the thief of Mary's blood.

"I'm telling you he didn't do it. I swear on my life," I answered him.

"But he has pled guilty. He admits doing it. It's his word against yours, and you both lay claim to the same crime. Unless, of course, there is someone else that helped you. If you did what you say you did, you surely had some help. Was it him? Did the two of you take the dogs together? Or is there someone else that can testify that this man did not steal those dogs?" he asked.

"There is no one else," I whispered. "But that man did not steal those dogs."

The prosecutor told the judge he was finished and took his seat, and the judge turned to me.

"I'm sure you are very emotional right now," he said softly, perhaps even kindly. "But he says he did it, and I have every reason to believe him. Go on home now, be a good girl, and don't let me see you back in this courtroom again, you hear?"

"It's the truth," I said. "He didn't steal the dogs."

"You know lying under oath is a crime, Ms. Heron. Now run along home."

The judge withdrew to consider his ruling and I obeyed him and went home. But not before my eyes found his face, and my heart kissed him goodbye. He never once looked at me. Keeping his downcast stare. Wearing the look of a man whose blood had been stolen.

Chapter XXXI

*I*t was the silences. They were his sharpened knife. His loaded pistol. Like with my momma. It wasn't really the locked door that had killed her. That was just the wounding weapon. What had finished her off was the silence. As she banged on the doors and windows begging for a response, his lips had pursed together, poised for the kill. I was my momma's daughter, so it was my turn.

"Father Heron," I begged him, "he didn't steal your dogs. I did. I'll buy you new ones. Or you can let me take his place in jail. I'll confess whatever you want me to at church. I'll do anything! Just please don't do this!"

And he sat cool and silent, finishing everything off.

"Please!" I grabbed his hand. "Father Heron, please! I don't care what you ask, I'll do it!"

One word from him could have freed Trout. It was a word that never came.

But I was the deacon's granddaughter. No better. I watched him and learned. I found my own cage. It was filled with bitter dreams. The ocean never came to me in my sleep anymore. But murder did. I dreamed of arsenic in his tobacco. Of Mamma Rutha's knife in his chest. Of a locked door as he lay bleeding on the other side.

Della knew. We'd sit in her momma's car and she'd tell me I was crazy. She was right. Mamma Rutha carried those dogs off because they killed without reason. She was crazy enough to get her revenge. I was her daughter too, and I was no better.

"You don't want to end up in jail. Sheriff Barnes would know it was you if anything happened to Father Heron. Father Heron's old anyway. A few more years and he'll be dead. Just let it go," she begged.

But it was all I had left.

"At least promise me one thing," Della asked. "Let me help? I've got a clearer head than you right now. And if we're gonna do this, we're gonna do it right."

I told her I would, so she would feel better. But I had slid beneath promises. Murder had entered my heart, leaving lies floating on the surface. Oh how Mamma Rutha prayed about it, sitting naked in the November cold. But it was no use.

"Mercy baby," she said, kneeling by my bed in the middle of the night.

"Yes."

"You mustn't feel all the hate."

"I can't help it. It's all I have."

"But you're doing the same as him."

"What do you mean?"

"He choked his baby's soul with hate. And now you're doing the same."

The baby, I thought, feeling confused. Not once had I thought of it. When I confessed in court, I never imagined what it would be like to be born in prison. Or have your momma locked away. The only thing I thought of was my innocent Trout. And how I wanted Father Heron dead.

"I don't believe you," I said bitterly. "I only feel death within me."

"There's more to you," she said, as she laid her hand across my belly. "It's a blessing and it lives. But it's choking on all the grief."

"I don't know what you want from me. There's nothing I can do for it," I muttered.

"You must keep it safe. From him. And from your hate."

I had Della buy a pregnancy test. She looked down at the test and smiled. "It's pinker than the Pink Panther." I didn't return her smile.

"You're gonna be okay, Mercy. I think 'Aunt Della' sounds pretty good, don't you?"

But how could it all be okay? I was carrying a baby, a baby who would be born in the spring. A baby whose father was locked away. And I didn't even know for how long. I wrote him a letter that night.

Dear Trout,

Someone else waits for you. A baby. Now you have someone else to dream about, when you get tired of dreaming about me.

Tell me the day to wait for. It doesn't matter how long. Rachel in the Bible had to wait fourteen years while Jacob labored for her. I'll be your Rachel. You are my Jacob. We will labor as long as we have to.

Your Mercy

For the next two weeks I fiercely guarded the mailbox. Until one day, my letter came back. "No such prisoner" was scribbled across it. *No such prisoner?* As though he had never existed. Had Prisoner 3902 vanished too? Had Father Heron done something more?

"Relax, Momma Mercy," Della said. "Remember how that guy at the jail said that they just assigned a number to him? He probably got a new number when he went over the mountain."

I needed that number. I needed to know what Trout's "name" was. It was my only way to find out where he was living and breathing. Della drove me back to the jail. The same pimply-faced young guy was working the desk.

"Hey handsome," she said as she walked in the door. "Remember me?"

He started giggling. "Sure I remember you."

"Thought you might be able to help me out again."

"What do you need?"

"Just some information. On a guy that used to be here. Prisoner 3902 Price. I need to know how to track him down," she said.

"I'll call down the mountain and see if they can track him down."

"Anything you could do to help will be greatly appreciated," she whispered sexily.

"Sure thing, sweetheart." He smiled as he picked up the phone.

"Hello, is this Roger?" he said in his serious "cop" voice. "Uh, Roger, this is Mike up on Crooktop. I was wondering if you could do me a favor . . . We brought a prisoner by the name of 3902 Price down to you because we couldn't track his legal name. Can you look and see what his new number is and see if you can find out how long he's gonna be there . . . ? Yeah, we brought him down a few weeks ago . . . Oh. Really? Well I didn't know that . . . Well, I'm sorry to hear that, Roger. You say they're laying a bunch of you off . . . ? Ain't that a shame. Well, thanks anyway Roger. Take care now."

"What's happened?" I asked.

"Downsizing. They're having to lay off a bunch of guards, so they sent off all the new prisoners."

"Where?" I asked. "Where did they send them?"

"To different jails. They divided them up and sent them wherever they could find a space."

"Well, don't they have a record of where they sent them?" I asked.

He shrugged his shoulders.

"But he's in one of the jails out there, so if I wrote to all of them he might get a letter?" I asked.

"Yeah, I guess he would if he was there. You might want to address it to Prisoner 3902 Price, originally from the Crooktop Jail, because that's probably the last jail that would be in his record. That might help 'em figure out which one it is. You gotta remember, lady, these guys are busy keeping society safe. They ain't too concerned with running a post office."

"I need the addresses. Of all the jails that he might be sent to."

"Lady, I gotta jail to run here. I ain't no damn secretary."

"But you gotta copy machine, don't you?" Della said. "It'd be pretty easy for you to just push a few buttons. Wouldn't it?"

"What's in it for me?" He smirked. "If I make the copies of the addresses?"

She laughed. "Won't my happiness satisfy you?"

"Not enough," he said smugly, his arms crossed.

Della's face reddened.

"No, Della. Let's just go."

But she was already around the counter, telling me to step outside for a few minutes.

"Don't, Della. It's not worth that. Let's just go."

"Mercy, this is my business now. I ain't asking your permission."

She was whoring herself. Not for the love of a man. Or for the fun of it. Or to rebel. She was whoring herself for me. For my child. And my addresses.

She came outside smiling, with a glint of shame and anger in her eyes. Waving papers filled with addresses. Her hair had grown out enough for her to shape into a short pixie cut. With her vanilla skin and golden eyes, she looked like a fairy that had lost her wand.

"Why did you do that?" I asked. "I hate it when you do stuff like that."

"I told you I'd do anything you needed me to do to

help you fix everything. And we couldn't fix it. Trout's off in jail somewhere. You're carrying his baby. Helping you write your baby's daddy is the least I can do."

The two of us sat up that night copying my letter over and over until our hands cramped. We wrote "Prisoner 3902 Price/Originally from Crooktop Jail" on so many envelopes my mouth puckered with the taste of glue. We mailed them the next morning, full of hope.

I walked halfway down the mountain each morning to meet the mailman before he came to the house. He only handed me my letters back. "No such prisoner" scrawled across each of them. Eventually the letters stopped coming.

I knew then that it was just me and the baby. And I knew I needed to take care of it. I tried my best. I would cover my face with a pillow when I sobbed at night so that the baby wouldn't hear. I would make my mouth sing a happy song when it wanted to call out his name. When it wanted to scream, *Trout! Where are you?*

I let Della take me to a clinic over the mountain where nobody would know me. The doctor had cold hands and impatient eyes. He gave me some vitamins and told me to relax and not to worry, because everything would be fine. *Everything would be fine?*

"Women give birth every day," he said with a laugh. "Don't worry at all."

I let my baby hear me say, "Oh, I know, Doctor, I'm not worried."

But it was all lies. I was sick with worry and grief. Because I knew that I might spend the rest of my life waiting for someone that would never come.

Soon I would show. My breasts were growing so large I was borrowing all of Della's bras. I laughed at myself in the mirror. Finally, after all the years of hating my willowy figure, I had nice round breasts. And now I had to work to hide them. I wore loose shirts over sweatpants and hid out at Della's. We would dream about beautiful nurseries and how we would decorate them. We would make lists of names. And I would feel like a good momma on those days. But the things that Mamma Rutha had warned me to protect my baby from were still there, pulsing inside of me. My blood was thick with it, and it was feeding my baby. I pushed it down and hid it from everyone. But the baby knew. There wasn't a corner of my heart it couldn't see. There wasn't a beat of my heart it didn't feel. It swam in the darkness of my soul.

Chapter XXXII

I had spent the day with Della helping her dream up revenge for Randy. Thoughts of punishing him amused us those days, when thoughts about my danger, the baby's danger, and its missing daddy were too painful. We sat and giggled over all the horrible things we could do to him until it was time for me to sneak back home. From the porch I could hear Rusty's voice inside. Level and polite. I stopped still to listen.

"Yes sir, I think a lot of your family. My folks used to talk about your pap when I was just a little tike. They said he'd stop by the diner after crawling out of the mines, black all over. He wouldn't come in, he was that polite. So my momma would carry his dinner out to him. And he'd eat it there in the parking lot. Yes sir, my folks always did respect the Heron name."

"How's business been lately?" Father Heron asked.

"Oh, it's been good. People 'round here are always up for some smoked pig."

"And your parents?"

"They're fine. I just thought I'd bring some dinner by, sir. See how you was doing."

"We're doing fine."

"That's good. I also wanted . . . I just wanted to let you know, sir, that, well, that I heard about Mercy's little trouble. And it made me madder than hell, pardon my language, to have some outsider sneaking in here and taking advantage of Crooktop's women."

Father Heron was silent.

"I know you think the world of her, and how worried you must be about her. Truth is, sir, I do too. Always cared for your Mercy. And if it was all right with you, I'd like the chance to show her. You know me and you know my family. I got my own business, I go to church. I'd like the chance to take good care of her, sir. Even after all her trouble."

I could hear Father Heron shifting in his seat.

"Deacon Heron, I know you can't force her to do anything. I know she's powerful headstrong. I know you've raised her right too. Always brought her to church yourself, even when her grandma quit. You've done good by her, sir. I can't pretend to know how hard it must be to raise a girl all by yourself. And I know you must be disappointed in her right now. But deep down she knows what's right. And I was thinking maybe between the two of us, we could steer her that way again. I'd be grateful to you if you'd give me that chance."

"I'll speak to her," Father Heron said. "Stability. That's what women like her need. It's what I've always given her. I'll speak to her, 'cause I trust you to provide a firm stable hand. Women the likes of her need it."

"I appreciate that, sir, I really do. I know she puts a lot of stock in what you say. Well, I better be off to help close the diner up. I brought your family some dinner here," he said, rustling brown paper bags.

"Much obliged. You tell your folks hello, and I'll see them at church."

"Yes sir, you take care."

I slid around to the side of the house as Rusty left. I watched him heave himself into his truck. Laboring to carry his weight and breathe through his smoke-filled lungs.

I walked quietly into the house, untucking my shirt as I went.

"Mercy," he called.

"Yes, Father Heron?"

"Come eat dinner."

I could smell it everywhere. Smoked pig. The odor of hickory and flesh filling the house. My stomach turned. And turned again. I gagged.

"Mercy?"

"I'm coming," I yelled, feeling hot from the crown of my head to my toes.

I watched him pull the pork from the bags. Shredded bits of gray flesh, drowning in a red paste. My stomach began to knot. *Stop it*, I told myself. *You cannot throw up in front of him. If you do, he will know. He will know and then he will kill you both.*

"Have a seat."

"I'll pour us some tea," I said, whirling around so I could gag. I had to get through that dinner without vomiting. I took a sip of tea. Sweet and familiar, nothing harsh or smoky there. I sat down, careful to keep my eyes off of him *and* off the food. Every muscle in my body was tense, pulled tight to keep it from the release it sought. Even my toes were curling tight in my shoes. I could feel my pulse in my stomach, throbbing out its anger. My skin began to burn. I watched him bow his head and mumble a prayer.

"Amen," I said, when he raised his head, unaware that I hadn't even closed my eyes.

"Saw your boss today."

"Oh, really?" I asked, not bothering to update him that I had been fired.

"Mhmm. He brought this dinner. Good boy, Mercy. Got his act together, that one."

"He's always been a real nice boss," I said, my eyes catching a glimpse of gray pork being stuffed in his mouth. I didn't know how to breathe. If I inhaled through my nose, I could smell it. If I opened my mouth to breath, I was afraid of what I couldn't hold back. So I did the best I could. I sat there with my jaw locked and teeth gritted, sucking air between the tiny gaps in my crooked bottom row.

"I think it'd be good for you to spend some time with him."

I sat there and counted the flies on the ceiling, to distract myself from the smell, the gagging, and my fear. One, two, three, four . . .

"Lucky he's interested in you at all, after whoring yourself out to that mater migrant," he growled.

One, two, three . . . the fourth had flown away.

"So you will spend some time with him," he said.

I was unsure of what to say. Was it a trick? To see if I was still *hot for men*, like he called Della? I stifled a gag.

"Did you say something?"

"No sir."

He eyed my plate. "Not eating much."

"Not too hungry. Once you serve this food all day you get to the point where it's hard to eat," I said, picking up my fork and swirling it through my food.

"Humph," he muttered. "Ungrateful. Rusty brought this all the way up here for us. Better than that mater migrant of yours ever did. But this Rusty fella, he's a different sort. Good churchgoing boy. Think it'd do you good to spend time with him instead of that whore Della."

I wondered what he was up to. He had never seemed concerned with what was good for me. Just what would make *him* look good. And after I had sufficiently shamed myself in the eyes of his friends, he had been content to wash his hands of me. But now there was a new interest, a new concern with what was *good for me*. What was good for Mercy now? Something that could make him look saintly? To manage to marry off his whore granddaughter even after she shamed him?

"I see him every day," I said.

He chewed and swallowed, chewed and swallowed.

"That ain't what I mean. See him outside of work, have him up for dinner sometime. Show people you ain't just a mater migrant's whore. He comes from a good family and he's taking a liking to you. I reckon if outsider trash is good enough for you, then you could manage to make yourself respectable with the best of Crooktop."

"Why should I?" I dared to whisper. What did it matter now that he had gotten rid of Trout? Now that I had confessed myself at church? He didn't answer, and when I stole a glance at him I saw danger in the lock of his jaw. Danger in the way he gripped his fork. Tightly, forcefully, like the fork had a life that he could choke.

"I'm not questioning you, sir, I didn't mean to do that," I retreated. "Guess I'm just surprised he's taken to liking me."

His jaw relaxed and he lowered his fork.

"Your momma . . ." he began, balancing his fork on the edge of his plate.

I sucked in my breath. My eyes locking on his, begging him to finish his sentence.

"Yes?" I whispered.

"Was about the same age when she did what you've done. There was no redeeming her. You made sure of that. But your belly ain't poisoned like hers. Least not yet. There's still hope for you."

He didn't want to have to kill me. That's what he was telling me. He wanted me to be the old Mercy, Deacon Heron's granddaughter. Killing was hard for him. I was learning that. In the way he sighed on my momma's birthday. In the way he shook his head over his barbecue. I wondered if the back doorknob scared him the way it scared me. If he dreamed about biting blood-filled apples from our tree, the way I did. If he could ever get her scream out of his ears. He had loved her, and killing her had been hard. *He was looking for a reason not to have to kill me too.*

"What was she like?" I whispered, daring to ask the

question that had been waiting on my tongue since her birthday.

He sighed and didn't look at me. I didn't think he was going to answer me, so I started stirring my pork again. He took a sip of tea.

"She was a good enough girl, I reckon. 'Til him, anyways."

I waited. Knowing there was more. Not wanting to pass over the things that I had always missed in him.

"A bright little thing," he said softly, the tips of his fingers tracing circles on the table. "She could climb a tree better than any wildcat. Once, when it was the first day of school and she didn't want to go, Rutha and I searched everywhere for that girl. She was just a little thing, barely over my knees." He was talking to himself now, unaware that I sat stone still across from him. "We found her up in the top of an old hickory. Somehow she had managed to shimmy her way up the trunk. And she would not come down. No matter what we said. I told her I'd wear her out. Rutha promised her cupcakes. But she would not come down out of that tree," he said with a hint of laughter in his voice. "She always did do what she pleased. The day wore on and soon it was growing cool. Still she wouldn't come down. So I climbed my way up in that tree and sat there with her. 'Til she agreed to go in and have some dinner. She was a mess. Bark all over her new dress. Knees all skinned up from the trunk. She always did do what she pleased." He looked at me. "I never saw you climb a tree a day in your life."

"I have," I said. "Lots of times." *I am like her,* I wanted to tell him. *It would be hard on you to kill me too.*

"Tell Rusty to come to dinner soon. I'll clear your grandma out of the house," he said, as he left the table and walked outside.

I sat motionless until I could hear him working in the shed. Then I let go. Spilling hot and sour, over my cold pork. I was trembling and hot. I laid my head on the cool tabletop and thought about what he wanted me to do.

He was asking me to give him a reason not to kill me. And I would, until I could figure something else out. I would be Rusty's girl.

Chapter XXXIII

*H*ey there," Rusty said, grinning, when I stopped by the diner.

"Hi Russ."

"What have you been up to lately?" he asked, still grinning.

"Not anything. You?"

"Just working. Come smoke with me." I followed him out to the back of the diner, where the smokers were boiling over with hickory. That's what it would mean to be Rusty's girl. A life of smoke swirling through and over me.

We talked about the weather and about the diner while I struggled to force myself to do what I knew I had to. He grew restless. He knew why I was there.

"Well, I got to get back to work," he said, rising to his feet.

"Wait," I called out.

"Yep?"

"Come to dinner tonight. At my house."

He grinned. "Well, sure thing, Mercy girl."

I could feel him watching me walk away, spying the new bounce in my breasts.

An hour before he arrived, everything was ready. The house was clean, the dumplings simmered, the collards were limp, and I had showered and put my lipstick on. It seemed like I cared. And the truth is, I did. Loose shirts and my puffy coat might be able to hide my belly from Father Heron. But Rusty could hide me from his interest.

Being his girl wouldn't be easy, because Trout never left me. I thought of him sitting in a dirty jail while I cleaned for another man. I thought of the way he fed me, as I cooked for another man. Of how he made my body blossom with life, as I got dressed for another man. There was only Trout within me. Everything else, the cooking, the cleaning, the pleasing, it was all a part of Father Heron. It sprang from my black eyes in a desperate attempt to keep Trout's baby safe.

Rusty pulled up, and I opened the door.

"Hey there, pretty girl." He had readied himself too. Hair freshly gelled and parted. The scent of heavy after-shave mixing with smoke.

"Good to see you," I said, trying to smile, trying not to fidget. Father Heron walked in the room.

"Come in Rusty, welcome."

They sat and talked as I set the table. Imagining how different my life would have been if I could have brought Trout home. How different everything would have been if Father Heron would have been willing to sit and talk with him.

"Y'all ready to eat?" I called from the kitchen.

I sat between them. My hands beneath the table, secretly rubbing my belly, my hidden connection with Trout. They ate well, taking seconds of everything. I felt no hunger. I rarely did. I lived in a world of grief and danger. There wasn't room for hunger where I hid.

There was more chatter around that dinner table than there had been in years. Probably since my momma was alive. They talked about church. About business. About the new threat of another coal strike. I studied them. Searching for what it was that they liked about one another. I looked at Father Heron as everyone else saw him. Neat and well groomed. With cautious table manners and rigid posture. He looked like a patriarch. And that's why people respected and listened to him. That's why people felt sorry that my momma had left him with me.

I looked at Rusty. Constantly grinning and nodding. Saying "yes sir" and "no sir" and "thank you sir." He was a church-boy, a good son, a business man. He was every patriarch's dream.

Father Heron took Rusty out to the shed to show him his new tiller. I was alone in the kitchen washing dishes, until Mamma Rutha walked in.

"What are you doing?" she asked.

"Washing dishes. There's some leftovers if you're hungry."

"What are you doing?" she repeated.

She was close to me, closer than I had realized. Smelling of cedars.

"Remember how you'd save the blood of Father Heron's hunting kills? How you'd drain the possum, or squirrel? And then when you knew he was about to go hunting you'd take it out and sprinkle it on a crazy path, round and round, and far away from any creature's nest. His dogs would lose their minds trying to track that scent. They'd run in circles and backtrack. 'Cause you'd thrown 'em off the real trail." I looked at her. "That's all I'm doing."

"Your grandpa said you could come for a walk," Rusty called through the door. I walked to him. He stood there waiting for me, with eager eyes and nervous hands.

"Where you wanna walk to?" I asked.

"Anywhere, I guess." He shrugged shyly.

We walked up the road. Past the few other houses that dared to defy the mountain. Neither one of us spoke much. Just stray comments about the weather or the diner. I thought back to the first time I walked with Trout. In the rain. Inhaling deeply to smell him. I walked with one hand on my belly.

"I didn't want to fire you from the diner," Rusty said.

"It's okay."

"It's just that, well, with your trouble and all . . . and I've got customers to think about . . ." he said, stopping in the road.

"It's really okay, Russ."

"And if it was all my business and not my daddy's I wouldn't have . . . I just have to think about things like that . . . I just have think about whether . . ."

"It's okay," I whispered, pressing in closer to him.

"But I didn't want you to think that I felt, or that

I thought . . . I mean I want you to know that I don't think . . ."

"Shhh," I whispered, softly placing my finger over his mouth.

"Mercy," he whispered. "You're trembling."

"I know."

"Mercy. Mercy," he whispered.

I let him touch me. There on the side of the mountain, I let him run his red knuckles through my hair. I let him press his smoke-filled body closer to mine. I let him taste my mouth. I thought about that day in the diner. How I shuddered when I saw his hand on my knee. I was so far beyond that.

The baby moved.

"You're crying," he said, stepping back from me and staring at my face.

"No I'm not," I said too cheerfully, forcing a stiff smile.

"You must be cold," he said. "Standing out here kissing in the middle of winter. Let me get you home."

We walked home with his arm around me. It felt strong and supportive, and warm. And that made me want to cry even more. That I would be left alone having to find support and strength in Rusty. My hands didn't leave my belly for the rest of the night. I laid in bed cradling the part of me that still held Trout. It was my living link to him.

I began seeing Rusty every Friday night. And the more I saw of Rusty, the less I saw Father Heron. I still hid from him. Rising before dawn and going to Della's. Or sleeping in until he had left. But he didn't seek me now that I was making myself a respectable woman. I was sprinkling the blood of my heart in circles around that mountain. And it was throwing Father Heron off track.

Dating Rusty wasn't the worst thing. It was better than thinking about Trout in jail. It was better than fearing that Father Heron would want to snoop out what I did with my days. Rusty the man was different than Rusty the boss. He was less assuming and less assured. And I was doing a good job hiding the truth from him. When he pulled me close, so that our bodies pressed against one another, he felt my belly. Round and firm. I even let him put his hand there, covering Trout's baby.

"Mercy, have you . . ." he began, his eyes tensing into little slits.

"Yes." I laughed. "And it's not nice of you to bring it up. Yes, I have put on a few pounds this winter. Must be all those dinners I cook for you."

His face relaxed and he began to tease me, calling me his little dumpling. It was gross, but it was safe. I wasn't going to tell him until the moment I had to.

That moment came when he surprised me with a "special" date. He had cleared the diner out early. There were little pink carnations on the center table. And candles. He pulled a chair out for me, and laid a napkin in my lap. He was treating me like a lady. *If he only knew.*

"I cooked this meal myself," he said, as he walked back to the kitchen. He came and arranged a covered dish in front of me. Then he lifted the lid.

"I hope you like it," he said softly.

Smoked pork ribs. The best part of the pig. Perfectly charred and basted. But as I looked at it, gray flesh in red paste, and smelled it, there was no damming the river. I bolted from the table to the bathroom. I didn't even have time to shut the door. As I knelt, retching, I felt his hands lift my hair, and a cool washcloth cover my forehead.

I started crying. Sobbing right into the toilet. I wished he wasn't so good to me. It only made me ache for Trout even more. It only made me remember when life itself had been good.

"Mercy," he said, kneeling down beside me in the bathroom. "What's wrong? What is it?"

"Don't you know?" I sobbed. "Can't you see?"

"What?" he asked.

"Why are you so good to me? You don't know me," I cried. I was shaking all over.

"What is it? I thought we were having a good time. Me and you, hanging out together. I thought we were having fun."

"You thought this was fun?" I cried. I was angry with him for being so nice to me.

"What's wrong?" he asked again, his hand grabbing mine.

I sat up and looked at him. How could I tell him that I had used him? How could I tell him that I could never, would never, be his? That all of his efforts were wasted? How could I tell him that I was beyond redeeming?

"Mercy?" he whispered.

I lifted my shirt. I lifted it high, exposing my roundness and my heavy breasts. I took his hand and laid it on my belly. His eyes wrinkled again, into little slits. I shook my head yes. He pulled his hand away and sat back on his heels.

"When?" he whispered.

"Late spring, I think."

"Is it the mat—" he began.

"Yes. It's his."

He sat there looking dumbfounded. Shaking his head no.

"What are you gonna do?" I asked him.

"What do you mean?"

"What are you gonna do now? Now that you know?"

He sat quiet. Looking at me. Looking at my belly.

"Well, I'm gonna take you home," he said calmly.

He didn't open the truck door for me, the way he normally did. But he did ask if I was cold. And he turned his heater vents in my direction, to help warm me. We sat in silence the whole drive home. When he pulled up to my house, I started to speak.

"Russ, I . . ."

"Just run along inside now. Just go on inside," he said lowly, without looking at me. I walked inside and packed a bag. I emptied my jelly jar into it. I had to be ready to run for my life in case he told Father Heron.

Two days later as I slept in, trying to avoid seeing Father Heron, he called through the door.

"Mercy?"

"Yes."

"Saw Rusty in town yesterday."

My feet hit the floor. I reached under my bed for my getaway bag.

"Good thing you're spending time with him. He's a good one."

He hadn't told. Even after I had used him. Even after

he learned I could never be his. His goodness made me seem bad. I had imagined that Rusty was almost as evil as Father Heron. But the truth was that Rusty was good to me. He was kind to me. The reason Crooktop called him decent and respectable was because he *was*. And he was still being good to me. He was still letting Father Heron think that I couldn't be out whoring myself because I was with Crooktop's best. And I don't know why. He owed me nothing. And I found myself owing him a lot.

I felt guilty, but I didn't regret it. Because dating Rusty was the only thing I did that was good for my baby. I didn't protect myself from the cold. I didn't let myself feel the hunger. And I couldn't stop the flow of grief and hate. Mamma Rutha had told me to, but she hadn't told me how. And it was everywhere in me. It flowed from my heart to my belly. Nothing could survive it. My belly was the reservoir of everything miserable. The place where my baby eventually drowned.

Chapter XXXIV

*I*t was a wild winter night, with snow and ice and cutting winds. I lay in my bed touching the expanse of my belly. A firm round growth. I was thankful it was winter. I could walk to the valley with my big puffy coat on, zipped up and covering my middle.

I hadn't seen Father Heron in over a week. I would spend entire days in my room to avoid having to see him. I would pee in a jar beneath my bed, so that I wouldn't have to open my door to go to the bathroom. At night while he slept, I would sneak to the kitchen. Steal scraps of food and fill a thermos with water, just enough to last another day in hiding. I didn't even go to church anymore. And he hadn't tried to make me. He was content to leave my redemption to Rusty.

But with the snow and the ice, Father Heron would be trapped inside. So I hid in my room and prayed for the snow to stop. But the weather wasn't my only worry that night. I touched my belly with more than curiosity. I touched it with worry. The baby hadn't moved in so long.

"Just give me a little kick," I asked it. "Will you squirm just a little for me?"

But there was nothing. For hours I lay there begging it to move. I scolded it. "Don't worry your momma like this. That's not a nice thing to do." I bribed it. "If you'll move, I'll make biscuits and gravy for breakfast." I begged it. "Please move. I haven't felt you in days. Please let me know you're there."

I waited and waited, but nothing came. I had drowned it. It wasn't Father Heron that had killed it. It was me with my bitterness, hate, and grief.

"No," I sobbed into my pillow. "No. No. No. Not this, God. I can't take this. Just let me have my baby."

I cried into the night. My sobs covered by the winds that whipped around the house. Tears shaking my body as the weather shook the house. There was no life in my belly and no rest for me. I didn't think there would ever be again.

At some point in the night, as I lay crying and moaning to my baby, begging it to move, Mamma Rutha came in and stretched her hands over my belly.

"Something's wrong," she said with worried eyes.

"I killed it. Not Father Heron. I fed it my grief and I killed my baby," I cried.

"Put your coat on," she said in a low stern voice. "Get out of that bed and put your shoes and coat on now!"

"I can't move, Mamma Rutha. I killed my baby. Don't make me move," I sobbed.

Her rough hands jerked me up.

"Mercy baby, you listen to me. You put your shoes and coat on now. Now!" she screamed, her eyes glowing.

She had never spoken to me that way before. She wasn't asking or pleading. She was ordering.

As I pulled my socks on I told her that a doctor was no use because I could feel its dead body, floating lifeless within me.

"You do as I say now. You're right. Ain't no doctor that can fix this. But you just do as I say," she said, helping me put my shoes on.

She dragged me out into a night of bitter, stinging snow. The flakes weren't big and soft like in Christmas movies. They were small, scaly bits that blinded me.

"Hold my hand," she commanded as she pulled me into the woods.

We walked straight up the mountain. Up and up and up. Until I collapsed on the ground.

"I can't go no further, Mamma Rutha. I can't even feel my feet I'm so cold," I cried.

Mamma Rutha took off her socks and pulled them over my shoes. "That should help some," she said, pulling me up.

We walked until I forgot that we were walking. I was being pulled through a dark stinging woods, but I didn't know it. The cold, the exhaustion, the grief, had eaten me alive. When I awoke I was lying on a dirt floor.

"Drink this," Mamma Rutha said as she poured something hot into my mouth.

I blinked the melted snow out of my eyes and looked around. I was in a one-room shack, but it was sturdily built, keeping most of the bitter wind outside.

"Where am I?" I asked.

"You're at the top of the mountain, Mercy baby, the very top."

"This is where you go?"

She smiled.

"Are there other people here? The rumors in the valley, are they true?" I asked.

"You can't ever tell anybody that you were up here. Promise me," she said solemnly.

I nodded my head.

A tall woman walked in the shack.

"This is her," Mamma Rutha said to the woman. "She needs his help."

The woman eyed me suspiciously. "She from the valley?"

"No. She's from me. My granddaughter. I'd be indebted to you for his help," Mamma Rutha said.

The woman nodded and walked out of the cabin.

"You rest here," Mamma Rutha said as she pulled off my shoes and began to rub my feet. "Just close your eyes and rest now. Mamma Rutha's gonna take good care of you."

When I opened my eyes again, there was a man standing over me. He had long gray hair and a clean-shaven face. He smelled like Christmas. Like pine trees and candle wax.

"She needs your help," Mamma Rutha said to him.

He nodded his head and knelt by me. He was staring at my belly. His eyes peering and intense. He pulled my coat back and he lifted up my shirt. My skin glowed in the firelight. He stared deep and hard. Did he see my baby, hanging lifelessly inside of me? He leaned over my belly and whispered to it, then sat back up and watched. Waiting for something. He leaned over again to whisper. And then he nodded. Had it answered him?

He spit into his hands and rubbed them together. Then he held his palms open, over my belly. I felt a strange warmth from them. Like I was standing with my naked belly near a fire. His hands moved closer, and the heat grew. And then closer. Until it was burning me. I began to whimper in pain. And felt rough hands hold me down. The open palms were burning me up. Inches from my skin. Then they touched me. His wet palms laid flat across my stomach.

I screamed as I felt my flesh melt and the heat pierce through my body. It was as though I had swallowed hot coals. And then my baby leapt. Filled with the heat it squirmed and kicked.

He smiled at me. A full, toothless smile. "Your baby good now."

I held my stomach with both hands. "You came back," I whispered to it. "You came back to me."

I was crying and laughing. Crazy joy had taken over me.

"Sleep now," Mamma Rutha told me. "Your baby needs you to sleep now."

I obeyed. I slept deep and hard until my baby woke me. Wriggling its little body. Still feeling warm. I knew then that it hadn't been a dream. Life stirred again within me.

I was ravenous. I hadn't felt the hunger of most women during my pregnancy. So much of me had been trapped in the cage of my heart, unconnected to my body. But my baby had escaped the cage, and was reminding me of its hunger.

I rummaged around for food, but I didn't find any. I walked outside and squatted on the ground, my round belly sticking out as I stuffed my face with snow. A girl, almost my age, stood watching me.

She looked like me too. Dark brown hair and black eyes. But she was younger, and happier.

"Hi," I said.

She smiled, her shy eyes darting away from me.

"My name's Mercy."

She smiled. "You came with her, the Song Lady."

I nodded. The Song Lady, that was certainly Mamma Rutha.

"She brought you to the seventh son," she said.

"What is that?" I asked.

"The healer."

"What?"

"The gift of the seventh son is the healing gift. It only happens when there are seven sons, and then the seventh son himself has seven sons."

"I don't understand."

"Well, the first seventh son, he doesn't have the gift.

He just has the ability to pass it on. But if he has seven sons, then his seventh son will have the gift. That man you saw last night, he was the seventh son of a man that was a seventh son. So he had the gift. Lucky for your baby too."

"What's it mean, the gift of healing?"

"You know." She smiled. "You had it last night. You know what it means."

It meant life. It meant a squirming baby that demanded that I feed it snow.

"Yeah, I do." I smiled back at her.

"It's like the Song Lady. She's a seventh daughter, you know. But her healing power is different. She soothes the spirit with her songs. When my daddy died and my momma about lost her mind over it, somehow the Song Lady knew. Nobody knew where my momma had run off to, and nobody went to tell the Song Lady. Somehow she still knew, though. She found her, carried her back here, and sang to her 'til she was feeling better."

Mamma Rutha, a seventh daughter? I remembered how rough hands and bitter herbs had carried me back from my plastic death.

"Only bad thing is they can't heal themselves. Their gifts don't work on them," she said.

"Why not?"

"Don't know. But the seventh son, we take good care of him, 'cause he can't heal himself. The Song Lady, though, your people didn't take care of her. She has a soul hurt she can't heal."

"Do you know what her soul hurt is?"

"No, but she spends days trying to heal it. She'll be in the heart of the mountain, naked no matter what season it is, pouring out her hurt. Her song is long and strange, about two dead children. One of them dies because they can't walk through a door. The Song Lady tries to heal its soul hurt, but she can't. We don't know why the other one dies. But we know that one's name. It was Naomi."

I shivered.

"Do you know what killed Naomi?" she asked.

I shook my head.

"I thought you might since you're from the Song Lady. Sad that she had two children killed. Well you better go inside before your baby gets too cold."

Two children killed? Me and my momma? In a way, the girl was right. When my momma died, she took everything that was supposed to be me with her. She took a child that would have always known it was loved. She took a child that would have looked at the world with curiosity and not fear. She took Naomi with her. And left me, traded down Mercy Heron. Lord have mercy on the bastard child. Call her Mercy, that's what she'll need.

As I walked home with Mamma Rutha, I saw it. She wasn't just a crazy old woman singing strange songs. She was a seventh daughter. A soul healer. And all of nature knew it, and loved her for it. I asked her about herself, what it meant to be a healer. We walked in silence for a great distance, until she spoke.

"When I was a little girl, my momma told me to sing. She said, 'Sing Rutha.' And so I do," she said. "I send out the gift and it's soaked up to heal. Except for one place.

Look under the apple tree, and see the pool of wasted songs. He couldn't soak 'em up. And once he killed her, she couldn't either. Even the song of forever won't work if a creature won't hear it." She paused and let her hand caress a tree.

"First time I loved him, I was younger than you. I loved him in spite of his crippled heart. And songs I had never dreamed of poured themselves into my soul. I sang to him. As I cooked his dinners. As I cleaned his house. As he sought me in the dark of night. As I brought forth his child. And I saw the puddle growing underneath the apple tree, but I loved that crippled heart. When he killed her I knew. It was the folly of my gift. For loving him. For wasting my songs on him. That day my heart grew a new skin. And his puddle ceased to grow."

I rested that day in bed. Trying not to think about Mamma Rutha's soul hurt. About how she had loved Father Heron, or about dead Naomi. Those thoughts made me feel sad and bitter, and I couldn't risk feeding my baby any more grief. So I made a new vow.

"From this day on," I whispered to my belly, "I'm gonna take care of you. All my thoughts won't be sweet, because we still aren't safe. But no more choking grief. So don't you leave again."

The baby stirred within me. It was a sign of the covenant between us. I wouldn't choke it with my grief. It wouldn't leave me. And together, we would survive.

To go to war with a murdering silence, I was going to have to find my own weapons. I had warned my baby that some of my thoughts wouldn't be sweet. But I could only guess how dark they might become. Could my baby swallow that? Without leaving me again? I needed protection for my baby. There was only one thing I could do. *I was from the Song Lady.* I would bless my baby, and she would grow.

Chapter XXXV

I *carry a child. She was there all along, nestled within. She makes my belly round and smooth, like a polished river rock. My belly rises. Like the swell of the moon over the mountain. It is filled with Eyes that see. Fingers that clutch. A Heart that pulses. She feeds off my bones. My blood. My breath. My soul. To give the world a new song. A song that hums like a steady August rain. And laughs like the flow of a mountain stream. She has eyes like sunflowers floating on deep river pools. She is love. She is her father. She is my new song.*

I knew I was having a daughter. She came to me nearly every night in my sleep. "Come on," she would call me. "Come into the ocean. It's warm here. And safe."

I would wake up from those dreams and whisper her song to her. We would hide during the day, like me and the Sally doll, hoping he wouldn't smell our fear. And I would think the dark thoughts that I needed to, in order to keep us safe.

The deep chill of the winter was beginning to thaw. Father Heron hadn't seen me without my puffy coat on in months. Spring was close. All of the earth knew it too. The sun hung around longer, warming the ground. The streams purred louder with the melted snow. And my baby grew big and strong within me. She stretched my womb and banged her fists against its walls. She was ready to sing for all of Crooktop.

With all the jelly jar money that I had saved up over the summer I bought supplies. Sweet little baby things that smelled clean and sugary. I sent Della to the Magic Mart to buy a blanket, a little pink dress, socks and a hat, sleepers, baby wash, lotion, and diapers. A whole summer's jelly jar spent in one trip. I laughed when I thought about how I had wanted to buy sexy jeans with it. At that point I could barely zip my oversized puffy coat, much less squeeze into tight jeans.

"Lord how people must be talking about me!" Della giggled. "One day I'm buying a pregnancy test, and the next day I'm coming home with diapers and a little pink dress. And I've still got my figure, too! Bet them old cats are chewing their tongues off!"

Della helped prepare for the baby. She was working odd shifts at Rusty's diner. He asked about me every day, and sent food that Della would have to hide and eat so that I couldn't smell it. She spent most of her money on me and the baby. Feeding us what we craved. Black licorice jelly beans. Molasses over cornbread. And biscuits and gravy. Always biscuits and gravy. And after my jelly jar money ran out, she bought some onesies, a story book about birds, and a little teddy bear. Her first toy. A little brown bear with a cream-colored face and brown-marbled eyes. He smelled like baby powder.

"What are we going to do about him?" Della asked.

"I'm still working on that. You know what has to be done. And it isn't just for revenge anymore. It's for safety. He'll kill my baby, Della. I swear to you he will."

"Shhhh. Couldn't you just beat him to the punch and announce to the world that you had a baby? Then he couldn't just get rid of it like it never happened."

"He has ways of killing that look legal. Like my momma. He never even had to touch her to kill her. And he'll find a way to do it to us," I said, rubbing my belly.

We had lots of ideas. I always fell back to the arsenic in the tobacco.

"First of all," Della said impatiently, "where in the hell are you gonna find arsenic? And secondly, it can be traced! They trace that stuff on TV all the time! You got a baby to raise. Both its parents can't be locked away in jail."

I winced. Since my promise to the baby that I wouldn't choke it with grief, I had tried not to think about its daddy, locked away in jail. The baby stirred and I thought that I could feel her gasp. So I whispered her song. A song that Della had learned now too, she had heard it so many times.

"Well what do you suggest?" I asked.

"I say we get somebody else to do it. Make it look like a robbery. Let 'em ransack the place, and beat him 'til he's dead," she said evenly.

"Who?"

"We'll hire somebody. There's lots of desperate people that are willing to do anything. Even kill an old man."

"But we don't have any money, Della. We've spent it all on diapers and black jelly beans!"

"There's other currencies," she said. "You know that by now."

"No, that's your momma's type of money. And it just leaves everybody more broke. Besides, this job is too important. I can't trust it to nobody else. It's going to have to be me."

I thought about how surprised he would be when I didn't dance around him. I was going to dance with him, through him, over him, until he was dead.

"Well how are you going to do it?" she asked.

"I'm going to drown him. There's a stream, not too far into the woods. It used to have wild morning glories growing around it. I'm going to drown him in it."

"How on earth are you going to hold that man underwater?"

"Sleepy tea. Mamma Rutha drugs him all the time. I'll make sure he's stone dead asleep. Then I'll drag him to the stream and lay him facedown. I'll bring his fishing pole too and lay it in his hand. It'll look like he's been fishing and just keeled over dead. It's perfect."

"You think you can drag him?" she asked.

"To keep my baby safe, I could drag this mountain."

I walked home that night with new energy. Finally, I had a plan to protect my baby. I started tracing the path to the stream every night. Memorizing its curves. Pushing back its brambles. Making it a smooth death walk.

Chapter XXXVI

*A*fter Father Heron left for church, I started crushing Mamma Rutha's hidden crumbles into a fine powder. I stared out the windows, at the dark clouds of a storm brewing. And I thought it was a sign. The stream would surely be full from the rain.

I brewed some extra-sweet tea. It was death tea. "Shall we dance, Father Heron?" I whispered as I slid it into the fridge.

But someone else wanted to dance with me that day. Tapped out with the pulsing rhythms of my womb. *Curl graze snap.* Twirled around the blood of my body. At first I thought I had just spilled the tea. A gushing flow down my legs. But the tea was still steady, not a drop had spilled.

You can't come yet! I wanted to scream to my baby.

It's not safe. Just give me one more day. I felt her tug at my womb. She was itching to dance.

"You've got to stop," I whispered to her. "You've got to give me more time. Just one more day."

I laid down in my bed, willing my body to get control of itself and make those dull pains disappear. "It's okay. There's no pain there. You're not having this baby," I whispered to myself. When the pains would leave I would celebrate. *That's it. Just a warning. Like a fire drill.*

But the alarm kept going off, and as the pain grew stronger I knew that it wasn't a drill. I got out of bed and began to pace. Back and forth I walked for hours. I counted the tiles in the ceiling. *One two three . . . fifteen, sixteen . . . twenty, twenty-one.* And then the pain would come and I would brace myself against my bed, moaning into my pillow. Then, *one two three . . . fifteen, sixteen . . .* More pain. Harder, longer. It was a hot pain, like the seventh son's hands but longer and sharper. *One two three . . . five six . . .* oh God the pain. I was in bed again. Flat on my back. Chewing on my hand as I stifled my screams. Blood trickled down my wrist. The taste of copper filled my mouth. There wasn't time to count between the pains.

"*I can't survive this. God, protect my baby,*" I whispered.

Mamma Rutha was there now, singing and moving her hands over my belly. But I only saw pain. I breathed it. I screamed it. I ate it. She started yelling for me to do something, but I couldn't hear her. Because with every pulse of my womb my baby was singing her song. *She was there all along, through all the losses.* Pain. Hot coals, filling my belly.

It is filled with Eyes that see. Fingers that clutch. A Heart that pulses. Pain. Gnawing my insides, ripping my body. *She feeds off my bones. My blood. My breath. My soul.* Pain. Spilling my blood over the bed. *She has eyes like sunflowers floating on deep river pools.* Pain. Tearing away the life that had rooted inside of me. *She is love. She is her father. She is my new song. My Song Baby.*

There was a cry that was really a laugh. A pain that was really a joy. As she clawed her way out of me, I saw bars swinging open. I saw the Fire Trout, free and swimming away. I heard his voice in her cry. *You got glory all around you, Mercy.* As she laid upon my stomach, with red hands covered in our blood, I saw him. He lived again. Because of her. I lived again too.

"Thank you. Oh thank you," I whispered. She was my feast. After all the great losses.

Mamma Rutha was standing over me. Blessing my baby and rubbing her down. We were loving her cry. So full of life. Little lungs belting an angry song. My beautiful Song Baby.

"She needs a name. What have you chosen?"

I hadn't chosen a name. She had picked it herself. Her father had picked it. I just whispered it over her. "Glory. Glory Trucha Price." *A holy moment.*

"That's a fine name, Mercy baby. A real fine name."

Mamma Rutha was smiling, and her eyes were shining. My Song Baby was a healer too. Easing our soul hurts. But we were still in danger. There was a noise outside of an old truck pulling in the driveway. And Glory was still screaming her song.

"Shhh. Shhh. Glory, please. We aren't safe. Please be quiet," I begged.

Mamma Rutha's eyes flashed wild and dangerous. She began grabbing bloody sheets and stuffing them under the bed. She half carried me into my closet and pulled the clothes around me and Glory. I was a jelly jar secret.

"You stay here 'til I get him sleepy. Then we'll get you and Glory to the top of the mountain. You'll be safe there 'til we figure something else out."

We hid in the closet. The smell of old pig smoke surrounding us. Glory was making soft little gurgling noises. Whispering her song. She sensed the danger that stood silent on the other side of the wall.

"Have some tea, Wallace," I heard Mamma Rutha say.

"Not thirsty, Rutha."

Glory made a sharp, squealing noise.

"What was that?" he asked.

"What?"

"That noise?"

"Oh, a bird. There was a bird's nest fell out of the oaks this morning," she said.

He walked into the living room. Heavy footsteps on an old wood floor.

"Didn't sound like no bird to me."

"Shhh, Glory," I whispered. "Sing around him, not at him."

But Glory wasn't like me, she was free. She opened her little mouth and sang. Loud and strong. Daring the silence to come find us. *Come find us*, she sang. *I am not afraid of the silence*, she screamed.

It was all a blur. The smell of rotted apples on old hands reaching out for me. Reaching for my Glory. "Shame!" he screamed. "Your bastard!"

"No!" I cried.

I ran out the back door. Just like I had run with my Sally doll. I was still half naked, blood running down my legs. But I didn't feel the pain, I just smelled the fear that swallowed me. *Please don't burn my Sally doll!*

I fell. Letting my shoulder smash into the ground to protect my Glory. She was screaming so loud. *Or was that me?* I started crawling away from him. My hands gripping wet grass, dragging my broken body up the death path. A boot pushed down on my back. Pinning me to the ground. My body pressed full against my screaming Glory.

"Hand her to me," he said.

"No," I cried. "I won't let you kill her like you killed Momma. Like you killed Naomi."

His boot pressed firmer.

"Hand her to me," he said. "I won't have this kind of sin in my house."

He kicked me in the head. I felt the blood squirt across my eyes. I felt Glory leave my hands. I heard her screaming. *Or was that me?* Where was he taking her? To a fire? *Please don't burn my Sally doll!* She was screaming so loud. And then stillness. A murderous silence. I tried to stand up, but I was so dizzy. I could only see out of one eye because of the blood that was pouring over my face. So I started dragging myself toward the silence. I could hear it all. Blood. Murder. Locked doors.

The woods began to hum, as the storm finally settled in

on the mountain. Washing the wounds of my body, thrashing the limbs of the apple tree. Through the blood on my eyes I saw him carry Glory to the back door. His hand was on the doorknob. And I screamed for him to wait. I knew that he was taking her inside, to his silent death cage.

His hand started to turn the knob, but it held still.

"What in God's name is going on here?" he muttered.

"An eye for an eye. A tooth for a tooth. A man for a child. A locked door for a locked door," Mamma Rutha sang as she appeared next to him.

"You're crazy, Rutha," he yelled.

"An eye for an eye. A tooth for a tooth. A man for a child. A locked door for a locked door," she sang loudly.

He ran around the house to the front door. It was locked too. He returned to the back door and banged on it. He kicked it. He screamed. *Open this door!*

Lightning crashed and instinctively he ducked. I started dragging myself toward him. And as lightning flashed again, I saw him run and crouch underneath the apple tree.

Mamma Rutha was screaming her song now, standing in the middle of the rain, arms stretched toward a sun that refused to shine. Glory joined her, and the two of them sang louder than the storm, while I continued to drag myself toward Father Heron.

I was close enough to see him clearly.

"You don't have to burn her, Father Heron," I heard myself say. "I don't love her more than Jesus. She's our gift from him. Fresh from his lap. Can't you smell heaven on her?"

He looked up at me, and behind the hatred in his black eyes I saw misery. Killing was never easy.

"She is Mary's child too," I whispered, dragging myself closer. "Look at her, the way she screams, already trying to do just as she pleases. Just like Mary. Give her time, she'll climb trees. Give her time, and she'll learn to fish."

He looked down at her and choked back a sob. He laid her gently on the wet ground. The coldness startled her, and she waved her arms as she screamed. I reached for her, pulled her beneath my body, never daring to look up at him. I crawled, slowly to keep the rain off her, into the shed. We hid behind the tiller. I swaddled her in old potato sacks.

It was a long dark night, with a storm even worse than the one when I was thirteen that twisted the old hickory. Glory slept, wrapped tightly in the dusty sacks, our birth blood still smeared across her little body. I shivered as I kept watch. With every crash of thunder I jumped. Wondering if it was him, hunting us down. With every flash of lightning, my eyes hurriedly searched our surroundings to see if he was close. And with every breath I took, I placed my hand upon Glory's chest to make sure that she took one too.

Eventually, the rain slowed. The wind grew calm. Glory woke and turned in to me, her little mouth open and hungry. I offered her my breast, and felt for the first time the tugging burn that accompanies the sweet joy of nursing a baby. I heard her swallow, and she began to suck greedily, my eyes watering with the burn. I cradled her in that filthy shed, dried blood caked on our bodies, and thought about the pure white milk that flowed freely between us.

"*On the day you were born*," I whispered, remembering Mamma Rutha and the withered fig, "*you were not washed in water to cleanse you, nor wrapped in cloths. You were thrown out into the open field. And when I passed by you, and saw you struggling in your own blood, I said to you, Live! Yes, I said to you in your blood, Live!*"

Chapter XXXVII

I brought myself to the apple tree that had been fed with so much of our blood. I stood over him and looked at his face, framed by young apple leaves. At his hands, clenching the heavy apple wood that fell across him. At the black eyes opened in surprise. Things look smaller when they're dead. It's like breathing gives more than life. It gives size too. And shape. The man whose danger had always loomed so large before me, looked small. As I stood looking down on him, it was hard for me to grasp, that *he* was what had terrified me. That he was what had killed my momma. Had almost killed my Glory. *He was so small.*

I looked at the apple tree. Its twisted trunk. The branches broken and scattered. And even though it shouldn't have, it looked like every other tree. With bright yellow wood, smelling of sap. Gray bark, soggy from the storm. As it lay across my Father Heron, there was nothing unique about that killing tree.

I left him, my felled Goliath. And when spring warmed the mountain I bought packets of seeds to sow at Father Heron's grave. Sunflowers and morning glories. I laughed when I read the inscription on the stone. The preacher had picked it. *Eternal Peace in Glory.*

The last time I saw Mamma Rutha was the same morning I found Father Heron. She waved to me from the edge of the woods.

"I'm going home now," she said. "I love you, Mercy baby."

I nodded, my hand still raised in the air long after she had disappeared. When she had been gone for two months, the police decided that nobody could survive that long in the wilderness. Especially not Crazy Rutha. Since I was the sole Heron survivor, I owned the square white cage. And I sold it. I waved goodbye to the apple tree trunk and the two gardens and tucked a twenty-seven-thousand-dollar check in my pocket.

Then I made the long walk down to the riverbottom, one last time. Things had changed so much since I walked it last. I wasn't a new bride anymore. I was a momma. Glory was in my arms, and Della was by my side.

We found the old brown truck. It was still parked in the same spot Trout left it. I searched around in the bed, where I knew he hid the spare key. It started on the first try, and headed smoothly off the mountain. It was as ready to leave as I was.

"What are you doing?" Della asked, when I slowed to a stop.

"One thing left. Watch Glory, I'll be back soon."

I walked straight into the woods and headed back up the mountain. My mind was buzzing with memories. And I was humming my song, the one that Mamma Rutha always sang for me. It all made sense then, why it said that love is just as strong as death, but not stronger. I had my living Glory, but I lost her daddy. Love goes on after death, but love can't stop it from coming.

I walked up the mountain until I saw it. The terebinth tree. I looked at the grave that held my momma's dying. It was still neatly groomed. Mamma Rutha had been by, maybe she was even watching me. I fell to my knees and started digging. Deeper and deeper. Until the earth became too hard and I couldn't dig any more. I leaned over the grave.

"Mercy," I cried out. "Mercy. Mercy!"

Then I ran as fast as I could off that mountain. Trees, animals, dirt, all blurred past me. I heard the call. Loud and strong. And I thought of Elsa. *Maybe he put you here, so he could call you to him there.*

Della was dancing around the truck with Glory in her arms.

"Where you been, little momma?"

"Saying goodbye to someone," I said, as I started the truck again. "By the way, did I ever tell you where we're going they got little huts on the beach that sell ice cream?"

I glanced in the rearview mirror and saw Crooktop looming behind me. I thought about how I really was looking in Trout's mirror after all. I searched deeper, and saw my own black eyes staring back at me. *Call me Naomi,* I whispered. *I am Naomi.*

1. As Mercy walks through the August downpour to the Miners' Credit Union she wonders whether she looks crazy and decides "sometimes crazy is just the best choice." How is this statement true as her journey continues? In your life, has "crazy" ever been the best choice?

2. Was Mamma Rutha a good mother figure for Mercy?

3. What did Trout mean when he said to Mercy, "Maybe what you think is all messed up is the reason why I saw glory all over you"? Compare this to Mercy's earlier comment about wild morning glories' being "weeds that didn't know they were beautiful."

4. Were you surprised to learn that Father Heron was once a beloved "daddy" to Mary? Why do you think he locked the door?

5. Mercy spends her childhood being punished for not living up to the "holy" standards set by Father Heron. Yet Mercy arrives at church with her "heart full of hope" and continues to ponder God's design and call throughout her journey. Why is Mercy able to separate her fear and hatred for Father Heron from her feelings and questions about God?

6. Why was twelve-year-old Mercy so desperate for Mamma Rutha's blessings that she was willing to give up food for two days in order to earn them back? Which hunger do you think was worse, the one for blessings or the one for food?

7. If she hadn't gone into labor, do you think Mercy would have murdered Father Heron? If so, would that have changed your feelings toward her?

8. How do some of the characters' names further explain the characters (Mercy, Trout, Mary)? Why does Mercy call her grandmother Mamma Rutha and call her grandfather Father Heron?

9. Father Heron says Mamma Rutha killed Mary, and Mamma Rutha says Father Heron killed her. How do you think Mary died?

10. Why did Father Heron lay Glory down under the apple tree? Did it make you feel more sympathetic toward him?

11. Della says, "Love don't run," while Mercy believes that love comes in many different forms. What circumstances in their lives cause them to define love the way they do? Whose definition do you agree with more?

12. Mercy describes Crooktop ominously ("I knew that Crooktop had its fist around me"). How is Trout's perspective of the mountain different? Why is it different? Do you think Mercy's relationship with Trout changed her perspective of Crooktop?

13. Did you agree with Mercy's decision to "be Rusty's girl"?

14. Mercy often felt alone and that she didn't belong, despite the crowds around her. Della talked about feeling similarly, yet she "glowed" among the crowds and behaved very differently from Mercy. Why? Who suffered more from her lack of belonging? Have you ever felt alone, despite the crowds around you? Do you hide like Mercy or work to "glow" like Della?

15. Why do you think the author didn't resolve Trout's story? What do you think the future holds for Trout? For Mercy?